PRAISE FOR
The Black Dragon

"More dragons, please, Ms. James!"
—*Night Owl Romance*

"The audience will relish this compelling entry."
—*Midwest Book Review*

"Dragon fans rejoice . . . tasty and tempting reading."
—*Romantic Times*

Dragon Heat

"A unique and magical urban paranormal with dragons, witches, and demons. Will keep you enthralled until the very last word!"
—Cheyenne McCray, *New York Times*
bestselling author of *Shadow Magic*

"Exciting and passionate, this story is gripping from beginning to end."
—*Romantic Times*

"[A] delightful romantic fantasy."
—*Midwest Book Review*

MORE PRAISE FOR
ALLYSON JAMES AND HER NOVELS

"Hot! A must-read."
—Rhonda Thompson, *New York Times* bestselling
author of *Confessions of a Werewolf Supermodel*

"[An] exquisitely sensual tale spiced with danger and fantasy."
—*Booklist*

"[A] delightfully charming paranormal."
—*Midwest Book Review*

"Instantly grabs the reader . . . explosively passionate . . . wonderful. Allyson James has done a great job."
—*Fallen Angel Reviews*

"Sweet, funny, and deliciously erotic."
—*Romance Reviews Today*

"Fine romantic fantasy . . . beguiling."
—*The Best Reviews*

"Sizzling love scenes keep things spicy in this adventure romance."
—*Romantic Times*

Titles by Allyson James

DRAGON HEAT
THE BLACK DRAGON
THE DRAGON MASTER

MORTAL TEMPTATIONS

MORTAL TEMPTATIONS

ALLYSON JAMES

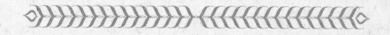

HEAT
New York

THE BERKLEY PUBLISHING GROUP
Published by the Penguin Group
Penguin Group (USA) Inc.
375 Hudson Street, New York, New York 10014, USA
Penguin Group (Canada), 90 Eglinton Avenue East, Suite 700, Toronto, Ontario M4P 2Y3, Canada
(a division of Pearson Penguin Canada Inc.)
Penguin Books Ltd., 80 Strand, London WC2R 0RL, England
Penguin Group Ireland, 25 St. Stephen's Green, Dublin 2, Ireland (a division of Penguin Books Ltd.)
Penguin Group (Australia), 250 Camberwell Road, Camberwell, Victoria 3124, Australia
(a division of Pearson Australia Group Pty. Ltd.)
Penguin Books India Pvt. Ltd., 11 Community Centre, Panchsheel Park, New Delhi—110 017, India
Penguin Group (NZ), 67 Apollo Drive, Rosedale, North Shore 0632, New Zealand
(a division of Pearson New Zealand Ltd.)
Penguin Books (South Africa) (Pty.) Ltd., 24 Sturdee Avenue, Rosebank, Johannesburg 2196,
South Africa

Penguin Books Ltd., Registered Offices: 80 Strand, London WC2R 0RL, England

This is an original publication of The Berkley Publishing Group.

This is a work of fiction. Names, characters, places, and incidents either are the product of the author's imagination or are used fictitiously, and any resemblance to actual persons, living or dead, business establishments, events, or locales is entirely coincidental. The publisher does not have any control over and does not assume any responsibility for author or third-party websites or their content.

First edition: January 2009

Library of Congress Cataloging-in-Publication Data

James, Allyson.
  Mortal temptations / Allyson James.—1st ed.
      p.   cm.
  ISBN 978-0-425-22369-7 (trade pbk.)
  I. Title.
  PS3610.A427M67 2009
  813'.6—dc22   2008032369

PRINTED IN THE UNITED STATES OF AMERICA

10   9   8   7   6   5   4   3   2   1

ACKNOWLEDGMENTS

I'd like to thank my editor, Kate Seaver, for giving me the opportunity to write this book and this new series. As always, her guidance and patience are amazing. Second to Allison Brandau, assistant editor extraordinaire, for all her hard work on this and all my books. Thanks to my husband for his unflagging energy and support. I don't know how he does it.

Last, thank you to Luna and Sandy, two new fuzzy friends in my life, for bringing back the laughter.

For more information on *Mortal Temptations* and other books, please visit my website, www.allysonjames.com.

1

Midtown, Manhattan

WHEN Patricia descended to investigate the noise in her antique store, she found a man with a broken wing stretched unconscious across the floor.

He didn't have white angel wings or transparent dragonfly wings; they were shining satin black, feathers gleaming and glistening in the dawn half-light as they spilled around his body. One wing cradled his bare torso as though cushioning his fall, and the other was broken.

Patricia played her flashlight over him, taking in muscled, broad shoulders, a chest dusted with dark hair, narrow hips hugged by blue denim, and a strong throat encircled by a thin gold chain. He had dark hair long enough to flow over the store's ugly beige carpet and a square, handsome face. His eyes were closed, lashes resting on firm cheekbones. His legs were twisted, one arm flung out to break his fall.

And wings.

The broken wing lay at a right angle from his back, the ends fanning across the floor. Strewn about the feathers were things he'd swept from the counters when he fell: an entire stand of necklaces, a box of sparkling pins, and a bisque doll who'd landed a few feet from him with her legs wantonly in the air.

Patricia couldn't blame her. He was sexy as hell.

Her two cats, Red Kitty and Isis, sauntered in from the back room. They sat on their haunches and stared at him, probably wondering whether he was overlarge prey or someone with the potential of filling the food bowl. Either way, they couldn't lose.

Were his wings a costume? But no costume-shop creation could match those glorious feathers and the perfection to which they fit him. When she crouched down to carefully touch the feathers, they were warm and alive, the tips fluttering beneath her fingers.

Being psychic, Patricia was no stranger to creatures of the night, but she'd never seen anything like him. His psychic aura was incredible: hot and wild, with lightning flashes that stabbed through the shields she usually kept in place. He didn't *feel* evil, but he didn't feel good, either. Most humans were a mixture of both, but supernatural creatures tended to be one or the other.

Her flashlight took in the bruise that stained his temple blue and purple. He was a big man, and anything that could take him down would be . . . bigger. She sensed a lingering taint of evil in the shop, like a faint odor of rotting meat. But it didn't come from the man, and he was alone now. The only auras in the place were his, hers, and the tiny, vibrant ones of the cats.

When she touched the bruise, he moaned but didn't wake. She fetched her first aid kit from the tiny bathroom and doctored the bruise, but she wasn't sure what to do about the wing.

It was broken halfway along, her fingers finding the thin middle bone bent. She had no idea how to treat it, but it couldn't hurt to carefully straighten the bone and wrap the whole thing with an Ace bandage.

The man twitched and moaned through the procedure, but the pain wasn't enough to wake him. She fetched a pillow and gently arranged the man's head on it, then covered him with a blanket.

That was all she could do for him. She was not a witch or a healer; her gift was the ability to read auras of people past and present and the psychic imprint they left on objects. That was why she liked antiques; she could feel their history and the people who'd touched them. Antiques weren't dead pieces of the past to her but shadows of living, breathing entities.

Patricia curled up on a Belter gentleman's chair and tugged a second blanket over her knees. Red Kitty joined her, the long-haired tom never passing up the chance for a warm snuggle. Isis, the black-and-white female, stayed next to the man to keep watch.

Patricia settled in to wait. Would the entity on her floor prove to be good or evil?

~ ~ ~

NICO woke to a pounding headache. He seemed to be on a hard floor, but he felt a pillow beneath his head and a prickly wool blanket across his chest.

He knew the Dyon hadn't been kind enough to leave him with a pillow and blanket. The Dyon had been doing its damnedest to beat Nico black and blue once they both figured out the ostracon and its inscription was no longer here.

The creature had thrown Nico across the counter, Nico hitting his head on the way to the floor, and the Dyon had dissipated. It wasn't allowed to kill him.

Nico raised his throbbing head and met the intense stare of a sleek black-and-white cat. Its gaze bored into his as though the creature were trying a spot of telepathy, but Nico knew it was just a cat. Nothing supernatural about it, thank the gods.

The stink of Dyon lingered in the room, quickly being covered by the aroma of percolating coffee. Nico tossed aside the blanket and painfully climbed to his feet.

He stumbled and caught himself on a glass counter, rattling the glitzy jewelry that glittered on its surface. He wasn't dizzy, despite the headache, but he couldn't get his balance.

He realized that his left wing was all wrong and saw in amazement that it was tightly bound. An Ace bandage crisscrossed it, crushing the feathers, held together with bright blue tape.

"Shit," he said out loud.

He heard running feet, and a woman emerged from the back room, a steaming mug of coffee sloshing in her hands.

Oh, fuck.

She was absolutely beautiful. Her hair was incredibly curly, a riot of dark blond ringlets that cascaded across her face and flowed down her back. She had a face neither too round nor too pointed, full red lips, and a lusciously curved body.

Her head would rest at his collarbone if she stood against him. He wanted her to, so he could lean down and inhale the warmth of her hair. He could whisper into her ear that he was there for her use; all she had to do was name her pleasure.

His cock began to lift, his balls warming and tightening against the fabric of his jeans.

He felt the familiar pull of longing, the compulsion of the spell kicking in. *Damn it, not now.* The curse beat on him at the most inopportune times, and this was a most inopportune time.

The woman started toward him, followed closely by a fluffy red cat. The black-and-white cat leapt to the counter, scattering more treasures, and sat down to resume her watch on Nico.

The woman reached Nico and looked up at him, and something stabbed through his heart. Her eyes were blue green, an incredible oceanlike aquamarine that sparkled like the sea in the sun.

"What are you?" she demanded.

Not *Who are you? What are you doing here? What do you want?* No hysterics. She simply wanted to know what kind of creature had landed in her store.

"A customer," he said, forcing a smile.

"I don't open until ten. How did you get in?"

She wouldn't believe him if he told her, so he just winked. "Through the keyhole."

"What were you expecting to steal? I don't have anything valuable in here, just sentimental jumble that reminds people of their grandparents."

"But you *had* something valuable?"

Her flush told him he was right; plus the thing's unmistakable presence still hadn't worn off. It had been here, but he and Andreas hadn't figured that out until too late. The Dyon hadn't known, either; he'd been following Nico to see what Nico was up to.

"I didn't call the police," the woman pointed out.

"I noticed." He'd also noticed she wore a tight-fitting T-shirt that nicely outlined her braless breasts.

"I thought I'd have trouble explaining the wings to the cops," she said.

"Probably."

"So, what are you?"

He took the coffee she handed him and sipped it. Did it taste better because she made it? The curse wanted him to believe so.

"A man with wings," he answered.

"I'm psychic; I can tell you're not human. Your aura is . . . strange."

"Is it?" He finished off the coffee quickly, needing it. He also needed her to touch him again. The curse was kicking in fast this time.

"Would you mind helping with the bandage?" He asked her. "I'm off balance like this."

She looked doubtful but set down the empty cup. "The bone was broken in half. I think you should keep it still."

"I heal quickly." He steadied himself on the counter and let her reach up and peel off the tape.

To unbind him, she had to step right into the flowing feathers of his wing. He couldn't stop himself from snaking the wing around her, liking how good she felt cradled in its embrace. He could feel every hollow and crevice of her body with the sensitive tips as she plucked at the tape and started to unwind the bandage.

Her breasts brushed against his bare chest, and he wondered if she could feel his pulse hammering under his skin. Her hair smelled nice, clean and fresh, like she'd just washed it.

His already inflated cock was throbbing by the time she unwound the last of the bandage and stepped away. Nico flexed the wing bone, which had mended as he slept. It was a little stiff but manageable.

"I can try to find a shirt for you," she said, her gaze fixed on his bare torso.

"That's all right. I brought my own."

Nico retrieved his T-shirt from where he'd dropped it when

he'd unfolded his wings to fight the Dyon. The ceiling was too low for a good stretch, but he fluffed his wings all the way out, the feathers sleekly erotic against his back.

The feeling didn't help his erection die, especially when he imagined pinning her against him with the wings.

There was a sharp pull in his shoulder blades, then the wings slid away, vanishing. He sensed her gaze on the sharp, black tattoo of wings that fanned over his back, the points of them disappearing under his waistband.

As he slid the T-shirt over his head, the cloth pulled at the hated chain, reminding him what he was.

"Andre's?" The woman read the logo that slanted from his right shoulder to his left pectoral. A large cat's-paw print splotched just under it. "Do you work there?"

Andre's was a trendy bar and club around the corner on West Fifty-sixth Street that had opened a few months ago. It was packed every night.

"I own it with my friend Andreas," he said.

"Oh." She looked at him in surprise. "I haven't seen you around. Not that I get the chance to get out much." She sounded regretful.

"Come tonight and talk to me. I'll waive the membership fee."

She fixed him with a stare as penetrating as her cat's. "Does everyone there have wings?"

"No, just me."

"I'll think about it."

Nico pulled a shining black card with white lettering out of his back pocket. The name he used, Nico Stanopolous, was printed at the bottom. "Show that to the doorman, and he'll let you in. Tell him I invited you."

She took the card, giving him a suspicious look. He flicked a more staid, matte-white card out of the little holder on her counter. *Patricia Lake, Proprietor.* "Nice to meet you, Patricia. Thank you for fixing my wing."

"You still haven't told me what you were doing here. Even if you didn't take anything, you knocked half my jewelry stock onto the floor."

Nico gathered up the pins and earrings and tangle of necklaces and replaced them on the counter. "I came to find something," he said. "It wasn't here."

"Would you mind telling me what?"

He hesitated. He could hear Andreas's roar if Nico decided to trust the woman, but that wasn't what made him reticent. He'd endanger her with too much knowledge, making her a target of things she couldn't possibly understand or fight.

She had magic in her, obviously, because she easily accepted that a man with wings had entered her store without breaking in or triggering the alarm. She hadn't called the police; she'd put a blanket over him and waited for him to wake up.

"Come to the club tonight, and we'll talk about it."

Patricia cocked her head, looking more adorable by the second. "And I should do this because . . ."

"You're curious." He tickled the black-and-white cat behind the ear, and the creature purred. "If you weren't, you'd have called the police by now. I took nothing. You can search me if you want."

He spread his arms, warming when her gaze flicked up and down him. She was a beautiful woman, and part of the reason he wanted to wait to tell her was so he'd have the chance to draw this out. His body throbbed with need, and his cock hadn't deflated since she'd walked into the room.

He knew damn well why he wanted to see her again, and the knowledge both excited and depressed him. She found him attractive, and she'd find him even more attractive tonight. It was an even bet that she'd want his hands on her, the compulsion affecting her, too. He looked forward to it and at the same time resisted it.

He suddenly wished with all his heart that with her, this could be real. But the thought only brought more depression, because he couldn't trust the voices of his heart.

"Come by if you're interested." He shrugged. "I have to go before Andreas rampages Manhattan looking for me."

A rampaging Andreas was bad. The man had a temper, and he'd give them away if he wasn't careful.

"I'll have to let you out."

The grates were still firmly over the doors. Patricia unlocked a box with a small key and punched a code. There was a loud click, then she opened the door and slid the grating back a few feet for him.

Nico turned sideways so he could slide through, letting himself brush against her as he went. She had a lovely, soft body, and he wanted to bury his face in her riotously curling hair and breathe her in. He craved it with an intensity that wasn't quite normal.

Outside, Manhattan was stirring. Early-morning commuters poured up from the subways and spilled across the sidewalks in a sea of black and dark gray. He had to go.

He brushed the tip of her nose with his fingertip and slid all the way out the door. She rattled the grating closed behind him without saying good-bye.

Nico chuckled as he moved into the crowd. Their relationship was going to hurt like hell when it was over, but first, it would be very, very good. He'd suck as much as he could from that and pretend it wouldn't break his heart when she was finished with him.

~ ~ ~

PATRICIA arrived at Andre's at nine, right before it opened.

Andre's was a private club, its memberships sold online and through other businesses. Patricia had debated all day whether to go, but in the end she knew she'd not be able to pass up the opportunity to see her winged man again. Nico had hit it right when he told her she was too curious to resist.

She still had no idea what he'd been looking for. She'd searched her record books for whatever valuable items she'd moved in the past few weeks but couldn't decide which one he'd come to find: the eighteenth-century writing desk; the ostracon, a small slab of limestone with Egyptian hieroglyphs on it; the carnelian earrings belonging to one of Queen Victoria's daughters; or the bone-handled letter opener from 1675? She'd found buyers for all of them from her list of people who paid her to keep an eye out for "special somethings."

Patricia handed Nico's card to the doorman, telling him that Nico had invited her. The women in line behind her wore tight dresses, which showed mountains of cleavage, and sharp-heeled shoes, which bared miles of legs.

In her neat black pants and blouse, Patricia felt woefully out of place. She'd put in antique earrings and a cobwebby antique necklace that earned a few envious glances, but the ladies behind her were surprised when the doorman nodded gruffly and opened the door half a foot so she could slide inside.

A second doorman, wearing an Andre's T-shirt and sporting a phone on his ear, took the card and jerked his head for Patricia to follow him. He led her through the dark club and up a flight of stairs. At the top he touched a buzzer beside a door and waited until the door clicked open. The doorman gestured her inside but didn't follow her in.

Nico waited for her at the end of a plush-carpeted hallway. His Andre's T-shirt was crisp and clean, and there was no sign of his wings. He'd obviously shaved since their last encounter, and his dark hair was damp from a shower.

He wore black jeans instead of blue, and sandals. Patricia had never liked sandals on a man, but she decided she'd make an exception for Nico. They seemed to go with him, giving him the aura of an ancient god.

He smiled at her, his dark eyes promising. "Hello, Patricia. I'm glad you came."

He took her hand and led her into the room behind him.

She'd expected an office but found a suite. It had a living room done in trendy minimalist decor and a small kitchen tucked behind a shining granite counter. Through an open double door she saw a bedroom with an iron-poled canopy bed and cubelike shelves.

A man came in from the bedroom, also wearing an Andre's T-shirt. He was not quite as tall as Nico, but his body was as well built and bulging with muscle. He had mottled black-and-white hair and eyes of clear ice blue. While Nico's eyes could melt a woman like ice cream on a hot sidewalk, this man's eyes chilled her through.

The one thing the two men had in common, besides powerful auras, was the thin gold chain around their necks.

The two of them looked completely wrong in this room, which must have been decorated before they moved in. This suite was for men in expensive corporate suits, not these beautiful males with auras of wild magic.

"This is Andreas," Nico told her. "At least that's what he calls himself. Andreas, Patricia Lake of Lake Antiques."

Andreas swept Patricia a dismissive glance and started talking to Nico like she wasn't there. "Does she have it?"

"Not anymore."

"Have what?" Patricia asked. "I can't help you find something if I don't know what you're looking for."

"The ostracon." Andreas fixed her with a chill blue gaze that had fiery rage behind it. "Give it to me, and Nico and I will fulfill your deepest desires. Anything sexual you've ever wanted to try, we'll do it for you."

2

PATRICIA blinked. "Oh, is that all?"

She thought of Nico's wings feathering around her while she had helped unwind the bandage, the warm, black silkiness against her skin. Her heart started to pound. She imagined his wings cuddling her naked body, the satinlike feathers touching every part of her.

Andreas stepped in front of her, dissolving the heady vision. Andreas smelled of male musk and spice, a little like Nico, but while Nico was enticing warmth, Andreas radiated danger.

"You know what we're looking for."

"Of course I do. The ostracon with the inscription from the Ptolemaic period. Not as good as Eighteenth Dynasty, and not very important historically, but my client wanted it."

"What client?" Andreas demanded.

"The one I sold it to."

"So, get it back from him."

Patricia's irritation rose, covering her uneasiness. "I can't just ask for it back. There is such a thing as client loyalty, and besides, I can't afford it."

"We will pay for it."

"That's not the point."

Andreas threw a glance at Nico, who watched with his arms folded. "Nico, leave us alone."

"No." Nico seated himself in an elegant armchair, drawing his knee up and planting his sandal firmly on the upholstery. He smiled, but his dark eyes were watchful.

Andreas's icelike gaze returned to Patricia. "I will pay you three times what your client paid for it."

"Really? Why do you want it so bad?"

"Will you get it back for me?"

"I don't know." Patricia folded her arms, pretending his stare didn't unnerve her. "I'm intrigued now. What is it about this ostracon that's so special?"

Andreas glared at her another moment, then swiveled away. "Nico."

Nico remained folded in the chair. "She's obviously not going to be moved by money."

"All humans will do anything for money," Andreas returned. "Especially their women."

"Insulting me isn't the best way to get me to help you," Patricia said. "I know the market; I can find another good piece for you at a decent price. As long as it's legit. I don't deal in stolen antiquities. But if you're going to be an asshole, forget it." She paused. "And anyway, what do you mean by *all humans*? I know Nico's not human, and you don't feel like it, either. Are you a winged creature, too?"

Andreas scowled at Nico. "How does she know?"

Nico shrugged. "She caught me with my wings down. It doesn't matter—she understands. She's magical."

"Magical, how?"

"Psychic," Patricia cut in. The way Andreas talked to Nico like she wasn't there annoyed her. "I can see the auras of people. And things—I'm best with objects. The psychic clutter that inanimate objects pick up over lifetimes is amazing."

Nico unfolded himself from the chair and came to her as Andreas's gaze locked on Patricia again. They both knew how to pin with a stare. Patricia held her ground, determined not to back away from either of them.

Her heartbeat sped, and not entirely with fear. Having two very muscular, large males hemming her in wasn't such a bad thing. Good cop, bad cop, or good winged man, bad . . . whatever. She could have fun dreams about this.

"What psychic clutter do you see on us?" Nico asked her.

Patricia looked at him, debating whether to lower her shields. She'd learned as a child to erect barriers between herself and what came to her, or she'd be so bombarded she couldn't function. When she'd found Nico this morning, she'd kept her barriers firmly in place, sensing he had enough psychic energy to knock her across the room.

Now she slowly lowered her shields. If she was careful and controlled it, she could look without hurting herself.

The white-hot blaze of Nico's aura sent her staggering. It was bright with awful power, stronger than anything she'd ever seen. She felt herself falling, then someone caught her—Andreas, she thought dimly.

Andreas's aura struck her from the other side. It was as strong as Nico's, but purple instead of white, sizzling with strength. Their collective power punched her like fists, and she screamed.

Nico's arms came around her, his body so bright and savagely beautiful that she had to squeeze her eyes shut. He cupped her cheek, his voice insistent and urgent.

"Block it out, sweetheart. You aren't made to stand this. Shut us out."

Patricia collapsed in on herself, huddling into a ball supported by Nico's strong arm. She instinctively started the exercises she'd learned as a child, chanting a string of sounds and picturing a screen rising to mute the auras around her.

Gradually the light died away, the wild purple hue of Andreas and the incandescent white of Nico dimming until they became hard-bodied males and nothing more. She drew a sharp breath that hurt her lungs, realizing she'd stopped breathing altogether.

Nico traced her cheek. "Are you all right?"

"I don't know." She gulped. "I've never seen anything like that in my entire life. What the hell *are* you two?"

"Trapped," Andreas said, suddenly somber. "Enslaved." He touched the chain around his neck. "That's what we are, Patricia Lake. Slaves who can't go home."

~ ~ ~

NICO spread the magazine open on the table, standing behind Patricia as she leaned over it. Her hair smelled like honey. The compulsion of the spell was making him crazy with desire, and he wondered if it was driving Andreas crazy, too. The spell would embrace the one Patricia was first attracted to, but a woman could be equally attracted to both of them.

Patricia touched the photograph of the ostracon he showed her. An ostracon was nothing more than a piece of stone or pottery with ancient writing on it. Egyptians and ancient Greeks had used them like modern people would use paper tablets. Many contained jottings of day-to-day notes by scribes and priests, or even school-boys' lessons.

The photograph's caption said the entire thing was about one foot wide by two feet high. The magazine showed one close-up section of it, and Nico could read what looked like a spell that might mean his and Andreas's freedom. Or it might mean nothing at all.

Patricia nodded. "This is the one I had. I bought it from a dealer here in New York. It was offered on the market by the Egyptian Museum in Cairo, not for very much, so it couldn't have been that important."

"I don't care where it came from," Andreas said. "I only care where it is now."

"But where things come from can tell us a lot about them," Patricia argued. "Objects retain impressions of where they've been and who touched them."

"And what did this tell you?" Nico asked.

"That it was old." Patricia looked up at him, those aquamarine eyes catching him. "Authentic, not a copy. From the Hellenistic period in Egypt—after Alexander the Great and before Cleopatra. It's fairly ordinary—as far as ancient ostracons go. I didn't feel it trying to give me a strange or urgent message or anything."

Andreas shoved himself away from the table. "We didn't need you to tell us this. It's in the article."

Patricia ignored him. "Anyway, a dealer bought it and brought it to New York. I thought it was interesting, so I picked it up."

"And sold it again," Nico prompted.

"I have a buyer interested in Egyptian artifacts. So yes, I sold it."

"To a person you keep secret," Andreas growled.

Patricia made a noise of exasperation. "If you're so anxious, I can ask my customer if you can at least look at it, as long as you don't do anything obnoxious, like try to steal it. If you're nothing but powerfully magical antiquities thieves, I'm not letting you anywhere near it."

Andreas's lip curled, but he subsided.

"If you can arrange such a thing, we'd be eternally grateful." Nico smiled, warming when her eyes softened for him. Andreas liked to dominate, to take, and make a woman enjoy his taking. Nico, on the other hand, very much enjoyed giving.

"I'll make phone calls tomorrow," Patricia promised.

Andreas grabbed a cell phone from the kitchen counter and shoved it at her. "Call now."

To Nico's delight, Patricia met Andreas's belligerent look with one of her own. "It's too late, and my client's elderly. Tomorrow."

The growl that came out of Andreas's mouth was primal. Nico expected the man to morph to his true self and force Patricia to do what he wanted, but Andreas clenched his hands and turned away.

"Is he always like this?" Patricia asked Nico, loud enough for Andreas to hear.

"You have no idea." Nico winked at her. "But sometimes he's a pussycat."

Andreas sent him a furious look. "Why the hell did I have to get stuck through the ages with you?"

"Fantastic luck," Nico answered.

Andreas's growl escalated, his fists tightening. But Andreas wasn't stupid. They needed to find the answer, and as volatile as Andreas could be, he'd not jeopardize things when they were so close. His dominant tendencies sometimes got in the way, but he'd learned—painfully—how to control himself.

"I'm going downstairs," Andreas said and slammed out of the room.

Patricia watched him go. "You have interesting friends."

"That's one word for him."

"Um . . . I have to ask. Are you two . . . ?" She looked embarrassed.

"Lovers? No, sweetheart. Old, old friends who got stuck with each other, is all. Why?" He grinned. "Were you thinking about it?"

Her furious blush told him he was right. Women they'd pleasured together had said what would please them most was watching Nico and Andreas naked on a bed together. Sometimes they obliged.

The two of them shared a friendship that spanned eons, and they could touch each other when they needed to without worry.

Patricia gazed at Nico in a gratifying way. He imagined her bare against his body, her sleek curls rubbing his skin. He'd like her looking at him like that while he lay flat on the bed with her straddling him. He could reach up and catch her breasts in his hands, lift his head to suckle her.

"Can I see your wings again?" she asked.

Nico's body tightened as her blue green eyes flicked over it. His cock began its little dance of hope. "My wings?"

She twirled one of her curls around her finger, her eyes soft and so damn sexy. "I want to make sure I didn't imagine them."

"Seeing my true aura didn't convince you?"

Patricia shivered. They'd had to feed her two cups of coffee before she calmed down after letting herself look at their naked auras. Nico had never met a human being who *could* see them, which made Patricia even more interesting.

"That's different. The wings were tangible; I felt them." She gave him a wistful smile. "I'd like to see them again."

Nico grinned, his cock dancing even faster, and moved to the center of the room to strip off his T-shirt.

He often let his wings free when he was upstairs, to keep from cramping, but never before had unfurling them been tinged with erotic excitement. It was almost like she'd asked him to do a strip-tease.

He tossed away the shirt and put his hands on his hips, determined to give her a show. He made a soft sound as his shoulder blades gave a jerk that was always slightly painful but somehow a pleasure, like the moment before climax.

The wings rippled from his shoulders, spreading in black smoothness out from his body. They were huge, curving up over his head and down his back to curl at his feet.

He stretched, loving the warmth of extending the tendons to the very tips. He couldn't fly much in Manhattan—too much risk of being seen—and he loved any opportunity to spread himself wide.

Patricia's red lips parted. "They're beautiful."

Her voice rasped, low and sweet, not releasing any tension from his erection.

He curved the wings in an arc in front his body. "So come here and touch them."

In wonder, Patricia left her chair and came to him. He tickled her cheek playfully, and she laughed, burying herself in the crush of his feathers. She rubbed her face against them, humming in her throat as she enjoyed the sleekness on her skin.

Her cheeks flushed, her nipples pebble-tight against her blouse. "They feel so good."

"You aren't bad yourself."

Nico slid his arms around her and gently drew her into his complete embrace. She came against him without a struggle, still buried in the warmth of his wings.

"My cats are fascinated with you," she said. "They think you're some kind of bird man."

"No." He cupped her face in his hands and brushed his thumbs over her cheekbones. "Some kind of god-man."

She gave him a startled look. As her lips formed a question, he leaned in and kissed them.

He kissed her slowly, sliding his tongue into the warm wetness of her mouth. She made a noise in her throat, her breath hot on his lips, then she opened to him like a flower.

Something jolted across his skin, a spark of awareness, an incredible joy. His heart beat faster, and a trickle of sweat moved from his shoulder blades down his spine to his ass.

With the spark of joy came sorrow. The curse had fully ignited. It was going to be good, so good. And then it would hurt like hell.

The kiss went on, her lips moving while she wove her fingers through his sensitive feathers. She was exploring him, getting to know him. He cupped her head in his hand, her warm curls spilling over his fingers.

"My," she murmured.

He'd like it better if she'd said *Mine*.

But she couldn't, of course. Part of the enslavement was that Nico and Andreas could give plenty of physical enjoyment, but they'd receive no love in return. No matter how much he delighted Patricia, she would never fall in love with him. In the end, she'd walk away and forget him, and Nico's heart would break.

He pressed the thought aside. "Do you like to dance?"

She blinked. "Dance?"

"Downstairs. This is a club."

"Oh." She looked like she'd forgotten. "No—thanks. I haven't danced in a long time, and I'm not really dressed for it."

Her face was red, and she wouldn't meet his eyes. Nico thought about the women who usually came here to ogle him and Andreas, dresses cupping their asses and mile-high shoes. Patricia didn't think she could compete, but she was wrong. She'd look fantastic in a tight skirt, but even more important, she'd look fantastic out of it.

"Sex, then?" he offered.

Patricia backed up quickly, only to be hemmed in by his wings. "You and Andreas toss out that offer casually enough."

Nico shrugged, pretending like hell that his entire body wasn't burning with need. "We'd be good together."

"I didn't come here to get laid."

He caressed her back with his feathers, softening his voice. "I'd make it so good for you, Patricia."

Her rapid breathing told him she believed him. But she firmly parted his wings and stepped away from him. "No."

She puzzled him. He knew she wanted him; her body gave all the signs. Yet she hugged her arms across her chest and turned away as though stopping herself from accepting.

"Are you going to throw me out now?" she asked in a hard voice. "Because I didn't fling myself on your bed and squeal, 'Yes, take me'?"

"No. You can stay as long as you like."

"Good, because I'd like to ask you more questions."

Nico felt a twinge of disquiet. The Dyons for the most part simply watched, but if they thought Patricia knew too much or was trying to help Andreas and him, they might attack, as had the one when Nico searched the antique store. Dyons couldn't kill Nico and Andreas, but they could kill anyone helping them.

Nico crossed his wings behind his back, letting the feel of them calm him. "What questions?"

"Like how did you get into my store?"

"I told you. Through the keyhole."

"I have dead bolts. Keyholes don't go all the way through these days."

"Don't they?" If Nico concentrated, he could slide through spaces that ordinary humans couldn't find.

She changed the subject. "Why is this ostracon so important? It's not very big, and it's not important historically, even as old as it is."

Now they were moving into dangerous territory. "Andreas and I want a look at it."

"Meaning you aren't going to tell me."

"There are some things it's safer not to know."

She chewed her lip. "Is it some key to a secret dimension or something? Where the bird gods live?"

Nico burst out laughing. "No. It's an ordinary piece of writing, like you said."

"You wouldn't be interested in it if it were ordinary."

He had to concede the point. "I just want to look at it. No harm to your elderly client."

"What about Andreas? Will he look at it without harm?"

Patricia couldn't know how much his senses were singing with her in the room. She wasn't the only one who could see auras. Hers was brilliant red and blue and smelled fresh, like crisp autumn wind. He'd love to spend a year in bed with her with them slowly getting to know each other. It would be a joy to teach her.

"Andreas isn't so bad once you get to know him," Nico said. "No, wait; yes, he is. But he doesn't harm innocents."

"Does he have wings, too?"

"No. I'd tell you what he is, but I promised I wouldn't."

Patricia subsided, still chewing her lip. The action made her mouth all the more red and kissable. "I guess I'll just have to find out for myself."

He sobered. "Be careful with Andreas, love. He won't harm an innocent, but it's not good to get in his way."

"Do you get in his way?"

"All the time." Nico lifted his wings overhead and reluctantly slid them back into place, letting the tattoo cover his back. He moved his shoulder blades as he adjusted his balance, then reached for his black T-shirt.

"If you don't want to dance, let me walk you home," he said, pulling on the shirt. "The streets are dangerous at night."

Patricia looked him up and down, her gaze lingering on his torso. "I have the feeling that I've met the most dangerous things in the city tonight: you and Andreas."

He let himself smile as he came to her and brushed a kiss over her lips. "You just might be right."

3

THE woman who'd purchased the ostracon for her eclectic collection was one of Patricia's regulars, an elderly lady who lived in an airy marble and gilt apartment on the Upper East Side. She'd outlived two husbands, was vastly wealthy, and loved to collect antiquities.

Patricia called her in the morning after a restless night thinking about Nico. When he'd gathered her in his feathers and kissed her, she thought she'd go into orgasmic shock.

He had a strong mouth and knew how to kiss. She'd felt the swell of his arousal even as she'd pulled away from him, knowing she was going too fast.

When he'd offered sex as casually as he'd offered to take her downstairs to dance, she'd felt a stab of disappointment. Maybe she was old-fashioned, maybe she expected too much, but she wanted sex to be special. Not *We have a few hours, so how about it?* She didn't want a fuck buddy. She wanted it to mean something.

So what did high-minded Patricia dream about all night? Nico in her bed, his wings spread so she could rub her naked body all over them.

In reality, Nico had walked her home, lightly kissed her good night, and left as soon as she'd entered her store. In her dreams, he'd carried her upstairs, stripped off her clothes, and laid her on the bed, his cock high and ready for her.

A big, beautiful cock, too, straight and tall, dark and rampant. Patricia's secret stash of nude male photos always included the cock; she loved looking at them. Asses were good, but there was something about a swollen I'm-here-for-you cock that always sent her over the edge.

She was dying to see Nico's, wanting to find out if the reality matched what she'd felt behind the zipper of his jeans.

Patricia tried to calm her libido by talking to Mrs. Penworth. Mrs. Penworth looked and sounded like a sweet, little old lady, but some of the stories she told of her years as a World War II army nurse made Patricia realize she'd had one hell of a past. Mrs. Penworth always got a wicked twinkle in her eyes when she talked about her wild days.

"Of course, dear, bring your friends by. I'll have Myrtle make drinks, and we'll have a little happy hour. Myrtle likes it when we have friends for drinks." Myrtle was the housekeeper who'd lived with Mrs. Penworth for forty years.

Patricia hung up, sensing that Mrs. Penworth would enjoy Nico. She wasn't so sure about Andreas, and she hoped Nico could keep the belligerent man in line.

The bell on the store's door jingled, and when Patricia came out of the back, a man was leaning his fists on the counter, studying Victorian brooches inside the glass case. He was strong and muscular, much like Andreas and Nico, and wore faded jeans and a sweatshirt. He'd braided his white blond hair into a tail that hung to the middle of his back.

When the man looked up at her, Patricia couldn't hold back a gasp. His eyes were wrong. She couldn't put her finger on why, as she stared into the yellowish gaze; then she realized his pupils were slits, vertical like a cat's—or a snake's.

Speaking of her cats, they'd vanished. She remembered their intense interest in Nico, and even with ordinary customers, they'd come out to investigate, but this time they'd deserted her.

She felt the man's aura tapping at her shields, and she refused to lower them. If he was anything like Nico and Andreas, his energy would knock her over.

"Where is the ostracon?" He spoke in a thin voice, almost hissing, nothing like Nico's warm baritone or Andreas's gravelly growl.

"The one from the museum in Cairo?" she asked as though unconcerned. "I'm afraid I sold it, but I can take your name in case I come across another one—"

How he got to her so fast, she never knew. One moment he was by the jewelry display, the next he had lifted her high and slammed her back onto the counter. His breath was foul, his slits of eyes terrifying.

"Retrieve it. Destroy it."

"Destroy it?" she gasped. "An artifact? I don't think so."

"You will." He shook her, and her head jounced painfully against the glass. "You must not interfere."

"Interfere with what?"

"She will punish you. Her wrath can reach across centuries."

"Who is *she*?"

Her heart pounded in fear. She couldn't reach the phone or the alarm button behind the cash register. This man was strong enough to kill her with his bare hands, and there was nothing she could do about it.

A low growl rumbled through the store. The sound went on and on, building in intensity, like a wild beast barely containing itself. In the back, her two cats started to howl.

Something blurred on her right, and the blond man dropped Patricia as a huge wild cat barreled at him. Patricia screamed and dove aside as the man and cat tumbled across the counter, everything left on it slamming to the floor in a heartbreaking crash.

Patricia got to her feet, wondering what the hell to do. Call the police? Animal control? Hose the cat down with the fire extinguisher? But the big cat had just saved her life, and she knew it. Police would shoot the beautiful thing dead or haul it away God knew where.

Red Kitty and Isis came bounding out of the back room, still howling. They danced around the fight, watching avidly, for all the world like they were cheering the big cat on.

The blond man managed to roll away from the cat. His clothes were in tatters, his shredded skin bloody. He hissed like a snake, then suddenly he became a thin column of smoke and disappeared altogether.

Patricia blinked in shock. But she didn't have much time to relax, because the wild cat halted in front of her, fixing his gaze on her from three paces away.

He was a snow leopard. His fur was white with mottled black spots, his eyes ice blue. His body was heavy, shoulders and haunches rippling with muscle, paws sporting razor-sharp claws.

"Nice kitty," Patricia tried.

Isis stalked around her and walked right underneath the leopard, rubbing her head against him as she went. The leopard glanced once at the cat, then back at Patricia. They faced off, woman to leopard, then the leopard yawned. His huge red mouth was lined with pointed teeth, his lips peeling back to reveal every one of them.

The leopard lay on her carpet with a whuff of breath. Isis butted his shoulder, and he butted her gently back before starting to groom his blood-smeared paws.

"Don't be afraid, Patricia."

Patricia bit back a shriek as Nico's black wings came around her. "Damn it. Don't you use doors like the rest of us?"

"Are you all right?"

"I don't know if you've noticed this, but there's a leopard licking its toes three feet in front of me."

Nico skimmed his warm lips over her ear, and she started to calm in spite of everything. "I asked him to come," he murmured. "We sensed the danger."

The leopard gazed up at her with cool blue eyes, and Patricia realized in shock where she'd seen that look before.

"He's Andreas."

Nico's hot breath touched her neck. "It is. You're the only human I've met who's been able to make the connection."

Patricia let a tiny part of her psi ability touch the leopard and saw the same purple-hued aura she'd seen at the club.

"He's a . . ." She groped for words. "A were–snow leopard?"

Nico chuckled. "Not exactly. Divinity trapped, like I am."

"Andreas said that last night, that you were enslaved. What does that mean? And who was the blond man?"

"A Dyon."

"What's a Dyon?"

Andreas, still in leopard form, growled softly at Nico.

"We've dragged her into it," Nico said. "She needs to know."

"Tell me," she said softly. "Please."

"Dyons are minions of Hera. Powerful. Old. We won't let them hurt you."

Patricia threaded her fingers through his feathers, loving the warm feel against her arms. "Why should they want to?"

"They want to keep us from breaking free, so they'll hunt any who try to help us. That is why, once we see the ostracon, we'll leave you well alone."

Patricia felt a strange compulsion to grab him and hold on tight, to tell him he wasn't allowed to leave. She was just starting to get to know her winged man and the were-leopard and their incredible auras, and she definitely wanted to know Nico better.

"Don't go," she felt her lips say.

Nico's hands skimmed her waist, then he gently kneaded her abdomen, circling with his knuckles. "We have to, to keep you safe. But before we go, maybe I could give you something to remember us by?" The sensuality in his voice let her know exactly what he meant.

This was all wrong. She'd just survived an attack by a strange man with snakelike eyes and had been rescued by a leopard who turned out to be Andreas, and all she wanted to do was take Nico to bed. No calling the police to report the break-in, no demands to know exactly what was going on. What she needed most right now was to be with Nico.

She gently disentangled herself from his wings, walked shakily to the front door, and turned over the Closed sign. She snicked the locks shut and pulled down the blinds against the crowd outside.

"All right," she said, holding out her hand to Nico.

~ ~ ~

NICO followed Patricia up her carpeted stairs to her apartment, leaving Andreas below to guard. The big cat sneered as Nico went.

Nico's heart beat swiftly, his blood already hot. He couldn't have Patricia for always, but he could at least have this. He'd give her the greatest pleasure she could handle, and when he was far away, he'd remember it, live it again in his dreams.

Patricia's apartment was tiny: a compact kitchen, a bedroom big enough for a bed, and a full bathroom grouped around a small living room. Nico stopped her in the middle of the living room and drew her close for a kiss. Her mouth tasted good, like fire and spice, and he licked his way around her lips.

Her hands tightened on his shoulders. "Nico."

"Mmm?"

"I didn't bring you up here for sex."

Yes, she had. Her body wanted it; he could feel it under his hands. She lied. "What, then?"

"I think you owe it to me to tell me what's going on. I find you wounded in my store, then this Dyon person tries to beat the whereabouts of the ostracon out of me, and now Andreas is a leopard. I'd like some explanations, please."

Nico leaned his forehead against hers. His body was on fire, everything pushing him to take her. He would have to soon, or the pain would become searing, crushing agony.

"Patricia, you don't need to be in this. Andreas and I have dealt with Dyons before, and we'll deal with them again. Without you getting hurt."

She gave him a grim smile. "Too late for that. Do you think this Dyon thing will leave me alone because you don't tell me anything?"

No, Nico really didn't. But he and Andreas might be able to draw him off. Once they'd seen the inscription, they could leave Patricia alone.

He threaded his hands through her hair and brought his wings around to enclose her. "Patricia, I need to touch you."

She put her fingers on his lips. "Not until you explain."

"No, I mean I *need* to touch you." His skin was burning, his cock so tight it hurt. "If I don't—" He broke off, his heart squeezing. "Let's just say it won't be pretty."

She gave him a speculative look. "Is that the line you use on all the women whose stores you break into?"

"Feel me." Nico took her palm and pressed it to his cheek.

She flinched when she felt his burning skin. "What's wrong? Are you feverish?"

"No. Cursed."

"I don't understand."

"Let me touch you, Patricia. Let me spread you and pleasure you—I have to. I need to." His heart was banging so hard it was making him sick. "Please."

"Why?" She pushed away from him, and he had to let her go. He couldn't force her. If she didn't want him, then he'd simply have to suffer.

"It's why we need to look at the ostracon. The writing on it could help us break the curse."

She looked bewildered but concerned. "What curse?"

He loved her eyes. That blue green like the sun-dappled sea drew him to her. He wanted to kiss her eyelids, lick his way to her throat, part her blouse, and arouse her with his tongue.

He kissed her palm and pressed it to his chest. "The pain won't go away if you don't let me fuck you."

She might not believe his words, but she must feel his heart beating like a piston, his skin on fire, see the pain in his eyes.

"Why are you—why do you feel like this?" she asked.

"The mother of the gods cursed us. Andreas and me. We must pleasure a woman like her slave, or we burn up. The curse won't kill us, but it will make us wish we were dead."

Patricia's eyes rounded in horror. "Why would someone do that to you?"

He tried to shrug, but his body hurt. "Some goddesses can take righteous indignation a long way."

"And I can help you by letting you give me sexual pleasure?"

He nodded, his throat too tight for speech.

She let her fingers soften on his lips. "All right, but if this is the worst pickup line since pickup lines were invented . . ."

His heart sped in hope. "You'll let me pleasure you?"

She smiled slightly. "Yes."

Nico let out his breath, some of the pain dissipating. "Thank all the gods. Put yourself in my hands, Patricia. You won't regret it."

~ ~ ~

SHE already regretted it. Not because she was about to have sex with someone she barely knew but because she already felt a pull toward him in her heart. They'd have a good time in bed, then he'd go, and she'd be left bereft.

That line in Shakespeare—"Better to have loved and lost than never to have loved at all"—was debatable. Wasn't it better to live pain free than break your heart over someone who didn't love you back?

Nico pulled her closer, his feathery wings enclosing her in warmth. The fear she'd seen in his eyes fled as he bent to kiss her.

She'd seen animals' eyes go fixed and distant when they were in pain, and she'd seen exactly the same look in Nico's just now. The pain tapped her psychic shields, pressing until she feared to lower them even slightly. If she could sense that black taint through her strongest shields, his pain must be incredible. And new. She hadn't seen it before, not when she'd first met him, not when she'd looked fully at him and Andreas.

The curse? If she could help banish it, well then, who was she to hold back?

He opened her mouth with lavish strokes. He tasted like musk and spice, his teeth sharp points on her lips. His palm slid to cup her buttocks, and the tips of his wings slid under her shirt, pushing it open and up.

The feel of the feathers on her bare skin was strange and incredibly erotic. Nico smiled as he pushed away her shirt and pulled her against his bare chest.

He unlocked her bra with his fingers and pushed it off. Still twining her in feathers, he backed up a step and looked down at her.

Warmth pooled in her belly as his gaze turned appreciative. He cupped her breasts in his hands, pushing them higher, the nipples tight and dark.

"Hold them for me," he said.

She gave him a startled look, then slid her hands under her breasts as he let go. The skin beneath them was hot, the globes heavy on her palms.

"Flick your thumbs over the nipples," he said, watching her. "Feel how hard and tight they are."

Patricia tentatively brushed her thumbs over the points, surprised at the fiery tingle that shot through her.

"Haven't you ever touched yourself before?" Nico asked her.

"Not on purpose," she said breathlessly. "Not like this."

"Really? How do you release yourself?"

"I don't. I just live with it."

Nico's perplexed look turned sly, and her heart beat faster. "I think we'll have to change that."

"Will we?" She let her hands go slack as a shiver went through her.

"We will. Keep touching your breasts, Patricia. Don't stop until I tell you to."

She had to be out of her mind. Nico was an otherworldly creature, not even a man, and she was letting him kiss her and touch her with *feathers* and give her commands.

But what the hell? When would she get the opportunity to play with a man with wings again?

"Unzip your pants," Nico said. "Pull them down for me."

Patricia's hand went to the button of her fly, but she hesitated. "I didn't lock the door to the stairs. What if Andreas comes up here?"

"What if he does?"

Patricia gulped. Right now Andreas was a leopard, but even so, the thought of him catching them, watching her strip and touch herself for Nico . . .

Excited her like crazy. Her hands warmed as she unzipped her jeans and pushed them down.

Nico grinned. "Now you're understanding."

She stood in front of him in nothing but her panties, thankful she'd put on cute blue-and-pink-striped bikinis this morning.

"Are you wet, Patricia?"

If she hadn't been before, she would be now. Patricia could feel the heat between her legs, pretty sure her panties were soaked with it. "I think so."

"I want you to know so. Put your fingers on your pussy, and tell me if it's wet."

4

Patricia's nipples were tight, dark points on her pale breasts. She was so beautiful, all luscious, compact curves, taut belly, sleek skin. Her curly hair escaped the ponytail she'd scraped it into, and blond ringlets cascaded down her back. Her legs were long, slim, and strong, the remnants of a summer tan staining her lower legs light golden brown. Her upper thighs were pale in contrast, showing that she liked to wear shorts.

She watched him with her lovely green blue eyes as she slowly dipped her fingers into the slash of blue-and-pink-striped panties.

"Go on," Nico said, standing back to watch. "Tell me exactly how wet you are."

Patricia made a faint noise as she moved her fingertip around. "Pretty wet."

"Show me."

She withdrew her finger, which glistened with moisture. Nico crossed the space between them and lifted her fingers to his mouth.

Delicious Patricia. Nico savored her, the smell of her musk strong. He could drink her all day.

He made himself release her hand. "Show me."

She gave him a shy look, but her eyes sparkled with excitement. She slid her underwear all the way off, then stood with her legs spread a little. The triangle of hair at her thighs was a darker blond but just as curly as the hair on her head.

"You don't shave yourself?"

She shook her head. "I never think about it."

Nico dipped his hand to her curls, liking how they caught at his fingertips. "I think I like that you don't."

He backed away again, knowing he wasn't here to touch this time; he was here to watch.

"Put your fingers on either side of your clit," he instructed. "Spread yourself out."

Patricia hesitated a moment, then she moved the first two fingers of her left hand between her legs.

Nico pulled a chair from the desk and sat down, making himself comfortable. Her fingers spread her so he could see the lips, pink and moist, peeking out from her thatch of hair. Her clit was a little bud, swelling slightly under the attention it was getting. Nico itched to get to his knees and flick his tongue over it, but he restrained himself.

"Touch yourself," he said in a soft voice. "Explore. Your body is beautiful, and you shouldn't ignore it."

"Inhibitions drilled into me from childhood." She let out a breathy sigh as her middle finger sank down to find her clit. "Nice girls didn't masturbate. Or even think about sex."

"I don't believe you never thought about sex."

"Of course I thought about it." Her mouth relaxed as she rocked her finger on her hood. "Mmmm. But I never followed up. I almost got married. Then I had a long-term boyfriend after that. I thought I didn't need to learn to please myself."

Interesting. He wondered what had called off the wedding, and where the long-term lover was now.

He resisted going to her and snaking his fingers in to join hers. She'd be moist and hot, swelling as she relaxed. "Press your thighs together over your fingers. Squeeze yourself."

Patricia put her feet together. Her muscles contracted, and she let out a little yelp of pleasure.

"That's it. Now, dip that finger inside you. Feel the wetness, draw it out to smooth over your clit."

"It's very wet."

"I can see that."

Her curls glistened in the sunlight from the one window. She stroked her fingers in and out, brow furrowing as she explored and tested herself.

Nico guided her with his voice, not letting her stop. Her breath came faster, her face relaxing, eyes drifting closed. As she became more used to what she did to herself, her hips moved, back arching.

"I'm thinking about you," she murmured. "How beautiful you looked lying in my shop downstairs with your wings—no, how totally *hot* you looked. I didn't know who or what you were, but I wanted to look at you . . . and touch you."

He leaned forward, watching her intently. "You bandaged my wing for me."

"You were hurt, and I wanted to help. But I wanted to touch you."

His heart beat thick and fast. "If that's what you want, I'm here to please you."

Her hips lifted, her hand squeezing tighter between her legs. He watched her wrist work as she rubbed back and forth.

"Touch me, now," she begged. "With your wings."

Nico felt a moment of surprise, then he slid off the chair and spread his wings, filling the little room with their sleek blackness.

"Yes," Patricia moaned. "Touch me. Cover me with them."

Nico came to her and slid them around her body, loving the feel of her nakedness. Patricia's hand worked, her body learning what she liked.

Nico stroked across her lower abdomen, fingers caressing and kneading. Her muscles tightened and pulsed, and he could feel the heat from her pussy without even touching it.

He stilled his hands and stroked his feathers down over her clit, twining them with her fingers, loving the wetness he found between her legs.

As his feathers penetrated her, she went crazy rubbing herself on his wings, and Nico clenched his fists to keep from tossing her to the floor and simply fucking her.

As much as he wanted to slide right into the pussy she'd opened for him and release deep inside her, he wouldn't do it. This was her pleasure, not his.

He could feel his control snapping, waking the famous wildness that had made women both human and magical run from him in his youth. They never ran very fast, happy to be caught and trapped in Nico's black wings.

His vision went dark, the bright window blurring. He wanted Patricia. His cock hated him for not falling on her and fucking her without compassion. There was something about her that made him want to lose all control, but that was forbidden.

He held his body rigid and closed his eyes, willing himself to remain still. He needed to keep this about her, to not hurt her.

Something warm brushed his face: Patricia's lips, soft and shaking. "Thank you," she whispered.

The sweet gratitude knocked through Nico's darkness. He opened his eyes to see Patricia's trusting face next to his own, her eyes warm with her smile.

"Thank you," she said again, then her expression turned to concern. "Are you all right?"

"I will be." He pulled her close, wrapping both of them in the warmth of his wings. Her nearness, the smell of her come, and her arms around him made him want to hold her like this forever.

He heard a faint noise and looked behind her to see Andreas, still a leopard, lounging on the sofa. He must have come in while they played, the big cat making no noise.

Patricia kept her face in Nico's shoulder, not noticing. Andreas yawned once, then laid his head down on his paws, the look in his eyes one of both amusement and satisfaction.

~ ~ ~

A cab crawled uptown a few hours later and deposited them in front of Mrs. Penworth's building. They rode up in an elevator that contained a cushioned bench and a man whose job it was to push the buttons for residents and their guests.

Patricia led Nico and Andreas down a marble hallway and rang the doorbell next to the double doors at the end. Myrtle, a sixty-something, rotund woman, opened the door, beamed a wide smile, and ushered them inside. Mrs. Penworth's two-story living room was crammed full of art and collections, but tastefully. She'd been collecting for decades, and her eye was legendary.

Patricia felt Andreas's tension behind her, his aura crackling like electricity. Nico was a little calmer but not by much. He stayed a step behind her, his fingers on the small of her back, a constant reminder of what she'd done earlier that day.

She needed to stop blushing. But she'd never done that before, never touched herself while a man watched her with intense eyes. Nico had left her after soothing her for a while, not demanding she pleasure him in return or proceed to her bed and finish what they started. He'd been rock-hard, but he'd let her go, kissed her, and left her to dress.

She wanted to ask Nico so many questions about himself and this curse he talked about, but when she'd returned to the shop below, Andreas had been growling impatiently about wanting to see the ostracon, and there'd been no time for discussion. Patricia's two cats had been sprawled across Andreas's lap, the big man absently petting them as they purred up a storm.

Now Mrs. Penworth greeted Patricia by enveloping her in a diamond-flashing, lightly perfumed hug. She was about five feet tall and very thin, her eyes glittering carbuncle blue. "Patricia, it is so good to see you. And your handsome friends."

Her gaze raked over Andreas and Nico with fervent appreciation, and Patricia thought with amusement that the woman wasn't dead.

Both the men looked normal this afternoon—at least as normal as a snow leopard shifter and a winged man could look. They wore dark blue jeans and sweatshirts, Nico's black, Andreas's dark red. The gold chains around their necks winked in chance beams of sunlight.

Myrtle brought out champagne on a sterling tray and served it in cut-crystal glasses. She scooted out again and returned almost instantly with a larger tray of canapés and other hors d'oeuvres, enough for a party of several dozen people.

"I love champagne." Mrs. Penworth smiled as she took a tasting sip. "When I lived in Paris after the war, my young men got me champagne every night. Of course, it wasn't allowed—all black market stuff. We didn't care. We were celebrating being alive."

Nico nodded in understanding. "Celebrating being alive—sometimes it is the best thing to do."

Mrs. Penworth deposited the glass on the table. "Now, you came to see your ostracon, not listen to an old lady reminisce. It's right over there. Will you bring it, Myrtle?"

Myrtle, who did everything with a good-natured efficiency, walked to a table full of polished stone objects, lifted the ostracon from its stand, and carefully brought it to them.

Andreas relieved her of it and set it on the coffee table himself. The ostracon was made of limestone and carved with a mixture of hieroglyphs and hieratic writing, the "shorthand" form of Egyptian writing. Some of the hieroglyphs were so tiny they needed a magnifying glass to read them.

Patricia let her psychic mind touch it, but as before when she'd stored it in her back room, she felt nothing unusual from it. The ostracon had been excavated from a site near Alexandria about ten years ago. Two thousand years before that, a scribe had tossed it negligently into a corner, where it had lain for two millennia, silent and untouched. She felt the peace of those centuries, then its shift to the dusty jumble of the basement of the Cairo museum and the tingle of its journey to New York.

She could tell that this was a broken piece of a larger writing, some of the carved letters at the jagged edges sliced in two. Andreas ran his fingers across the tiny writing, blue eyes fixed. Nico leaned forward with him, utterly still.

"Can you read it?" Patricia asked Nico.

"Some of it."

Andreas couldn't stop touching the stone. He traced the hieroglyphs with his fingertips as though he'd force their meaning out then and there. "It doesn't make any sense."

Mrs. Penworth watched with interest. "It's the inscription you're interested in? Not the ostracon itself?"

Andreas nodded absently. Nico's breath came faster, as though the writing excited him.

"I could take photos of it," Patricia offered. "Then we can lay out the whole inscription and study it. I've learned to read some hieroglyphs, but we can get an expert in to translate the rest. I don't know any of the hieratic."

Andreas at last took his hand from the ostracon. "Yes. Do it."

The man didn't have a gracious bone in his body. "Say please," Patricia said in a sugary voice.

The glare he flashed at her was pure leopard. She half expected him to snarl and bare his teeth.

"Peace," Nico said. His silky voice soothed Patricia almost instantly. Andreas growled a little in his throat but subsided.

The ever-efficient Myrtle brought out a digital camera. Patricia set up the ostracon on the magnificent dining room table and took a series of overall photos and close-ups that could be put together later.

Mrs. Penworth watched with enthusiasm, but Andreas paced restlessly. Nico was just as impatient, but he helped hold the stone steady while Patricia worked.

It was a little unnerving to have him so close, to brush against him and catch his warm eyes on her. She wondered whether, once they had their inscription, the two of them would depart. They could easily call a university or museum themselves and find an expert to help them translate the hieroglyphs and hieratic script. They wouldn't need Patricia anymore.

She clicked the last photo and wiped her brow. Myrtle took Patricia to a computer in another room where she uploaded the photos, printed them out, and brought them back into the living room.

Mrs. Penworth looked at the sheets spread across her costly mahogany table as Patricia labeled them so they could match the close-ups to the overall picture. "What do we do now?" Mrs. Penworth asked brightly.

The doorbell chimed, and Patricia felt a prickle of unease. "Were you expecting someone?"

"No, dear."

Myrtle ducked out to answer the bell, but Nico swung around, alert. "Myrtle," he called. "Don't open the door."

Myrtle paused, looking back at Mrs. Penworth for confirmation.

"What's wrong?" Mrs. Penworth asked. She looked excited rather than afraid.

Patricia felt a twinge of the same aura she'd sensed this morning, the dark red and black swirls that surrounded the blond Dyon.

Andreas took Myrtle by the shoulders and shoved her back into the safety of the living room at the same time something slammed against the front door. Myrtle screamed. Mrs. Penworth gave a little shriek and dashed through an archway that led to the back hall.

"Dyon?" Patricia asked Nico. He nodded grimly.

Patricia took up a stance behind him as the door continued to be battered with massive force.

"That door's a hundred and fifty years old," Myrtle said, distressed. "They'll ruin it, and Mrs. Penworth will be so upset."

"Go in the back with her," Nico said sternly.

Myrtle looked at him in anguish, then back at the door. Finally, she turned and scuttled through the archway to the hall.

She met Mrs. Penworth coming out. At the same time, the door crashed open, and the Dyon who'd confronted Patricia this morning burst in. His face bore red streaks from Andreas's attack, but otherwise, he looked whole and strong.

He went right for the ostracon. Andreas tackled him, swinging the Dyon away from the table. Nico remained in front of Patricia, protective but ready to fight.

The Dyon managed to break Andreas's hold just as Mrs. Penworth stepped right in front of him, a huge revolver in her tiny fists. "Hold it right there, buster."

The Dyon stopped in sudden surprise. For a moment, no one moved. The Dyon stared at Mrs. Penworth, Nico and Andreas froze, and Myrtle watched from the archway, openmouthed.

The Dyon snarled and lunged at Mrs. Penworth. Mrs. Penworth fired four times, her body jerking backward until she toppled over. The Dyon gaped at the four slugs in his chest, then he fell to the floor, blood splattering the two hundred-year-old Turkish carpet.

"Did I get him?" the old lady asked, jumping to her feet.

"Yes," Patricia croaked. She put her hand to her head, trying to catch her breath, as she stared down at the Dyon, who lay motionless in a pool of blood. "I think you got him."

5

PATRICIA couldn't tell if the Dyon was alive or dead, and had no way of knowing whether such a being could be killed by a conventional gun. She wondered what this was going to look like to the mundane police.

The Dyon jerked, and Patricia's heart jumped into her throat. Then, as he had this morning, the Dyon dissolved into a thick column of smoke. The smoke dissipated as they watched in silence, the blood with it.

"Well," Mrs. Penworth said with a breathy sigh. "At least we don't have to worry about getting rid of the body."

Myrtle firmly removed the revolver from Mrs. Penworth's grip and emptied it of bullets. "We'll have security up here any minute now," she said. "You know what they've told you about shooting off your gun in the house."

Patricia sank to the sofa, her ears still ringing from the shots. Nico and Andreas seemed unaffected. They faced each other over the spot where the Dyon's body had lain, arguing about something, Patricia could not tell what. She suddenly felt drained and exhausted.

"Did that kill him?" she asked in a loud voice.

Nico and Andreas turned together, two gorgeous men eyeing her in very different ways. Nico's gaze was dark and laced with the memory of what they'd done in her apartment. Andreas's was cold and clear, assessing her.

Patricia wondered if Andreas felt the same compulsion to pleasure her that Nico did. Or perhaps it worked only if she showed interest in him first, or maybe he had to have an inclination toward her from the beginning.

The fear in Nico's eyes when he told her he'd writhe in agony if he didn't pleasure her had been real. Once he'd made her orgasm, he hadn't insisted she pay him back or they go to her bedroom. This made him different from her past boyfriends, who had pretty much wanted to screw until *they* were satisfied, whether she felt anything or not.

So why hadn't Andreas shown the same compulsion?

She had the sudden vision of Andreas approaching her as soon as Nico was done, telling her he needed to pleasure her, too. Nico could watch, or join in, as he liked. She imagined Nico smiling at her with his warm eyes while Andreas sank to his knees to lick her pussy.

She gasped and jerked her eyes open to find Andreas glaring at her.

"What?" he asked irritably.

She gulped. "I said, did the bullets kill him?"

"Probably not," Nico answered her. "He was created by a goddess, so he lives and dies at her pleasure. But it probably put him out of commission for a while."

"Long enough for us to get the inscription translated?"

"Maybe. But she'll send others."

Patricia blew out her breath. "We'd best get on it, then."

Nico looked at her for a long time, emotions flickering through his eyes. She knew what he was going to say, even before he started.

"We have what we need, now, Patricia. The Dyons won't bother you anymore. They won't interfere unless you do something to help us, and you've done all you can." His eyes went bleak. "I enjoyed meeting you."

Patricia stood up. "So that's it, then?"

"That's all there can be."

"Oh, really? Can I talk to you in private, Nico?"

Nico glanced at Mrs. Penworth, who was happily reenacting the shooting for Myrtle. Someone buzzed the outer door, and a worried voice said, "Are you all right in there, ma'am?"

As Myrtle hurried to the door, Nico followed Patricia down the narrow back hall to the kitchen. The spacious chamber gleamed with granite and stainless steel, the profusion of copper pots and pans putting most restaurant kitchens to shame.

Patricia faced him in the middle of the slate floor and put her hands on her hips. "So, this morning meant nothing to you?"

He didn't pretend not to understand. "It can't mean anything to *you*."

"You're so certain, are you? I don't pull my panties down for just anyone, you know. I was surprised you didn't take it further, but I figured you didn't want to rush it on the first date."

"Patricia."

He sounded patient. Men always sounded patient when they wanted to break up. Saying he didn't want to hurt her—well, of course not, because if he thought she was hurting, he might have to feel guilty.

She rushed on. "Why do you think I helped you, Nico? Fixed up your wing and arranged this visit? Put up with Andreas's bad temper and even being attacked in my store?"

"Because you were curious?"

"Only partly. This morning you begged me to let you give me pleasure, and suddenly you're saying, 'Thanks for the inscription, good-bye.' Hell, I played with my nipples for you. I've never done that before, for anyone."

His eyes darkened. "Do you want more? I suppose we have time for a little more. You command me."

"That's not what I mean. I meant . . . maybe we could get to know each other. You're fascinating. I want to know all about you."

He gave her a little smile. "Get to know your pleasure slave?"

His eyes were bleak, but the sudden vision of him as a pleasure slave was heady. To have Nico lying on her bed with his black wings spread under him, naked for her delight, would be absolute heaven.

He touched the gold chain around his neck. "These are fused on by such powerful magic that we would destroy ourselves if we tried to remove them. When I am with you, you hold my chain."

The idea of having such power over a man like Nico made her shiver. She couldn't quite believe that he would be her *slave*; she couldn't imagine herself mastering this strong, strong male who'd made her feel so joyful. "And you don't want that, I take it."

"On the contrary. I'd love it." He stepped close to her, his warmth bathing her. "I'd love every minute of it, even if being with you meant destroying myself. I'd love it and want more."

"I'd never hurt you," she said, startled. "I'm not a cruel woman, Nico. I never could be."

"Curses aren't meant to be cruelty free."

Patricia touched his mouth, liking the firmness of it. "Then we'd better get that inscription translated, so we can get to know each other with no pesky curses between us."

Nico's expression remained neutral. "You're going to insist."

"Afraid so."

He looked away, some emotion flickering across his face she didn't understand. When he looked back at her, his eyes held naked hunger and a touch of the fear she'd seen before.

He snaked his hand to the nape of her neck and pressed a kiss to her mouth. It wasn't like the greedy, hot kiss he'd bent on her in her apartment; this one was warm, almost sweet. He kissed her cheek before he pulled away, his whiskers scraping her skin.

"I'm bound to you," he whispered. "It's too late for me."

She started to argue again that she didn't believe in enslaving anyone, but he touched her lips and shook his head. "Let's go translate hieroglyphs."

Without another word, he took her hand and led her back to the living room.

Andreas had resumed intently studying the ostracon at the dining room table. Mrs. Penworth was demonstrating for the startled security guard and Myrtle how she'd shot off her revolver, bam, bam, bam, bam.

Of all the people in the apartment at the moment, Mrs. Penworth looked happiest.

~ ~ ~

PATRICIA knew they couldn't simply show up at a museum or university campus and demand to speak to someone who could translate ancient Egyptian. First, she had to track down an expert. Second, she had to make sure he was available and somewhat easy to reach. Third, she had to contact him and make an appointment at his convenience.

Both Andreas and Nico were certain that Mrs. Penworth wouldn't be bothered again by the Dyons. Dyons weren't killing machines, Nico explained, but enforcers of Hera's curse, made to prevent Andreas and Nico from breaking the spell. They weren't very smart creatures, and if Nico and Andreas behaved as though Mrs. Penworth could help them no more, the Dyons would leave her alone.

This explanation didn't make Patricia feel much better, but she was less reluctant to leave Mrs. Penworth. The elderly lady took Patricia aside before they left and thanked her for the wonderfully exciting afternoon.

"I don't envy you having to choose between those two," she said, giving Andreas and then Nico another appreciative once-over. "They're both to die for. If only I were forty years younger." She sighed but with a twinkle in her eyes.

Patricia's cheeks warmed as she left the apartment. Nico walked beside her, again with his hand on her back, guiding and protective. Andreas prowled behind them, moving like the big cat he was.

She returned with Nico and Andreas to their club, where Nico said she could use their state-of-the-art computer to research hieroglyph experts. It was just after dark, the in-between time in Manhattan when the day commuters had scuttled down to the subways and the nighthawks hadn't yet emerged.

Nico showed her the office that opened off their suite, then disappeared to get ready for the club opening. Patricia started her searching, beginning with museums and universities she knew had good archaeology or anthropology programs on the ancient world.

She soon became aware of Andreas behind her, his gaze intense on the back of her neck, while she typed and clicked.

"I can work the Internet," she told him a little nervously. "I've been online since online was invented."

Andreas put one hand on the desk and leaned over her shoulder to peer at the screen. "You're Googling archaeologists?"

"I'm looking up university faculty and museum directories. I'll make a list of those closest to us, then start calling tomorrow. It's not brain surgery."

Andreas made a sound of agreement, but he wouldn't go away. He hung over her shoulder as she typed in search terms and clicked on the results. As she wrote down her list, Andreas's hot breath trickled across her skin.

"You don't have to watch," she said.

"I'm curious. You know, like a cat."

His breath transferred to her ear as his blue eyes fixed on her. She cleared her throat. "Have you always been able to shift into a leopard?"

"I was born a leopard. I learned to shift into human form later. My mother taught me."

"I see."

"No, you don't. Why are you teasing Nico?"

She blinked, trying not to be unnerved that his intense eyes were so near hers. "Teasing him? What are you talking about?"

"He likes you."

"I like him. What woman wouldn't?"

His voice grated. "Sweetheart, you have no idea what kind of fire you're playing with."

His gaze was chill, but she sensed heat deep inside him, the same kind Nico possessed.

"I told Nico I was happy to help you get free of whatever this curse is," she said. "Then we can get to know each other, like a normal couple."

Andreas leaned closer. "Like you and he could ever be a normal couple. Let him go, now. What you're doing is cruel."

Patricia forced herself to meet his light blue eyes, which were infused with diamondlike flecks. "I'm not a femme fatale, Andreas. I'm not out to hurt anyone."

"But it does hurt him."

"You mean because he has to give me pleasure or else he experiences pain? By the way, why don't you feel that way?"

Andreas sank to one knee beside her, not a conciliatory gesture but one that let him get closer than ever. "He wants you, he'll be tortured because of you, and you'll never be able to feel about him the way he feels about you."

"You're making no sense. I'm attracted to him. I've already said that."

"He didn't tell you, did he?"

"Tell me what?"

Andreas's voice went harsh. "The entire truth. That he'll fall in love with you, but you'll never be able to fall in love with him. He'll burn up, and you'll go back to running your antique store like nothing happened."

She stared at him, mouth open. "What are you talking about?"

"It's the curse, dear Patricia. When we feel an attraction, we have to pursue it all the way—I mean, *all* the way—but the woman will use and discard us without giving a damn. It's Hera's very female way of getting back at us."

She blinked. "Good Lord, what did you do to her?"

"Nico and I were typical demigods way back when. We had power and immortality and did whatever we damn well pleased. If that meant chasing a pretty little priestess who was perfectly willing to be caught, we did it. When we refused to become her devoted slaves, she complained to Hera, who cursed us to the slavery of all women. She wanted to teach us the meaning of a broken heart, she said."

Patricia watched him in shock. "Seems a bit extreme."

"The little priestess never had a broken heart. But she was angry with us, and Hera simply projected her own brokenheartedness over men onto her. She brought down divine wrath."

"If I remember my mythology right, Zeus was never exactly a stay-at-home husband."

Andreas didn't look happy. "I should know. He was my father. But Hera wasn't my mother. Zeus took the form of a snow leopard to seduce my mother, and the result was me."

Patricia listened in fascination, wondering whether to believe any of it. She'd never heard a story about Zeus as a snow leopard, but there were many tales of him turning into animals or rainfall or something to have his way with whatever woman caught his eye.

"What about Nico?" she asked. "He's a demigod as well?"

"A son of Dionysus, the god of joy and laughter, sex and wine. That's why he's so damn charming. His mother was a nymph, which is where he got the wings."

"I like his wings," Patricia said, remembering how *much* she liked them.

"The interest you feel for him is false. You'll break his heart, but he won't break yours."

"And what about you?" she asked.

"What about me?"

"Why will he break his heart over me, but you won't? Or can only one of you get smacked by the curse at a time?"

Andreas's gaze was as palpable as a touch. "I won't because you haven't shown interest in me yet. Nico is the nice one. I would show you a different kind of passion, one you're not ready for."

Her pulse quickened. "What do you mean by that?"

Andreas leaned closer, his face nearly touching hers. "Nico will show you playful desire; he'll show you how to love every minute of it. You will only want me if you want something stronger, more powerful. Some part of yourself you're afraid to surrender to."

"I think you're optimistic," she said faintly.

"It will happen. I'll be your slave, but you'll want to surrender everything to me. Everything. And then I will teach you what you never suspected you wanted."

A shiver began deep inside her. She told herself this was utter nonsense, the magic of this curse couldn't work on her. She was psychic, too aware of the supernatural world to succumb to its tricks.

She liked Nico because—well, she *liked* him. She liked his warm eyes, his touch, his sexy wings. She didn't need anything more than that.

Something in the back of her mind laughed at her. Her sex life had always been a bit mediocre. She'd been engaged at nineteen, when plain sex was so fresh that neither she nor her fiancé was very experimental. Later she'd begun a five-year relationship with a man she'd met in college, whose idea of daring sex was the missionary position with the light on.

She'd never gone beyond the ordinary, never had the chance to try the things her fantasies and best sexual dreams conjured. With Andreas's body heat covering her, her mind urged her to examine a few of those fantasies a little more closely.

But with Nico.

She touched Andreas's face. "I'm sorry. I want Nico."

Andreas's smile was hot and sinful. For a moment she wondered what he'd do if he weren't bound by the curse, if the slave chain broke. She envisioned him naked, his penis hard and huge while he touched her body and decided what he'd do to her.

"When you're ready," he said, his voice deceptively soft, "you'll come to me, and I'll show you what gives you ultimate satisfaction."

It was a heady thought, all the more frightening because she thought she might like it.

"Don't you have a club to run?" Nico rumbled from the doorway.

Patricia jumped. Nico leaned against the doorframe—how long he'd been there, she couldn't tell. He had showered, and his dark hair was damp, and he'd dressed in a clean Andre's T-shirt and jeans.

Andreas took his time getting to his feet. "As a matter of fact, I do. Why don't I go run it while you help Patricia do her search?"

Nico turned his gaze fully on Andreas, eyes speaking volumes that Patricia didn't understand. "Thank you."

"Hey, I'm your best friend." Andreas clapped Nico on the shoulder as he passed him.

"You're a pain in the ass," Nico told him.

"Like I said." Andreas banged out of the room, leaving them alone and Patricia very hot and confused.

6

Nico remained where he was, watching Patricia stare at him with her beautiful blue green eyes. Her hair tumbled down in thick curls that he wanted to furrow with his hands.

Her face was beet red. "Andreas was just—"

"I know what Andreas was doing." Nico locked the door Andreas had just banged behind him, the click loud in the stillness. "He was finding out whether you wanted him, if he would be up here pleasuring you with me."

Patricia left her chair. Damn, she was a sexy woman. He could feast on her. He could teach her things she couldn't imagine, sex so powerful she'd be in a stupor for days. He had the gift of Dionysus for pleasuring, and he could give pleasure beyond mortal understanding of it. He could hurt with pleasure, or he could heal with it, whichever way she wanted it.

Her voice was strained. "He told me that anything you feel about me is part of the spell."

"Partly. But I can't imagine a man not falling for you, love."

She watched him steadily, keeping herself from softening to his flattery. "He also told me I could never fall for you."

He shrugged, pretending to be matter-of-fact. "When you're done with me, you'll tell me to go. That's how it works."

"And I'm not allowed to have any say?"

"You won't want me anymore, and you'll be surprised you ever did. It's a powerful curse. What I feel isn't going to matter."

"It matters to me," she said stubbornly.

Nico went to her and put his hands on her shoulders. "I'll give you the greatest pleasure I know how to give. I'm happy to do it, not only because I'm compelled to, but because I think you deserve it. But you shouldn't pretend it will be any more than that."

He rested his hands lightly on her shoulders, letting his thumbs play along her neck. He was skilled at seduction and soothing a lady in distress, but right now he only hoped she wouldn't pull away.

She reached up and lightly kissed his lower lip.

The telltale pain began in his gut, the need to pleasure her before agony took him. Nico fought to slow down so he could savor her. Pleasure didn't equate with speed; slow was best.

Through the ages he'd been forced to service women who used their power cruelly, delighted they'd ensnared Nico as their pet. In ancient times, they'd known about and accepted his divine nature; as the world changed, he'd been forced to hide it more and more. Now came this woman who could see his divinity and wasn't frightened by it, who told him she loved his wings and was sorry he'd been cursed.

He breathed in the sweet scent of her hair as he leaned to kiss her fully. She exuded confidence that the inscription would be the key to setting them free, and once free, they'd be able to pursue what he felt between them. But Nico knew damn well nothing would be that easy.

Patricia gently suckled his lip, and his already rock-hard cock leapt. He needed relief and release, and he needed her. But he had to do this on her terms.

She dipped her tongue inside his mouth, licking behind his lip before she eased away. "This time I want you out of *your* clothes. Strip for me, Nico."

His blood went hot. She wanted to play.

He moved to the speaker positioned above the door and turned up the monitor, which let them hear the music playing in the now-open club below. The gritty beat of Nine Inch Nails filled the room, and Nico started a striptease to it.

He hid a smile at the way Patricia's gaze fixed solidly on him as he skimmed off his shirt and tossed it aside. He let his hips gyrate like a male exotic dancer's, while he moved in a circle around her. He didn't look at her, letting the movements of his body show her how much he wanted her.

She laughed, a light sound in the middle of the harsh music. Nico skimmed his hand through his wet hair, letting it fall haphazardly. He danced plenty downstairs in the club, and he'd always been able to quickly learn the dance rhythms of each decade. It was all much the same: the energy of moving to a beat, using the body to entertain and entice.

Patricia's smile was huge. "Take it off, Nico." She laughed.

Nico unbuttoned and unzipped his jeans. He teased her by holding the fly open but keeping his back to her, working his ass back and forth to the music.

She cheered. At last he shoved the pants down his legs, letting them rest on his thighs, while he laced his hands behind his head and kept dancing.

"This is better than Christmas," Patricia shouted over the music.

Nico enticed her for a while with his pants half down, then he kicked out of his jeans and faced her, wearing nothing but a thong. Patricia's laughter died, but her eyes retained a hot glow.

He danced up to her, gyrating his body against hers, still not looking at her. He wound one of her arms around his neck and placed his hand on her hip, making her dance with him.

She was warm and soft, and he could smell her excitement. The tips of her breasts grazed his chest through her shirt and bra, and he was so hard his tip was poking above his waistband. His body wanted him to take her down, strip her, fuck her, but he forced his need back.

He teased and danced, fitting her supple body against his, enjoying the feel of her against him. She laughed. "Do you do this in the club every night?"

He bent her back over his arm in a parody of a ballroom dance, and smiled into her face. "No, sweetheart. This is just for you."

"Well, good, because you'd probably get arrested."

Her blue green eyes sparkled with excitement, but her smile was slow and lazy. As the music charged on, he laced his arm behind her neck and scooped her up for a kiss.

She was beautiful all over; he'd seen that when she displayed herself for him this afternoon. A woman made for sex and loving, but she'd never learned how to open herself to it. He would enjoy teaching her how.

"Nico," she murmured against his mouth. "You haven't finished stripping."

He placed her fingers on his waistband. "Take them off me."

Patricia grinned. She kissed him, slanting her mouth hungrily

over his. Then, in one smooth movement, she yanked his underwear down to his calves.

She remained on her knees, her gaze resting on the enormous
cock in front of her. "Oh, I think I like this," she breathed.

Nico was very glad to hear it. "What do you want me to do,
love? I'm all yours."

"Get out of that underwear."

He kicked it off and stood in front of her in his skin. Her gaze
roved slowly down him, a warming stroke that was almost as good
as her touching him. Her breath came faster, and he stood very
still as its warmth touched his cock.

His body thrummed with joy when she flicked her tongue over
his tip. It thrummed even harder when she opened her mouth and
gently slipped her lips over the flange.

He clenched his fists. Patricia slid him into her mouth as far
as she could before drawing back. Wet, hot, lovely mouth, and a
woman interested in giving him pleasure.

Patricia nipped the skin beneath his tip, sharp teeth scraping.
He loved it. Then she wrapped her lips around him again and began to suck.

Her lashes curled against her cheek as she closed her eyes. A
strand of lighter gold curled across her hair, attracting his fingers
to brush it straight. His hand stayed on her hair, furrowing it, letting the silken curls flow through his fingers.

Patricia was enjoying herself. She cupped his balls, fondling him
until he parted his legs to let her get at him more fully. Her mouth
worked with her suckling, lips curved tight around him.

She looked up at him and smiled around his huge cock in her
mouth, and he felt the buildup surge of his climax.

She withdrew, but before he could register disappointment, she leaned lower to lap the underside of his stem to his balls. Every hot stroke of her tongue built his climax higher, and when her fingers joined her mouth, he knew he was going to explode.

He wanted to see his seed on her face, wanted her to laugh at him while she was wet with it. But that wasn't meant to be. The cold links of the chain at his throat burned, not allowing him what he wanted.

She looked up at him, eyes glowing warm, oblivious of the torture inside him. "Touch yourself for me," she said, her voice breathy. "Like you had me do for you."

Not as good as her touching him, but not bad. Having her watch him . . . He moved with sudden pleasure.

"Wings and all," she whispered.

Oh, gods. Make him insane.

He let his wings lift from his shoulders, displacing the tattoo. He fanned out the wings, then brought them around to close himself and Patricia in their warmth.

He wrapped his hand around his erection, stifling a groan. A dark shudder went through him as he began to stroke himself, his grip burning. His cock didn't want him, it wanted Patricia, but he had to do this her way.

Patricia's green blue eyes rounded as she watched him, the sinews on his arm bunching and twisting as he pulled at himself. His wings slithered across his thighs, the sensitive tips dipping between his legs to warm him.

He kept his gaze on Patricia as he pumped himself, his body rocking a little in rhythm. The music blared on from the speakers, a terrific counterpart.

Nico loved Patricia's eyes, that aquamarine sparkle like the sun on warm sea. Her lips parted as her breath quickened with his.

Her pulse flickered in her throat, and he wanted to lick it just there, tasting her salty skin.

Patricia unconsciously nodded her head a little, as though silently encouraging him. *Come for me, Nico.*

He wanted her under him, her sweat-soaked body begging for it. Or maybe so incoherent she could only make sounds that weren't words. Her head would drop back, and she'd groan her pleasure, her breath sweet on his face . . .

He shouted as his seed roped out around his fingers, wet and warm. Her eyes rounded as the liquid dripped all over his hands.

Nico closed his eyes and rocked back as sensation after sensation chased through his body: hot, cold, longing, satiation, the need to crush her against him and kiss her until he bruised her lips.

"Here."

Nico opened his eyes. His body was scalding hot, his hands shaking. Patricia stood in front of him holding a towel.

That simple, practical gesture made him want her like crazy. Even coming didn't keep him from needing to shove her onto the couch and delve into her clothes. His penis was still hard, and it craved her.

She could run while he chased her like a cat hunting his prey, and when he caught her they'd tumble together to the soft grass. She'd open her legs for him, and he'd find his joy inside her.

He longed for it with every breath.

Patricia was smiling at him, eyes glowing. "You came for me."

"Did I?" He took the towel and shakily wiped off the gob of come. "I guess I did."

"I liked it." Her smile contained both shyness and triumph. "I like that I can get you hot and bothered."

"That was easy. I've been craving you."

"Have you?" She cocked her head, giving him a teasing glance. "You don't just want me for my ostracon?"

He stroked one finger through her hair, loving the feel. "You found me passed out in your store, and instead of shooting me, you fixed my wing. I think that's incredibly sexy."

She laughed. "For your next turn-on, I'll give you a Band-Aid. You won't be able to keep away from me then."

He leaned to her and ran his tongue around her lips. "There are so many things I can teach you, Patricia."

Her smile was wicked. "I look forward to learning."

"You brought me off. How about I return the favor? With my mouth? Or my hands?"

She looked him up and down, face flushed. "With your wings," she said.

~ ~ ~

PATRICIA wondered how she'd ended up here, spread-eagled on Nico's huge bed while Nico knelt at her feet and gently moved her ankles apart. She wondered even more that she'd agreed to let him tie her hands to the bedpost with soft silk scarves.

He was beautiful: all naked, glossy muscle, his cock rigid and dark. The bed filled with the feathery goodness of him as he tickled and touched and slid strong feathers between her legs.

Her mind flashed to the feeling of him inside her mouth, the joy of watching him masturbate himself. She thought of how his wiry hair curled around her fingers as she cupped his balls, thought of the firm length of his cock and what it had tasted like.

Smooth. Hot. Like the best melted chocolate.

That thought led to a vision of coating his cock with melted chocolate and licking it off.

"Mmm." She wriggled on the bed, liking the feel of the covers under her bare butt, the smooth silk around her wrists.

Her legs were spread wide with him between them, cool air touching her pussy. She brought one foot up to caress his back, liking the smooth warmth beneath her sole.

"That's it, love," Nico whispered. "Feel me."

"I don't feel anything *but* you."

"Good."

Her pussy was hot and full. She started to reach for him but was pulled up short by the silk tethers and made a noise of frustration.

Did Nico take pity on her and loosen her hands? No, he kept pleasuring her with his feathers, never touching her with his hands.

"I'm going to come," she cried. "I want your mouth on me. Please."

"Are you sure?" Nico the torturer asked.

"Yes. *Please.*"

He smiled, his feathers still rubbing her, tickling, teasing. Just when she thought it would be too late, he leaned straight down and fastened his mouth over her. He sucked on her nub, nibbled and teased, then delved his tongue straight inside her.

Patricia jerked at her bonds, feet going crazy on the bed. She came and came, pressing her pussy to his wonderful mouth, crying out as his tongue tantalized and rubbed and sucked.

Patricia writhed one last time, Nico holding her hips in his strong hands while he lapped her.

"Thank you," she gasped, then she crashed down onto the bed, the waves of her climax rolling over her.

Nico laughed again, his voice so dark. He rose, his hair tangled, his eyes burning with a strange light. He wasn't human—the bed filled with feathers was evidence—and the fire in him was different. Powerful, heady, dangerous. It was like touching lightning.

"You're beautiful, Patricia," he murmured. "You taste like ambrosia."

"Thank you," she whispered again. Or thought she did. Oblivion hit her within moments of her climax, and she fell into the hardest after-sex sleep she'd ever experienced.

When she woke again, her hands had been untied and a sheet pulled over her body. The shower pattered quietly in the bathroom, and a bedside lamp cast a small circle of light over the bed.

Andreas was leaning against the bedpost at the foot, smiling at her.

7

"Y OU look happy," Andreas said.

Patricia gasped and tugged the sheet to her chin. "What are you doing here?"

"I live here. This is my bed." He lounged even more negligently, his light blue eyes tracing the outline of the sheet.

"What time is it?" she asked.

"About four. Club's just closing."

"Oh, shit. I need to get home." Patricia started to sit up, then clutched the sheet closer, remembering she was naked beneath.

"I'm sure Nico would be delighted if you stayed," Andreas said.

"What about you? Would you be delighted?"

"Oh, yes." His look turned predatory. "I think I would."

"I was joking."

"I'm not."

She studied his hard body in jeans and a T-shirt, the Andre's logo stark on his chest. The paw print meant him, she realized. His leopardness.

"You'll want your bed," she began, hoping he'd take the hint and leave so she could get dressed.

"Not necessarily. There's another bedroom upstairs, in case we need it."

She looked at him in surprise. "Do you and Nico usually sleep in here together?"

"Sure." He shrugged massive shoulders. "Why not? It's a big bed."

The thought of the two of them curled up, large, muscular bodies filling the bed, made her mouth dry.

"Nothing. It's just that . . ."

"I've been hanging around with Nico for over two thousand years. There's been plenty of times we had to sleep together for warmth and protection. Not that we hit the sack at the same time every night. There's always something to do."

"Inscriptions to find. Dyons to fight."

"Something like that."

Patricia drew her knees to her chest and circled her arms around them. "Why do you think this particular inscription will help you?"

Andreas's eyes went bleak, as though he were trying not to hope. "Because there are hieroglyphs on there that might refer to Nico and me. I'm willing to have this Egyptologist you find translate it and find out."

"It's worth a shot, you mean."

He nodded, his white black hair catching in the lamplight. "It may be nothing. We've had false hopes before."

She hugged herself a little tighter. "I'm sorry this happened to you."

"Part of it was our own damn fault. We liked to enjoy our-selves too much. Like now."

"You think Nico is enjoying himself too much with me?"

"No. I think I am."

She stilled. "And what do you mean by that?"

"I'm enjoying thinking about snatching that sheet from you and looking at your lovely body."

Her hands automatically clenched the sheet. "That wouldn't be fair to Nico."

"I said *look*. Not touch."

Patricia's entire body heated. Andreas was already gazing at her as though he could see right through the sheet, and she didn't know why that excited her so much. She liked Nico and wanted to be with *him*, not Andreas. She liked Nico's laugh, his smoldering eyes, his touch, his caring.

But she suddenly wanted Andreas to look at her.

Slowly she skimmed the sheet from her torso, then leaned back on her elbows and pushed the covers all the way off. She stretched out her legs and lay there, stark naked, for Andreas to see.

His blue eyes flashed, quick volatility that was instantly masked as his gaze roved her from head to foot. He lingered at her breasts, and she felt the nipples rise for him, then his gaze dipped to the dampening tuft between her thighs.

Patricia parted her legs and let him look, going so far as to lick the tip of her fingers and touch them to her clit.

His erection was evident in his pants, but he simply leaned on the bedpost, folded his arms, and studied her.

"Very nice," he concluded. He pushed himself away from the bed and ran his tongue over his lips. "Keep the bed," he said softly. "I'll sleep upstairs."

Giving her a final, lingering look, he turned and left the room.

Patricia let out her breath and scrubbed her hand over her face. That had been—incredibly erotic. She'd come close to orgasm feeling his admiration on every inch of her. She'd never let a man look at her like that before, and now she'd played with one man and spread herself in front of his best friend not an hour later.

Then she realized that the shower had stopped—had stopped some time ago.

She looked up in alarm. Nico leaned against the bathroom doorframe, a towel around his waist and water droplets all over his shoulders.

"Nico," she whispered.

Hurting Nico was the last thing she wanted. She didn't understand why she'd wanted Andreas to look at her body; she understood none of this.

"I'm sorry," she said, remorse biting her. "I couldn't seem to stop myself."

"I know." Nico flicked off the light in the bathroom and came through the darkened room to her. He sat down on the bed and slid one hand across her bare hip. His towel-wrapped body was incredible, and her own body throbbed for him again.

"This is how it happens," he said. "You want me first, then you'll draw Andreas in until he becomes fixed on you. You'll have us both until we're so tangled we can't get free without pain. And then it's over. You move on, and we eat our hearts out."

She listened in dismay. "That is *not* what's going to happen."

"It's the way of things."

"I am going to find a way to set you free, Nico. So that if we want each other, there's nothing in the way, and we know it's real."

"Maybe."

Patricia started to scramble up. "It will be real; I swear it. Now, I have to go. I have cats to feed, a store to open in a few hours—"

His hand on her hip tightened. "Stay." His eyes went dark. "Sleep with me tonight. I know a great place for breakfast, best bagels in Manhattan."

The incongruity of a demigod, son of Dionysus and a nymph, on the lookout for a really good bagel made her laugh.

"All right," she conceded. "I'll stay. My cats will never let me hear the end of it, though."

"I'll send Andreas to look after them. He likes cats."

She started to smile again, then Nico pulled off his towel, and she got lost in admiration of his body. "I hope you mean he likes to pet and feed them."

"I do." Nico slid under the covers with her and shut off the bedside light. "He's a pussycat at heart, I told you."

"Sure," Patricia said numbly. "I believe you."

But she had to admit snuggling down in the warm bed with Nico, kissing him good night, and spooning back against him, was worth the price of a couple of pissed-off cats.

~ ~ ~

NICO's great place for breakfast turned out to be outstanding. It was one of those incongruous storefronts that didn't even try to compete with the trendy restaurants of the day and served its customers in a small space of home-baked goodness.

Nico ate a full breakfast while Patricia nibbled a bagel, both as comfortable with each other as though they'd been together for years. Patricia still was not sure what she felt about her encounter with Andreas or about Nico's proclamation that she'd ensnare them both and leave them high and dry.

Patricia knew she had faults, but being a siren wasn't one of them. Breaking up with someone because they'd grown apart or couldn't get along was one thing; using and discarding someone was something else.

She'd also not been sure how good a cat minder Andreas would be, despite Nico's assurances. But when she'd popped in on the way to breakfast with Nico, she found the water bowls topped off and Red Kitty curled tightly around his favorite toy. Isis sat guard as usual, sphinxlike on the bottom stair.

"He likes cats," Nico repeated after they'd left Patricia's apartment again. "Cats like him."

"You do know that I've never met anyone as bizarre as the two of you, right?" she asked as they sat across the booth from each other. "Even when I dated another psychic."

Nico sipped his coffee. "Glad to know I'm unique."

"That's one word for it."

"And I treasure you," he said, giving her one of his smiles that made her blood heat. "I've not met a woman in eons I can show my true nature to. It is not easy for us, remaining hidden. We were thrust here against our will, yet we can't openly be what we are. Most mortals don't want to believe in the supernatural, not really. Not alive and walking among them."

"I've never had the choice."

"How long have you been psychic?" He leaned toward her, his attention intoxicating. When Nico looked at her, he truly looked at *her*, and it was obvious his mind was on nothing else. She'd never had that kind of attention from a man, and it was heady.

"I was about eight when I found out," she said. "I'd always felt presences lingering on things and in places but never thought much about it. One day when my grandmother was visiting, she explained it was a talent not many people had, and that I shouldn't talk about it too much. But it was a gift, and I should use it wisely."

"Your grandmother was psychic, too?"

"I didn't know it until that day. When I talked about her visit later that day, everyone looked at me oddly. She'd died the night before."

Nico's brows rose. "Interesting."

"For some reason it didn't scare me. She'd needed to talk to me, to pass on her knowledge before it was too late. I never saw her after that. It's not like I can conjure ghosts or carry on conversations with dead people whenever I want. I'm just good at reading auras and figuring out what happened in rooms where there were strong emotions or reading the vibrations on a piece of furniture. Comes in handy in the antiques business."

"Which you love." He smiled, and her heart squeezed again. "I see it in your eyes."

"I do enjoy the work," she said, trying to sound offhand. "I like the excitement of a good auction; I like tracking down obscure pieces for clients, like the ostracon for Mrs. Penworth."

"Why did she want it?"

"She'd heard about one that belonged to Cleopatra. She couldn't get that one but wanted one like it. So I searched the market."

Nico traced the edge of his mug. "If Andreas and I had come to you in the first place, you might have been able to find it for us."

"Or the Dyon might have prevented me from finding out about the ostracon at all. You might have gone straight to the dealer, and I'd never have met you."

Nico caught her gaze in one that was half amused and half anguished. "And I wouldn't be in this deep."

She laid her hand on top of his warm, strong one. "I don't know what kind of women caught you in the past, but I don't go through men like a hot knife through butter or leave a trail of broken hearts behind me. I think women who do that have intimacy issues. Or not enough to do."

"Or they refuse to be hurt," he suggested.

"You mean it's easier to end a relationship before you start caring too much? I suppose." She sighed. "But I don't think it's healthy to go through life never getting close to someone, no matter how much it might hurt later."

He was laughing at her, his dark eyes dancing.

"What?" she asked.

"I notice that most of you humans can't say the word *love*. It's *relationships* and *intimacy issues*." He pushed his coffee aside and leaned forward. "Everyone is afraid of love—deep, gut-wrenching, heartbreaking caring for someone else more than for yourself. Love, pure and simple. No analyzing the hell out of it, no sitting with a third person discussing *issues*." He put his fist on his chest. "It's raw, simple emotion, and without it, the world would have been a dead place a long time ago."

"Oh." Patricia liked how his eyes had gone dark and intense. "I've never heard it put quite like that."

Nico lifted his coffee, breaking the spell. "Call me old-fashioned."

Patricia called him sexy as hell. In her thirty-two years of life, she'd had male friends as well as female, and she'd seen that her men friends could love as deeply as her women friends.

But she'd never heard a man declare that love was as important as Nico just had. The fact that he could still think such a thing, after being so long buffeted by the whims of a goddess, warmed her.

He didn't believe she'd be different from whatever women he'd had before, didn't believe she could be. But she intended to show him. What she felt for Nico already went beyond sexual interest—although that interest was pretty strong.

She intended to prove to him that she wouldn't be fickle, spell or no spell. She'd do anything to wipe away the sadness she saw deep in his eyes.

~ ~ ~

THEY walked back to Patricia's apartment so she could call the Egyptology professor she'd located at Cornell. Nico slid his hand in hers as they strolled along the busy Manhattan street, and she enjoyed his strength and the feeling of protection he wrapped around her.

Once the call was made and the meeting arranged, Patricia packed a few clothes, put the cats in their carrier, and left with Nico for the club. They found Andreas up, in a T-shirt and jeans and drinking coffee, his white black hair mussed. He insisted he come with them to Ithaca, to her surprise and consternation, and not long later, the three of them plus cats were in a rental car heading north out of town.

The only Egyptology specialist Patricia had found with both the expertise and the time to talk to them was Rebecca Trimble, a postdoc at Cornell. The university's website said that Rebecca had taken her doctoral degree at the University of Chicago, had plenty of experience at excavations, and had won several prizes for her hieroglyphs and hieratic expertise, including the fellowship she currently held. She'd agreed to see Patricia late that afternoon.

Patricia had planned to drive up, talk to Dr. Trimble, spend the night, look through promising antique shops, and cruise on home the next day. Her store could stand to be closed that long; her walk-in business was nowhere near what her behind-the-scenes business was. She'd not been surprised when Nico wanted to accompany her, but she wasn't sure what Andreas's motive was.

Andreas stretched himself out in the backseat next to the cat carrier, tucked earbuds into his ears, and closed his eyes. The cats squished themselves to the front of the carrier to be close to him and fell asleep.

She left city gridlock for packed freeways, which thinned out a little as she drove north. The early fall air was crisp, and Patricia drew a heady breath of it. She'd grown up in the middle of Michigan, where winters were dark, but spring, summer, and fall were fresh and alive. She loved living and working in Manhattan, but the countryside always held a special place in her heart.

Nico watched the scenery or watched her. She could feel his dark gaze on her, which reminded her of the warmth of sleeping curled up beside him in bed. Every time he looked at her was like a heated touch.

She glanced into the back to see Andreas, eyes closed, mouth relaxed in sleep. If she was daring, she'd pull over to the side of the road, skim down her pants, then start up again, inviting Nico to lean down and lick her as she drove.

The idea made her pussy throb, but she knew she wasn't anywhere near that daring. A noise of frustration escaped her throat.

Nico looked over and slanted her his sexy smile. "Are you wet, Patricia?" he asked in a low voice.

Patricia gripped the steering wheel. Her nipples must be sharp outlines against her blouse, but she was too busy driving to check. "I remember what happened last time you asked me that."

"Good." His voice went darker as he snaked his hand to her thigh. "I want you to be dripping wet for me, your panties soaked with your come."

She swallowed and glanced quickly into the backseat, but Andreas lay unmoving, tinny sound emanating from his earbuds.

"I think I'm pretty much there," she said.

Nico curled his fingers on her thigh, nowhere near the join of her legs, but her pussy squeezed, and squeezed again. "Stop it," she half laughed. "I need to drive."

"I don't want to touch you, Patricia. I just want to know that you're wet for me, that if I unzipped your pants and dipped my fingers inside, I'd find you wet all over. That my fingers would slide over your clit, that it would swell for me, and you'd drip on me even more."

Patricia squirmed in her seat. "Oh, God."

"Your patience will be rewarded, love. I promise you."

"If you make me come while I'm driving, it may be the last thing I ever do."

"Don't worry. I won't touch you. Not yet."

"You make me want to touch *you*."

Nico squeezed her thigh again, hunger in his eyes. "Why? What do you want to do to me? Tell me."

"I want to open your pants," she said rapidly. "I want to find your cock hard and huge. I want the tip to wink at me."

"That could happen."

"I want to stroke you all the way down to your balls. I want to fit my hand under your butt and play with your balls where they're warm from hanging inside your pants. I want to feel the hair there rubbing my hand, and feel your balls all hard. I want you to lift your cock toward me, with you dying for me to put you in my mouth."

Nico's gaze was intense, his eyes black-dark. She resolutely watched the traffic.

"What else?" he prompted.

"I want to tickle your cock with my fingers, then bend over and lick it everywhere I've touched it. I want to suck the tip in my mouth and wiggle my tongue over it."

"That sounds nice."

"I want to suck you until you can't stand it, until you're dying to come in my mouth. And then I want to slide my own pants off, straddle your lap, and slip your cock into my pussy, which is so, so wet for you."

He rubbed his hand once along her leg. "I'd like that."

"And then you'd fuck me. You'd thrust your huge cock inside me until I screamed, because it's so big. You'd fuck me hard, and I'd keep coming while you screwed me."

"I'd like that *very* much." He didn't move, but his gaze was so fixed on her she could feel it.

"Then you'd come. You'd come so high inside me it would burn me up, and I wouldn't care. And then I'd . . ."

She pressed her brakes hard, screeching the car to a halt before she climbed the red taillights of the one ahead of her. "Damn it."

Nico burst out laughing. He couldn't possibly realize how sexy he was when he laughed, his brown throat exposed, his hair falling like black silk. "Maybe you'd better stick with driving," he said.

"Maybe so." She did a quick nipple check, but nope, they weren't relaxing at all.

As she started moving again, she heard a noise in the backseat. Andreas rose like a god from the sea and leaned forward between them, sinewy arms resting on either seat. He said, "When you're done doing all that to him, would you consider doing it to me?"

Patricia gasped and almost had to slam on the brakes again. "Shit. I thought you were asleep."

Andreas regarded her in the rearview mirror with lazy blue eyes. "You were mistaken."

Nico continued to laugh, not disturbed in the slightest.

"You see?" he said to Patricia, weaving his fingers together. "Tangled."

8

Nico spent the rest of the trip uncomfortably hard from Patricia's fantasy until he was afraid the zipper of his jeans would fly apart. He knew damn well that if he opened her pants as he'd described, he'd find her slick and wet and wanting him.

Whenever they reached where they were going, he'd reward her by spreading her and licking away that sweet honey until she shuddered with release. She needed to release, and Nico could do that for her.

He knew Patricia had a place inside her where desire waited to be caressed to wakefulness. She was shy about it, but as she'd shown him, her buried desires were dying to break free.

He'd teach her that there was nothing wrong with releasing her inhibitions. Before this was over, he would teach her everything, and even if she couldn't respond to him emotionally, he would have the satisfaction of knowing he'd helped unlock parts of herself that she kept hidden deep down. It was really all he could have from this.

Patricia had booked them into a bed-and-breakfast on a hill overlooking the town, the inn surrounded by trees loaded with September yellow, orange, and crimson foliage. The air was cool but not yet biting. Beautiful.

Patricia asked for two rooms, one for herself and one for Andreas and Nico. The innkeeper, Mrs. Blake, was a bright woman with short white hair, and showed them around with enthusiasm. The house was nineteenth-century, and Patricia looked around as though she were feeling the auras of the many people who'd passed through.

"I've given you boys the Helen Monroe room," Mrs. Blake said. "She was the original owner of the house. Don't worry if you hear something scuffling about in the night. The whole place is haunted."

Nico caught Patricia's twitch of lips as she turned away. He wondered if it was because she knew for certain whether or not the house was haunted or because of their diminutive host calling him and Andreas "boys."

Patricia settled into her room with her cats, which she'd brought because the inn was pet-friendly. Isis and Red Kitty weren't used to staying on their own at night, she'd said.

The resident cat, Peachy, was large, gray, and orange-eyed, and supervised all proceedings with a bored air. She did, however, condescend to stalk to Andreas and rub her face against his leg. Isis and Red Kitty hovered around him, too, while they prepared to drive down to Cornell and interview Dr. Trimble.

They met Dr. Trimble in a tiny office in a redbrick building in the middle of campus. Rebecca Trimble was younger than Patricia, maybe in her midtwenties, and wore her yellow brown hair scraped unattractively back from her face. Her clothes were shapeless and baggy, and she wore no makeup.

Nico wondered if she deliberately tried to make herself unattractive, and why she would. She couldn't hide the fact that her face was delicately boned or her eyes were soft and brown, but the frown she gave them was stern to the point of rudeness.

"I don't have much time," she said. "What is it you wanted me to look at?"

Patricia set the folder of photos on the woman's desk and opened it. Dr. Trimble leaned over the desk, her sloppy blouse parting at the neck, and her annoyed look vanished. "Where did you get these?"

Patricia described the ostracon, and Rebecca listened, her face animated, which betrayed her prettiness. Andreas's ice blue eyes watched the woman's every move with his predator-sizing-up-prey look.

"I agree that the ostracon is Ptolemaic," Rebecca said when Patricia finished. "But the text on it is far older. I see references to gods here that were pretty much forgotten by the time the Greeks took over. It was probably copied from an older source, and I'm betting the copier didn't even know what it meant."

"How can you tell?" Patricia leaned forward, just as interested, her blond ringlets catching the sunlight from the room's one window.

"The inscriber got the names just a little bit wrong. A common mistake by copiers of the later periods. Some of the gods got changed into Greek-Egyptian hybrids, but these names would be familiar to the pharaohs of the Eighteenth Dynasty and earlier."

"Can you read it?" Nico asked her.

"I think so. It will take me a little while to study it and do the best translation possible—"

"How long?" Andreas asked abruptly.

Rebecca glanced at him, then immediately away, her cheeks staining red.

"I'm not sure," she said. "I have a lot of commitments, but I'd be happy to work on it whenever I have a spare moment. Perhaps by the end of this semester?"

Andreas rose, his tall frame filling the office. "Drop all the other commitments and do this for us. We will pay you whatever amount of money you require."

Rebecca stared up at him, her pale mouth open. "It's not that easy. I'm here on a fellowship, and I have obligations."

"Which you can fulfill after you translate this." Andreas tapped the pile of photos. "How long will it take if you spend all your time on it?"

"I don't know. Depends on how much I have to look up. A week, maybe more."

"Good. Start now." Andreas shoved himself away from the desk and out of the small room, anger rolling from him in waves.

Rebecca stared after him, openmouthed. "Is he always like that?" she asked Patricia.

Nico flashed her a smile. "My dear, you have no idea."

Rebecca swallowed and looked quickly at the photos again. "I probably can take a few days and see what I can come up with."

"Excellent," Nico said, crossing his long legs. "We'll wait."

Patricia stood up. "No, we'll leave her to it." She flashed Rebecca an apologetic look. "Don't let these two bully you. You do what you need to do and take the time you need." She sent Nico a glare. "I'm sure the rest of us can find something to do while we wait."

~ ~ ~

NICO insisted Rebecca stay at the inn with them, which Patricia took to be worry about the Dyons finding Rebecca now that they'd showed her the inscription. Patricia called their hostess and learned she did have an extra room available, then Patricia and Nico went with Rebecca to her apartment so she could pick up what she needed for a few days' stay.

Andreas had disappeared completely, but they found him waiting at the inn, the cats all over him.

The four of them had a quiet dinner at the B and B, Patricia and Rebecca finding common ground talking about artifacts and the antiquities markets, legal and illegal. Nico and Andreas didn't eat much and remained quiet, Andreas particularly tense.

Patricia was a little surprised that Nico didn't try to follow her when she retreated for the night. He brushed a light kiss to her forehead before Patricia left the sitting room, but other than giving her a seductive smile, he made no indication he wanted to follow.

She wasn't certain if she was disappointed or relieved as she crawled into bed by herself. The four-poster was comfortable and warm, made more so by Isis and Red Kitty curled up on either side of her.

She felt the cats leave as she began to drift to sleep, probably off to find Andreas, their new best friend. She wondered sleepily why the cats were so attracted to him. He did his best to be rude and gruff with humans and then let the cats climb all over him. Maybe cats had a secret snow-leopard fixation.

"Patricia."

Patricia jerked awake. She tried to roll over, but Nico's warm body nestled protectively alongside her, penning her in. His face was dark with unshaved whiskers, his hair disheveled from sleep.

"What are you doing in here?" she whispered.

The room was dark, a sliver of moonlight leaking through the gauzy curtains. The house was silent, outside equally so.

"I like watching you sleep."

He skimmed his hands down her body and inched up the hem of her nightshirt. She hadn't bothered to wear panties to bed. Anticipation?

His hands were big and warm on her back. He slid his fingers to the cleft of her buttocks, making little circles there that drove her crazy.

"Where's Andreas?" she asked.

"Hmm? Patrolling." He paused a moment. "Do you want me to fetch him?"

His eyes were unreadable in the dark, his fingers gentle.

"No, I want you." She touched his lips. "Why do I want you so much, Nico? I never think about sex like this. Not this constant wanting."

"Spells are like that."

"It has to be more than that." She stopped, frustrated. "You say you're drawn to me by the curse; you have to pleasure me until I've had enough. But I don't want that. I don't want you coming to me just because you're compelled to."

He kept on stroking her back, fingers soothing. "It is more than just the curse," he said softly.

"How do you know that?"

"I don't." His eyes went darker still. "I want it to be more. It goes both ways, Patricia."

"And if we break the spell, what happens then?"

He stroked her hair, his hand warm. She felt his wanting clearly through the fold of nightshirt that had slid between them, his cock hard and heavy.

"I don't know," he said. "I don't even know if it's possible to break it. All I want is to be with you right now, in case I can't ever be with you again."

Patricia went silent, watching the flick of his lashes as he looked at her, the moonlight making shadows of his eyes.

"I've never believed in casual sex," she said.

"No? But it happens all the time."

"Not to me. If I'm not emotionally engaged, I can't do it. I don't want it."

"Patricia." He touched her cheek. "Do you want me?"

"I'm dying for you."

"Then let's enjoy each other. We'll worry about how we feel tomorrow when tomorrow comes."

He stopped her next words with a kiss, lips sliding over hers and driving out of her head what she'd intended to say. He slid hands down to pull up her nightshirt again, skimming it all the way up until he cupped her breasts.

"Let me give you joy," he whispered.

She nodded, seeking his mouth again. His tongue and lips were masterful, and she thought she could kiss this man forever.

He had other ideas. He pulled her up until he could suck her nipple into his mouth, and then he suckled, his teeth and tongue doing a wonderful dance. Hot tingles wove through her, and she cradled his head in her hand.

"Harder," she begged.

He obeyed. He opened his mouth wide, drawing as much of her breast into his mouth as he could, then withdrew, clinging to the tip with his teeth until the last minute. He did it over and over, lavishing attention on each breast, licking and sucking like he couldn't get enough.

She pushed him onto the bed and burrowed her face against his chest, liking the way he groaned when her mouth found his flat, male nipple.

She'd always heard that men liked being played with almost as much as women, but this was the first time she'd had the chance to test out the theory. She moved in between the areolas and sucked his skin sharply into her mouth, wanting to leave a love bite.

He groaned and laughed. "You like me."

"I like every bit of you."

"Especially the wings?" he teased.

"I'd like you with or without wings. Although, with wings is better. Can you fly with them?"

He chuckled, his chest rumbling beneath hers. "Yes. They work." He moved his mouth close to hers. "I'll take you flying one day, sweetheart. I promise."

"Can you fly and fuck me at the same time?"

His laughter cut off, his eyes going darker than ever. "I don't know, but it would be fun finding out. Not tonight, though—too dangerous with Dyons looking for us. Plus I'd hate for some stray hunter to take me for an overlarge goose." He pulled her closer. "But one day . . ."

Nico skimmed his tongue across her lips, then took her hand and closed it around his hard, hot cock.

~ ~ ~

ANDREAS, a leopard once more, could smell the sex going on in the bedroom next to him. Patricia was hot for Nico, and her rampaging pheromones made his fur tingle.

Patricia would want Andreas soon. He'd glimpsed the inkling of it in her eyes, the unearthing of fantasies that she'd kept long buried. Her longings had flared when she'd bared her body for him in his and Nico's bedroom, but she'd snapped the lid over them again.

It wouldn't be long now. Both he and Nico were stripping away her inhibitions, and soon she'd be ready for what she'd never dared before.

Andreas had opened the window before he'd changed, and his big cat form easily slid out to the huge maple tree that spread across the side of the house. The branches sagged under his weight, but he quickly leapt from limb to limb to the ground.

To his annoyance, he heard Patricia's two cats springing after him. Not really the threesome he'd had in mind.

He worried a little about Nico. Nico always tried to remain stoic about the women he serviced, but this time, he wasn't. Patricia was cute, no denying it, and the woman had a certain something. But if they couldn't unravel the spell, and Patricia dumped Nico—and she would—Nico was going to get kicked in the balls. Nothing Andreas could do about it, but he didn't want to see his friend in pain.

Andreas padded around to the ground-floor room Rebecca had been given. She was the most vulnerable of them, but she'd refused to switch rooms with Patricia.

Rebecca's room was the smallest in the inn, its only amenity being a little private porch overhung with vines. Rebecca had argued that she wanted to stay up late and look at the inscription, and tucked in the back of the house she'd keep no one else awake.

Andreas had volunteered to watch out for her rather than have to explain exactly why they wanted her more secure. He approached the porch slowly, admonishing the cats to keep silent. They slunk about his ankles but obeyed.

Rebecca was still up. She sat at a tiny desk at right angles to the porch door, the photos spread across the desktop. She'd loosened her clothes, blouse half unbuttoned as though she were trying to be comfortable. Her hair was still pulled back, but honey blond wisps had escaped to straggle down her neck.

Rebecca would never be beautiful in the way that humans in this country in this time regarded beauty, but she had a solid earthiness that appealed to Andreas. The tilt of her head, the animation in her eyes as they flicked over the photos attracted him. A dangerous thing, this attraction.

Dangerous, too, was the way she sat in full light without closing the curtains. She likely thought nothing of it; the inn was far off the road with no other houses around it. But Dyons were creatures of darkness, at their most powerful during the night.

Andreas climbed to the porch and lay down just outside the door, the cats draping themselves around him.

If Rebecca heard the soft thump on the porch floor, she made no sign. Nor did she hear the moan that came from the window above, where Patricia and Nico were starting in. It took all Andreas's willpower not to climb onto the porch roof, put his paws on their windowsill, and watch them.

~ ~ ~

PATRICIA's face was in shadow, but moonlight outlined her breasts, which pushed up against the nightshirt, her nipples tight points stretching the light fabric.

Nico straddled her on his hands and knees, excited and hard. He helped her tug the nightshirt up and over her head and toss it to the floor.

She was so beautiful bare. He recalled what she'd looked like in her apartment when he'd told her to strip. Her body was slim and taut, breasts large enough for him to catch in his hands and enjoy the warm weight of them.

Thighs strong, belly tight. The tuft of hair between her legs glistened with moisture. She gave him a lazy smile, her ringlets of golden hair haloing around her face. Did she know she was driving him insane? Breaking his heart?

Probably not. She was caught up in wanting, and for now, that was fine.

He caught her under her knees and lifted her legs, opening her for him. The slit of her pussy shimmered in the moonlight, the golden hair surrounding it glistening with her dew. His penis wanted to slam inside that intriguing dark opening, to pound until he came.

That wasn't what he was here to do. He had to pleasure her, never mind his own needs.

Patricia smiled and reached for him, and his body warmed. She still didn't really believe in the curse, though she would in time. She didn't understand what it was to have an all-powerful creature at her mercy, as Hera wanted him to be. Patricia just wanted Nico.

He knew what else she liked. He closed his eyes in pleasure as he let his wings break free, and she laughed as she caught feathers in her hands.

"Yes," she whispered, clutching the black feathers tight, then she cried out as he leaned down and began to pleasure her with his tongue.

~ ~ ~

REBECCA woke with a start. She had fallen asleep at the desk, her head resting on her bent arm, the pencil still in her fingers. She sat up, rubbing the stiffness in her neck.

A snow leopard sat at her feet, watching her with unblinking blue eyes.

Rebecca went very still. The creature's face was white with

patterns of small black dots, while his legs and back bore the large, circular spots common to leopards. The fur on his chest was nearly pure white, and his eyes were like chips of blue ice.

The two cats Patricia had brought with her wove around his feet, and the inn's cat sat on her haunches just behind him. All three cats were purring, but the leopard remained silent.

Interesting dream. "Hello, you," she said. "You're pretty."

The leopard's eyes narrowed. Maybe a male leopard didn't like to be called "pretty."

"Handsome, then," she amended. "Can I pet you?"

The leopard lowered his head toward her hand. She laid it on his fur, marveling at how sleek it was. He turned his head into her palm, and she rubbed behind his ears, enjoying how his eyes closed in pleasure.

He put his paw in her lap. She flinched at its weight, but his claws were sheathed. He hoisted himself to half rest on her thighs, his breath warm through her shirt. She continued to rub his head and scratch along the side of his face, and he let out a little whuff of contentment.

As she rubbed, he leaned forward until his large nose pressed the opening of her blouse, his breath hot on the bare skin beneath.

"Stop that," she said, but she couldn't help laughing.

Her laughter ended abruptly when his hot tongue lapped between her breasts, catching in the lace of her bra. She tried to push him away, but he was too heavy.

"All right, this is too weird, even for a dream."

The leopard looked up at her, a smug look in his eyes. *You like it.* His words, tinged with a growl, rang in her brain.

"No, I don't. I draw the line at leopards."

You have needs, Rebecca. I feel them. You're burning up with them.

His voice sounded so like Andreas's, that strange white-and-black-haired man with the same blue eyes. Dear God, was she manifesting him in her dream as a leopard? Was she that desperate?

She put both hands on his chest and pushed, but it was like trying to move a brick wall. "I have rules." She panted. "No animals."

He rumbled in his throat. *I'm different.*

He pushed her back, and Rebecca found herself falling from the chair to the soft carpet, the leopard on top of her. Her gasp was cut off when he licked her face with a broad, hot tongue.

His breath was surprisingly sweet, much better than she'd expected from a wild animal. But then, this was a dream.

His weight on her was warm and dense, and made her feel . . . protected. He licked her again, his tongue lingering on her lips.

"Really, you have to stop it." She pressed a shaky hand to his face, and he playfully nipped her fingers, keeping his razor canines in check. "I wonder what Freudian kink makes me dream about being licked by a leopard."

It depends on the leopard.

He licked her once again, slowly, and she let him. His whiskers tickled her throat, his breath so comforting and warm.

His tongue dipped between her breasts, lapping the sweat there. The bra kept him from touching her skin, but his leopard tongue found where her nipples pointed through the fabric. The licking aroused her nipples even more, and she tried to push him away again.

"No, I *really* can't do this."

But you're enjoying it. His nose wrinkled like he was laughing.

"No, I'm severely horny, and Andreas is hot."

You like Andreas, do you?

Her face heated. "No. He's rude and domineering, and everything a strong woman hates." She sighed. "I wish he weren't so damn hot."

I'll tell him.

"You'll do no such thing . . . What am I saying? This is a weird, kinky dream, and I still can't believe I'm having it."

He thinks you're sexy.

She burst out laughing. "Now I know this is a dream. I'm a major geek. No man thinks I'm sexy."

Andreas does, he said softly. *Sleep now, Rebecca.*

She tried to resist the command, but her eyes grew heavy, the dream drifting away. The leopard dissolved like smoke, and the next thing she knew, the sun was up. She lay on the floor with her blouse open, and Isis the cat was staring at her with curious green eyes.

~ ~ ~

PATRICIA swam to wakefulness, smelling coffee brewing and sausage frying downstairs. Delicious.

She was pleasantly tired, every muscle relaxed, her sexual play with Nico having left her contented to the deepest part of herself. She wasn't sure what she'd liked better: his feathers warm and soft all over her nakedness, his skillful tongue and hands, or just touching his lovely large cock.

They hadn't had full sex, not him inside her, which both surprised and delighted her. She'd never known a man and woman could have so much fun without actual intercourse.

She felt his warm weight beside her and smiled as she opened her eyes. Except the eyes that looked back at her weren't sinful dark brown but ice blue.

9

PATRICIA stifled a shriek. Andreas had stretched out next to her not wearing a stitch, his gaze that of a bad-tempered leopard.

"Damn it, Andreas, this is *my* bed."

He rolled half onto her, his body hard and heavy. "You want me here."

She put up her hands, but instead of pushing him away, her treacherous fingers caressed his shoulders. "No, I don't."

"I've been trying to avoid coming to you, even distracting myself watching over pretty Dr. Trimble. But you're thinking it, Patricia. You're thinking, *What would it be like with both of them?*"

Her face heated, but she couldn't deny the forbidden fantasies dancing around in her brain. "I don't want to hurt Nico. I don't want to be like that."

"He already knows. He told me this morning he knew it was time for you to take it to the next level."

Anger stirred in spite of her excitement. "I'm so glad the two of you decided for me."

His smile turned feral. "*You* decided, Patricia. We only watch . . . and wait."

"I don't want to hurt Nico," she repeated stubbornly.

Nico's voice came from the doorway. "You won't."

He walked inside, fully dressed, then shut and locked the door behind him. He looked not at all angry or dismayed that Andreas was there, though some suppressed emotion flickered across his face.

Staying dressed, Nico climbed onto the big bed and lay down on the other side of her. "What do you want him to do?"

Patricia's limbs felt watery and cold, her body hot and shivery at the same time. Andreas's breath warmed her face, the firm muscles of his arm heavy on her shoulder.

On her other side, Nico was all that was protective. She liked the feel of his jeans and shirt against her bare skin. Having a man on either side of her was an unfamiliar, delicious pleasure.

"Am I really doing this?" she asked in wonder.

"You are," Andreas said.

Nico laid his hand on her abdomen, once again the smiling, sinful, seductive Nico. "Give in to what you truly need, love. What do you want us to do?"

Patricia took a deep breath. Her most buried fantasies, the ones that made her blush and wonder if she was quite normal, started knocking for her attention. Nico's question loosened the desires that she'd wanted to fulfill for a long, long time but never imagined she'd have the chance. Now two men were at her service, their gold chains meaning she could ask them to do anything she wanted.

"I want Andreas licking my pussy," she said rapidly, "while I suck on your cock."

Andreas's blue eyes sparkled. "That's an arrangement I can take."

Nico smiled like a wine steward pleased with a patron's choice. Then his look turned as feral as Andreas's, and he ripped the covers from Patricia's body.

Patricia was still naked and damp from their play, and she'd slept hard. "Not yet," she gasped. "I have to shower."

Andreas rolled away from her, conceding. "We can do this *in* the shower."

"If it's a big enough shower," Nico added.

"We can scrub her down, anyway." Andreas sauntered into the bathroom, morning sunshine through the blinds' slats throwing stripes across his body.

"Nico," Patricia began.

He was on his feet, his hand at his fly. "Go," he said, his dark eyes shuttered. He didn't want to talk; he wanted to *do*.

Patricia scrambled out of bed and scurried into the bathroom, where Andreas had already turned on the water. The bathtub was a long whirlpool tub with a showerhead above it. It was large enough for two; a tight fit for three.

"It's warm," Andreas announced. "In you go." He snatched Patricia off her feet and easily deposited her in the shower.

His big body was warm and already wet. She hadn't liked Andreas at first, but she'd begun to warm to him. He was as trapped in all this as Nico, and his bad temper stemmed from that. Now her warmth for him was turning volcanic.

Nico walked into the bathroom, unclothed, as Andreas slid to his knees in front of Patricia. Andreas snatched a cake of soap from the holder and started to rub it over her thighs and pussy.

There was a second bar of soap on the counter in a box. Nico tore it open and dropped the little boutique soap on his large palm.

He reached into the shower and smoothed the bar over Patricia's back and shoulders.

The double massage felt wonderful. Patricia leaned her head back, letting the shower wet her hair, and Nico moved his hand to soap down her breasts.

"Every woman's dream," she murmured. "Two gorgeous men washing me all over."

Andreas chuckled. "We're just getting started."

Patricia hummed in her throat as four hands, slick with soap, moved over her breasts, her nipples, her clit. "I don't think the innkeeper would be too thrilled with us having a noisy threesome in her best guest room. Not to mention Rebecca. We don't want Dr. Trimble to run away in disgust."

"They'll never hear us," Andreas said.

"No? I'm sure sound carries in this old house."

Nico laughed softly. "We do have some powers, love. The ability to mask sounds to give us some privacy is the least of them."

Patricia shivered, despite the hot water, wondering what some of their greater powers were.

They both stopped soaping her and rinsed her off, then Andreas bent forward and started licking her nipples. She groaned, and Nico leaned forward to catch the sound on his lips.

The layout of the bathroom prevented them from enacting her scenario, so Andreas shut off the water, and the two of them dried her off and carried her back into the bedroom. There Nico sat her on a chair, and she tentatively spread her legs.

Andreas sent her a dark smile as he sat back on his heels in front of her. The shower had darkened his white black hair and dotted his shoulders with beads of water. He didn't seem to care as he leaned down and fastened his mouth on her pussy.

"Oh, God," Patricia moaned. While her mouth was still open, Nico bumped it with his cock.

She turned her head and seized it with her lips.

Nico made a soft noise in his throat and rocked back on his heels. His fists rested on his thighs, brown skin tight.

Patricia loved the way he tasted. She remembered what she'd told him she'd do in the car: take him into her mouth and feel every inch with her tongue, while she cupped his balls with her hands. She ran her fingers up the base of the cock to his balls, which hung tight and heavy between his legs.

Andreas proved he was the master of the tongue. He pressed her thighs open with strong hands and buried his face in her, his mouth doing all kinds of wonderful things. He was going to take her over the top in no time, and she wanted to come at the same time Nico did.

She mimicked the movement of Andreas's tongue with her own on Nico. He moaned and jerked, and then she felt his hands in her hair. She liked him caressing her, showing her that he liked what she did.

She couldn't believe she had two men pleasuring her. She, Patricia Lake, who felt more at home with bits and pieces of the past than with living beings of the present, was having two men at the same time. This had to be some giddy, wonderful dream.

She held on to Nico's cock with one hand, and with the other, ran her fingers through Andreas's hair. His hair was sleek and soft, probably like his leopard's coat.

Andreas certainly knew how to give pleasure. He alternately suckled her clit and licked it, nibbled lightly with his teeth, and tickled with his thumbs. When she feared she'd climax too fast, he slowed down; then, just when she'd caught her breath, he'd suckle her again and have her crying out.

"Patricia, love." Nico's voice was throaty.

Patricia was too far gone to sort out her feelings, but she knew she wished the *love* to be true.

Andreas suddenly sped up his attack, licking and suckling hard and fast. The room seemed to spin, nothing certain but Andreas's mouth on her and hers on Nico.

In a masterpiece of timing, Andreas had her hips rising with her climax just as Nico groaned and shot his seed into her mouth. Then Nico was pumping into her, stroking her hair and moaning her name while Andreas's mouth drove her climax on and on.

When things quieted, she opened her eyes and found Nico looking straight at her, his gaze so intense with emotion that she nearly melted off the chair. He quickly masked his expression and picked up a towel to gently dab her mouth clean.

Andreas sat back, his blue eyes wicked. "There. One fantasy, come true."

"Maybe she has another." Nico could make her hot and bothered with just his voice. Patricia should be sated—Andreas had done such a fine job—but she found her heart speeding at his suggestion.

Andreas laughed at her. "I think she does."

Andreas's cock was huge, sticking out of a thatch of dark hair, nice and hard. Nico beside her was only half deflated and growing again with the thought that she might want to do something else.

What Patricia wanted she barely dared let herself think. But something about the atmosphere around Nico and Andreas, something about their auras, electrified the passions she hid in her heart.

"Don't be afraid to tell us," Nico said. "No inhibitions before breakfast."

Patricia gulped. "But it's something . . . I never understood or thought I'd really want. Until I met you two."

Nico stroked her hair back from her face and leaned to kiss her cheek. "What is it, sweetheart?"

She drew a shaking breath. "I'd like you to suck Andreas off."

"Mmm." Andreas's usually cold eyes warmed. "Aren't you the wild one?"

"Not if you don't want to," she said hurriedly. "I wouldn't make you—"

Nico cut off her words with a kiss. "Hush, love. No inhibitions, remember?"

"But this is different. It's not about me."

"Yes, it is." Nico kissed her again, his lips warm and silken. "It's a different kind of need."

Andreas sent her a lazy smile. "You'd be surprised how many women want to watch two men putting on a show for the lady."

They weren't dismayed. She realized, watching them, that they'd done this sort of thing before.

Why did that make her more excited still?

"Well, get on with it," she said breathlessly. "I'm starting to want my breakfast."

"Listen to who's giving orders," Andreas said, eyes sparkling. He was still laughing at her, still arrogant, still in control. So was Nico. They might be compelled by this curse, but she had the feeling they managed to do exactly what they pleased.

Nico pulled a straight-backed chair next to Patricia's and straddled it backward. Andreas rolled nonchalantly to his feet, his penis stiff and hard and ready.

Patricia held her breath, unable to believe they would really do it. Nico slid his hands over his friend's hips, expertly positioning him, then Andreas tucked his cock neatly inside Nico's mouth.

Patricia sat so close she could see every lick, every suck, every bite that Nico gave him. She saw Andreas's hands clench and his body go rigid, saw his erection press the inside of Nico's mouth.

She gasped herself and pressed her finger to her clit as Nico had taught her. Watching Nico expertly pleasure his friend, eyes closed, sent waves of wild excitement through her. It was better than anything she'd ever imagined, raw and stark and real.

Andreas rested his hands in Nico's hair and Patricia's, stroking them both as Nico pleasured him. Patricia turned her head and licked the base of Andreas's cock, tasting Nico's lips along with the dark saltiness of Andreas's skin.

He liked it, urging them both on. Patricia kept on licking, her tongue and Nico's sometimes colliding. Andreas was groaning out loud, thrusting his hips at them as Patricia licked and Nico sucked.

Andreas's moans turned to animal-like growls, then he shouted, "*Fuck,*" and roared his release inside Nico's mouth.

10

BREAKFAST was tense. Nico joined Andreas, Patricia, and Rebecca in the sunny breakfast room after he'd caught a quick shower. The four of them sat at a corner table, the inn's eight other guests taking up the rest of the room.

As soon as Nico sat down, Mrs. Blake and her two helpers brought out French toast in a decadent fruit syrup, scrambled eggs with sausage and potatoes, muffins the size of Nico's hand, and coffee. Lots of hot, fresh coffee. Nico attacked his loaded plate, hungry after the morning's debauch.

Neither Patricia nor Rebecca would look at him. Rebecca shot sidelong glances at Andreas, her cheeks pink, and Patricia would not look up from her plate at all.

Andreas, on the other hand, leaned back in his chair, stretching out his long legs and sipping coffee, as though he'd done nothing more decadent that morning than read the newspaper.

"Did you sleep well?" their hostess asked cheerfully as she refilled coffee mugs.

Both Patricia and Rebecca jumped. Andreas yawned placidly. "I did."

"As did I," Nico joined in. Snuggling with Patricia had been sweet.

"Good. The cats like you, Andreas, don't they? I think Peachy stayed with you all night."

The three cats were even now winding around Andreas's feet, looking up with hopeful eyes. Andreas ignored them.

"They think he's their mother," Nico said.

Andreas gave him an evil look. "Their protector," he corrected coldly. "They know I will protect them."

The cats at the moment looked like they hoped he'd feed them. Andreas surreptitiously took a bit of sausage from his plate and crumbled it to the floor for them.

Mrs. Blake smiled at them. "You look lovely this morning, Dr. Trimble. I think the little porch room is good for you."

Without waiting for reply, she moved off, leaving Rebecca redder than ever. Nico noted she'd not pulled her hair back this morning but let it float across her cheeks in soft yellow waves. Instead of wearing a plain blouse like she had yesterday, this one had a little white embroidery on the collar.

"How is the translation coming?" he asked her.

Rebecca jumped half a foot and flushed deeper. "Translation?"

"You know," Andreas rumbled. "The one on the ostracon. The reason I'm here letting lackeys run my club."

"Of course I know which translation . . ." Flustered, Rebecca dug into a slim portfolio briefcase at her side and withdrew a small sheaf of papers.

Nico stacked the used breakfast plates in the middle of the table, and Rebecca spread out papers and the photos of the ostracon. Patricia finally looked up with interest, but she refused to meet Nico's eyes.

"It's a most curious inscription," Rebecca said. "I understand about half of it, but the other half is gibberish. I copied it out the best I could."

She spread out papers covered with hand-drawn hieroglyphs, jottings of hieratic script, and words written in English letters.

"Some of the words are easily recognizable," she said. "Others I'm not as familiar with off the top of my head, but I can look them up. But these . . ." She touched a row of hieroglyphs she'd copied out. "I can't make head nor tail of them. Some of them I've never seen before, and I've read most of the texts available. In other words, they aren't really hieroglyphs."

"Or they're so old, no one knows what they are?" Patricia suggested.

Rebecca shook her head. "No, we have examples of writing going all the way back to 3000 BCE. It's a completely different writing, or else whoever copied them onto the ostracon carved them absolutely wrong. I'd love to see the original inscription."

"On the ostracon?" Nico asked, studying the lettering. He could read some hieroglyphs, as many as he'd bothered to learn, but he couldn't read the odd ones Rebecca had pointed out.

Rebecca's embarrassment faded as she warmed to her subject. "Remember I said that it's likely whoever carved the inscription had no idea what he was copying. There are words and symbols here that are from far before the Ptolemaic period, Eighteenth Dynasty, I still think. Plus, your ostracon is only a fragment of the entire carving. It's likely the archaeologists on the dig found it in pieces, and the museum in Cairo still has the others. Or they sold all the pieces to different collectors."

Andreas listened with barely concealed impatience. "So you have to have all the pieces to figure out what it says?"

"It would be best. I can translate much of what's here, except the odd parts, but there will be gaps."

"Shit," Andreas growled.

"The other pieces shouldn't be too difficult to locate," Rebecca said calmly. "Archaeologists are manic about keeping records, at least in this day and age, and the museum will know exactly where all these pieces went. Also, if this inscription is a copy from something older, like a temple wall or tomb, there will be records of that, too."

"Unless the other pieces were destroyed or never found," Patricia said glumly. "It happens."

"We can but try," Rebecca said with confidence. "I know a lot of people in the archaeological world, and those people know people. Let me make some calls. You'd be surprised how much we can unearth, pardon the pun."

Nico hid a smile. Their translator was a little geeky, but she was smart, optimistic, and capable. Patricia had made a good choice.

Andreas caught Rebecca's eye and waggled his tongue at her. Instantly she subsided into incoherent blushing, and Andreas grinned. It made Nico wonder just what his friend had gotten up to in the night.

~ ~ ~

REBECCA scolded herself as she entered her snug room to start making phone calls. She'd had a dream last night, was all. Nothing to get all flustered about every time she saw Andreas.

But looking into Andreas's chill blue eyes, she understood why she'd dreamed him as a snow leopard. His mottled hair, his gleaming smile, and above all, his eyes, so beautiful and cool and arrogant, made her think of a beautiful wild cat. She'd seen a snow leopard only once, a sad specimen in a zoo, but her dream leopard had been strong and sleek.

She vividly recalled the cat's strength as he'd climbed onto her, his breath hot between her breasts. He'd known exactly where to lick . . .

Rebecca found her face heating again, and she banished the memory. It was a silly dream, but she realized what it meant. She'd wanted *Andreas* to do those things, and her dream had put him in the form of a leopard to keep herself from admitting it.

She made herself work hard in the autumn sunshine on her room's little porch. She liked problems like the strange hieroglyphs, unraveling inscriptions no one else had unraveled before.

Rebecca had made her name proving that the uninteresting could be important. A minor priest's account of what happened at a temple could solve the mystery of where a lost queen might be buried. She'd won awards for her work.

But spending days hunched over her desk or scorching weeks in the desert brushing dust from a piece of stone disrupted her love life—what there was of it. She hadn't been laid since . . . Oh, God, she'd forgotten.

She looked across the grounds and saw Andreas out on the grass, tossing a football back and forth with Nico. Just an ordinary guy in tight jeans and a sweatshirt, except that she'd turned him into a leopard in her dreams.

It was Saturday, and she didn't have a class to teach until Tuesday. She could spend the next three days here dawdling in this nice B and B with sexy Andreas. She hummed softly as she worked, enjoying the nice weather she missed shut up in an office.

A shadow obscured her papers, and she looked up in annoyance. Andreas leaned on the porch rail watching her, the three cats twining around his feet. He'd abandoned the football and Nico, who was walking away with his arm around Patricia.

"Andreas." She gulped.

He leaned over the porch rail and peered at the papers strewn across the table. Rebecca didn't let herself look at the way the blue jeans hugged his hips or at his zippered fly and speculate what his cock looked like lying snug inside.

"Getting anywhere?" he asked.

"What? Oh, the translation. It's moving ahead."

"How long will it take you?"

Her nervousness turned to irritation. "I don't know. It's not like scrubbing a bathtub. There are nuances, and I don't want to miss anything."

"Do you scrub many bathtubs?"

What was he talking about? "I live by myself, so yes. There's no one else to do it."

His eyes took on a mischievous glint. "I think I'd enjoy watching you scrub a bathtub."

She couldn't imagine why, and the way he looked at her embarrassed her and irritated her.

"I had a dream about you last night," she said sharply. "Or I think I did. You turned into a leopard."

His brows rose. "Really? What did I do?"

"You just . . . were a leopard. The cats were in it, too, following you around like they always do."

"They can't get enough of me."

Isis and Red Kitty were practically binding his ankles with their tails. Peachy perched on the porch railing beside him, closing her eyes as Andreas scratched her chin.

He looked too good. His sweatshirt stretched across hard shoulders, his throat strong and tanned. Blond hair covered muscular forearms that were crisscrossed with little scars. He'd shaved this morning, a faint scent of aftershave clinging to him.

"Maybe if I help, it will go faster," he said. He invited himself up the porch steps and scraped a chair out from the table.

"You read hieroglyphs?"

"Some. I can read enough to know that the inscription is about us."

Rebecca blinked at him. "About you? How could it be?"

He put his finger on the picture of a wild cat and the hieroglyphs next to it. Transliterated, they sounded like *ndr*. Egyptians didn't include vowels when they wrote; the reader filled them in.

"That's one of the words that makes no sense to me," she said.

"It's the name Andrei, the Greek form. I changed it to Andreas as times changed, because people could spell and pronounce it easier."

He pointed to a picture of a man with wings. The copier had drawn detailed feathers that flowed down the man's back and curled at his feet. The inscription transliterated as *ncls*.

"Nikolaus," Andreas said. "Which he shortened to Nico."

Rebecca laughed at him. "Andreas, this inscription is several thousand years old. I'll know exactly how old if we can find the original. As egotistical as you are, it can't be about you."

"It doesn't matter what you believe." He lounged back, clasping his hands behind his head. "As long as you find an answer for us. Soon."

"I don't work for you," she said in irritation. "I'm doing this as a favor to Patricia. You and Nico are the ones who insisted I stay here with you, but you keep interrupting me. I'm getting it done as fast as I can."

Andreas slanted her an unreadable glance. "I'll make it up to you." His voice went dark. "Promise."

"What do you mean by that?" she asked nervously.

Andreas leaned forward, putting his face near hers. "I know you like being licked between your breasts. I can do that for you."

Her face flamed. "You can't know that."

"Afraid I do." He tapped the picture of the wild cat. "It wasn't a dream, sweetheart. You tasted nice."

Her throat went dry. "You can't possibly know everything I dreamed."

Andreas skimmed his fingers down her throat and brushed the hollow of her collarbone. "You're awake now. Isn't it better this way?"

Rebecca wanted to stop him. She opened her mouth to tell him she would never finish the translation if he distracted her so much, but she seemed robbed of words.

She closed her eyes as his warm fingers continued downward, then he tugged at the lace of her bra. "Take this off."

Her eyes popped open. "You mean right here?"

"Take it off and put it on the table."

Rebecca glanced quickly over the porch railing, but she could see no one in the yard. The room was tucked into a corner, the porch shielded from the front of the house by two big trees.

She wet her lips. The Rebecca she knew would never dream of obeying him. She was practical, disciplined, smart, and sensible.

Her fingers seemed to move of their own accord as she slowly undid the buttons of her blouse. Andreas watched with flattering interest while she loosened the shirt enough for her to reach around and unhook the bra.

She'd mastered the art of removing her bra without taking off her shirt, wanting to rid herself of its binding spandex the instant she came home. She slid the shoulder straps down her sleeves and over her hands and then pulled the black lace bra away from her chest and laid it on the table.

Her blouse still covered her, but Andreas's gaze raked her as though he could see everything underneath it. "How long did it take you to learn to be so coy?"

"Is this being coy?"

"You're a tease."

"I can't be a tease. I have no one to tease."

"Open your blouse and show me your breasts."

She gasped at the abrupt command. "Why should you want me to?"

"*You* want to," he said flatly. "But you're waiting for permission." He gestured to her shirt. "Come on, show me."

The Rebecca she knew would snort in derision, tell him he was full of himself, and that she had things to do.

No, wait—the Rebecca she knew would never even get this kind of request.

Her fingers shook as she slid the rest of the buttons free. She closed her eyes briefly, then threw her inhibitions to the wind and slowly pulled open the blouse.

Cool air touched her breasts, which had never been bare outdoors before. Her skin tingled, and something inside her squeezed in excitement.

Andreas tilted his head as he studied her breasts, and she felt the absurd hope that he'd like them. The approval that flickered in his eyes made her want to give him more.

She pulled the blouse apart and slid it from her shoulders, letting it rest halfway down her arms.

Andreas growled. He slid his chair back from the table, and

before she knew what was happening, he had her out of her chair and on his lap, straddling his legs.

He leaned her back, and as the leopard had, licked between her breasts all the way up to her throat. Rebecca sucked in her breath, her quim going hot and wet. She loved the way he'd spread her legs around him, and for some reason she wanted to rub herself against his thighs.

Andreas traced circles on her neck, then licked all the way up to her lips. He danced his tongue around them, reminding her of what the leopard had done last night.

"This can't be happening," she said against his playing tongue. "I'm dreaming."

He cupped her bared breast, rolling her tight nipple between finger and thumb. "Does this feel like a dream?"

"The best dream."

He kissed her. His lips opened hers, his demanding tongue delving inside her mouth. It had been so long, so long, since a man had kissed her, and then they'd never kissed her like Andreas. She was coming in her pants, her hips moving back and forth like she was fucking him.

"Easy, darling." Andreas slowed the kisses, licking inside her mouth again. "You don't want to use me up too soon."

She had no idea what he was talking about. She suddenly wanted to kiss and kiss him, to drag him against her while he fondled her breasts.

She dipped her head and caught his thin gold chain between her teeth. She didn't know why chewing it was so satisfactory, but she was beyond reasoning.

"You'll get it, sweetheart," Andreas rumbled. "I'll give you all you want. But not yet. Things I have to do first."

"What things?"

He took her hands and held them still in his strong ones. His eyes glinted, something dark lurking behind the blue.

"Unfinished business. But soon." He pushed her from his lap, and she landed awkwardly on her feet.

She stared at him, her blouse unbuttoned and half open, the autumn breeze cooling her breasts. What would it be like, the devious imp inside her wondered, to be naked for him out on the grass? What would it be like to lie on the prickling green and spread her legs, inviting him to take her right there?

It would be incredible.

A sudden gust of wind made her shiver, and she dragged her shirt closed.

Andreas got sinuously to his feet and took the black lace bra from the table. "I'll keep this."

Rebecca's eyes widened. She tried to snatch the bra back, but Andreas folded it and stuffed it into his pocket. "Don't wear it the rest of your stay."

"I brought two more," she said faintly.

"Did you?" Andreas swung around and entered her bedroom, rifling the drawers until he found where she'd stashed her underwear. He lifted out two more bras, one white and one cherry red, and wadded them in his hand.

"I'll give them back when you go home," he said, then he walked out and banged the bedroom door behind him.

Her breasts suddenly itched, and Rebecca cupped them in her hands, feeling dew trickle between her thighs. No man had ever turned her on like this, and she wasn't quite sure if she could take it.

His high-handedness about the bra—about everything—

annoyed her, but at the same time it excited her to obey him. She sat down at her table again, pulling up the blouse, the fabric against her bare skin making her feel more wicked than she had in her life.

~ ~ ~

IN another part of the grounds, screened from view by a thick stand of trees, Patricia and Nico lay together on a blanket. They hadn't undressed, it being a little too chilly, but Nico had wrapped them in his lush wings, which kept them warmer than an electric heater.

"What will you do," Patricia asked, "if this inscription helps free you from the goddess? What are your plans?"

He nuzzled her, dark eyes enigmatic. "I've learned not to have plans. I never think ahead too much."

"You know that once you're free, you'd be free of me."

He shook his head. "I don't know what will happen once the curse is off, if it ever can be. I might leave this world and never come back."

She blinked. "What do you mean, leave this world?"

He touched her face. "The old gods have been pushed out as the world changes. They live apart now, away from the mundane world. It's harder now for the gods to move back and forth. Most have given up."

Patricia rubbed her face on his soft feathers. Nico wasn't human, as the wings she loved reminded her. He was half god, half nymph, tied to human beings only by the curse.

"I'd miss you," she said.

"You already have me enslaved. You could keep me here by destroying the inscription before Rebecca can decipher it."

"I wouldn't do that to you."

"You'd have nothing to lose."

Patricia tried to sit up, but he held her too tightly. "I hate that you're so sure I'll hurt you. Please believe that I won't."

He watched her for a long time, his eyes unreadable, then he kissed her forehead, feathers tickling her. "Like I said, I try to never look too far ahead, love. I'm only looking as far as tonight, and I have so many ideas about that . . ."

Patricia longed to hear them, watch him tell her with his seductive smile, but at that moment, Rebecca screamed.

11

Nico could move like lightning when he needed to, and he reached the porch room well ahead of Patricia. Andreas already had the Dyon in a headlock on the porch, the hissing, struggling creature trying to rake Andreas with his talons.

Rebecca had retreated to the doorway, watching with wide eyes. Nico sensed Patricia come panting up behind him, and at least she, too, was sensible enough to stay out of the way. All three cats stood on the porch railing, fur spiked, howling their encouragement.

"I was working," Rebecca called. "He just—appeared—and started grabbing my notes."

Papers were scattered over the floor, some ripped. Nico joined the fight, and the Dyon glared hatred from his yellow eyes.

Hera's being was strong, and Andreas was having trouble holding on to it. Nico ripped his shirt from his back and let his wings explode out of him. His strength and agility increased when he didn't mask himself, and he leapt at the Dyon.

Andreas released it, but only long enough to morph into his leopard form, teeth and claws ready.

The Dyon betrayed no fear. He fought hard, but Andreas's leopard strength coupled with Nico's god strength bested him quickly.

"Tell your mistress she's defeating herself," Nico said, his arm around the Dyon's throat. "We won't let her hurt those we're enslaved to."

"I tell her nothing," the Dyon spat. "I am hers to command."

Nico's rage boiled over. "Fine." He snapped the Dyon's neck.

Rebecca shrieked and clapped her hands to her face. Patricia, knowing how dangerous the Dyons were, relaxed in relief.

The Dyon dissipated into smoke, and suddenly Nico held nothing. The cats hopped down from the rail, tails high, purring loudly as they made for Andreas.

Rebecca's face was pasty white, and she leaned heavily on the doorframe. "I want to wake up," she panted. "Why can't I wake up?"

Andreas growled softly and butted his large head against her legs. Rebecca stared down at him in anguish.

"Oh, God, this is real. You really are a leopard, and I let you . . ."

Patricia passed Nico, her hand firm in his for an instant, then she all but shoved Andreas aside and led Rebecca back into the bedroom. "We need to have a talk," she said. "A long talk."

Patricia shut the door in Andreas's face. Suddenly drained of adrenaline, Nico hid his wings away and sat heavily on the porch stairs. He heard the crackle of bone and fur as Andreas resumed his human shape.

Andreas sat next to Nico and pulled on his jeans, his hard body covered with a sheen of sweat.

"This is getting fucked up," Andreas said in quiet voice.

Nico nodded agreement, his heart heavy.

The cats, perfectly happy with everything, draped themselves across Andreas's legs, their purrs like buzz saws. At least someone had gotten entertainment out of it, Nico thought. From inside the bedroom, he heard Rebecca burst into tears.

~ ~ ~

THEY stayed at the inn for the rest of the weekend while Rebecca made phone calls to archaeologists all over the country and outside it about the ostracon.

Patricia knew Rebecca had trouble believing, despite the evidence of her own eyes. But it was a lot to take in—Andreas was a leopard; Nico had wings; Dyons wanted the ostracon and turned to smoke when Nico killed them.

Rebecca could at least focus on the ostracon and the inscription, which she said was meat and drink to her. She doubled her efforts, letting the challenge help her deal with her shock of Nico and Andreas. She could barely speak to Andreas, shooting sidelong glances at him like a schoolgirl with her first crush. Once, when Rebecca had turned around quickly, Patricia saw that she'd taken to not wearing a bra.

Patricia left Rebecca to her work, only to find Nico's tension wound high.

He became as restless as Andreas, impatient with everything and worried another Dyon would find them. He said nothing more about what would happen if they found a way to get him free or what would happen if they didn't.

Whenever Patricia tried to start any conversation with him, no matter how innocuous, Nico would distract her with sexual play.

That meant her body was well sated by the end of the weekend, but she could get no closer to him.

Another thing that ramped up her frustration was that she and Nico still hadn't had full sex. Nico had brought her to some of the most profound pleasure she'd ever experienced, but they hadn't actually completed the act. Was he trying to make her so hungry for it that when they finally did consummate their relationship, it would be spectacular? She never could ask, because after their play, she'd drop into deep slumber, and Nico would be gone when she woke.

She'd thought that him being her slave would mean he'd do whatever she wanted, but he said no, it meant he'd bring her profound pleasure, his way. So far, she couldn't argue with his technique, but it left her emotionally unsatisfied.

The only one at ease was Andreas. The big, growling man spent the weekend reading newspapers with his feet up or talking on his cell phone to his assistant running the club back in Manhattan. He usually had a cat or two draped over him, and when he prowled the grounds at night as a leopard, they followed close behind him.

On Monday, Rebecca asked them to come to her porch so she could tell them what she'd found. Nico pulled Patricia to sit with him on a wooden bench, his arm around her, while Andreas lounged against the railing.

Rebecca lectured them from her table spread with papers. The ostracon had indeed been one of three fragments found in a Greco-Roman site in Alexandria. All three pieces had been studied, then sold by the Egyptian Museum in Cairo. One fragment now resided in Mrs. Penworth's living room, and Rebecca talked to an archaeologist who was certain the other two fragments were in the British Museum in London, where they'd lain for a hundred years, brought to England in a day and age in which they didn't want to share the artifacts with the country they came from.

Rebecca called the British Museum, but the person she spoke to could not be certain they were the right fragments, and apparently they didn't have the staff—or the interest, Rebecca said with disapproval—to photograph the fragments and fax them to her. Rebecca would have to go and look for herself.

"And anyway, it's better to look in person. A photographer or copyist might get it wrong." Her eyes were sparkling with excitement that told Patricia she was ready to continue the hunt.

"What about your job?" Patricia asked. "Your classes?"

Rebecca waved it away, a complete turnaround from the day they'd met her. "I only teach on Tuesdays and Thursdays. If we leave Thursday afternoon and get back by Tuesday morning, I shouldn't miss a thing. It is for research, after all. I could get a good journal article out of it."

Nico and Andreas seemed perfectly happy with this plan. Patricia expected Nico to tell her she'd be safer left behind, but he only looked at Patricia with pain in his eyes and advised her to come with them.

He was plainly torn between protecting her and needing her with him, the curse gripping him. Patricia supposed it would be kinder to remain behind, but she couldn't bear the thought of him going off without her. The curse must be gripping her, too.

Andreas and Nico offered to fund the tickets, which Rebecca accepted with the graciousness of a chronically poor graduate student. Patricia tried to pay her own way, but Nico insisted, then tortured her with pleasure that night for even suggesting it.

"You belong to me," he said, his voice dark with need. "Your pleasure and well-being is my charge."

He even gently tied a silken gag around her mouth as he played with her, preventing further argument.

Andreas bought the tickets online for Friday, the earliest they could find a flight, and on Friday morning, Patricia drove them all back to the city to catch the flight. The cats stayed behind at the B and B with Mrs. Blake. The innkeeper was happy to take care of them, which relieved Patricia, who hadn't wanted to leave them alone or put them in a kennel. The cats knew Andreas was leaving, and they sulked.

Andreas had booked first-class tickets, Patricia and Rebecca discovered when they reached JFK. He and Nico behaved as though this was normal, settling into the first-class lounge like they owned the place. Patricia usually flew as cheaply as she could when she went on buying trips and had gotten used to squishing shoulder to shoulder with strangers.

Rebecca, too, was used to bare subsistence travel as a student and doctoral fellow, and looked around in awe when they boarded the first-class cabin. Andreas had secured himself the seat next to Rebecca, with Nico and Patricia across the aisle from them.

"This is . . . cushy," Patricia said as she leaned into her generous seat on takeoff.

"Andreas likes to travel in style," Nico answered.

Andreas was busy saying something to Rebecca that made the young woman red and uncomfortable. When Andreas got up to wander to the bathroom, Patricia slid into his vacated seat.

"You can tell him to leave you alone, if you want," Patricia said. "He'll have to."

Rebecca tried to shrug it off. "I'm just not used to men. I mean, men who look at me as a woman instead of an academic."

Patricia grinned. "It happens."

"Not to me, it doesn't. I spent the past ten years trying to make men notice me for my mind. I was valedictorian, summa cum laude, top honors with my PhD. Universities are fighting to get me."

"Sounds like hell."

"No, it's wonderful," Rebecca said seriously. "I've achieved all I set out to and then some. Now I'm starting to want men to look at me for my body, and it's too late."

Patricia looked at her with a critical eye. "I don't think so. You have good material to work with."

Rebecca sighed. "I have no idea how to work with it. Look at me." She gestured to her baggy khaki pants, her pale pink top that made her complexion sallow, and her flyaway hair pulled again into a high ponytail. She wore no makeup as usual, but her face had good bone structure, and her lips were full, her eyes a soft brown.

"Leave it to me," Patricia said. "A few touches, and you'll be transformed."

Rebecca did not look convinced but let the matter drop.

Patricia got up as Andreas came back and returned to her own seat. Andreas put his lips to her ear as she passed him.

"You have a great ass, Patricia. Let me know when you want me to fuck it."

Sudden heat flooded her, and to her dismay, she had a vivid vision of him behind her, hard and ready to slide inside her. She felt her nipples pearl and her quim fill.

She dropped into her seat beside Nico without answering, and Andreas lounged back in his own chair, turning his full attention to Rebecca.

"What did he say to you?" Nico whispered. They couldn't snuggle very well in the state-of-the-art individual seats, but Nico leaned to her, running a caressing hand over her arm.

"Nothing important."

Nico watched her, his look turning dangerous. "I said, *what did he say to you?*"

He would get it from her, or Andreas, sooner or later. But she was struck with the sudden desire to tell him. It excited her to tell him.

She whispered what Andreas had said, and Nico's eyes darkened. "Do you want him to?" he asked.

"Well, of course not."

"Don't lie to me, Patricia. If you want it, that's what you'll have. You know this."

Patricia gulped and lay back in her reclining seat. "What I know is Rebecca had better hurry up and get that inscription translated."

Nico watched her a little longer, his eyes as dark as sin; then he chuckled and turned to look out the window. But he wouldn't forget the matter, and neither would Andreas, and she knew it.

~ ~ ~

WHEN they reached London, Rebecca discovered that the man they needed to talk to about the fragments at the museum was finishing up a holiday and would be back the day after tomorrow.

"They couldn't tell me that when we were still in New York," she growled as she hung up the phone in the suite they'd booked near the British Museum. "I suppose I could go over there and do some research while we wait."

"No, you can't," Patricia told her firmly. "Remember what I said on the flight? You're going shopping with me."

Rebecca brightened, as though offered a rare treat. "Shopping?"

"We're going to leave our boys and indulge in the frivolous, feminine sport of shopping. We deserve it."

Rebecca nodded, still hesitant, but her eyes showed her eagerness. "I suppose we do."

Patricia intended to find Rebecca an outfit that went with her trim little body and make her wear it. The woman was too used to the habitual slovenliness of the career academic, but she had potential, and Patricia intended to bring it out. *Like her fairy godmother.*

Plus, Patricia wanted to sightsee. She'd been to London before, but she usually only had time to go to antique auctions, ship her findings back home, and fling herself onto a plane, exhausted, for the return journey.

Now she and Rebecca strolled the streets and looked at what she'd only glimpsed from cab windows: the neoclassical glory of Buckingham Palace and the quiet of Green Park, Georgian houses that were an antique lover's dream, the Tudor remnants of Saint James's Palace. She pressed her nose to the window at Christie's and sighed over the beautiful antiques inside, pretended not to gawk at the wild characters in Piccadilly Circus, and walked with Rebecca out across the river to gaze back at the London skyline.

And they shopped. She and Rebecca browsed shops until Patricia found Rebecca an adorable skirt and jacket outfit, the skirt sexy-short and the jacket made to hug her figure. Rebecca perked up considerably looking at herself in the mirror, but she refused to accept it unless Patricia found something for herself. No conservative pantsuits or formless skirts, either; Patricia had to go for it.

Patricia tried on minute skirts and a dozen tops until Rebecca picked out a bright red skirt and a black sleeveless sweater with a halter neck for her. Nothing for it but they got thigh-high stockings and high black heels to go with it.

"Nico's eyes will pop out," Rebecca said as they walked out armed with shopping bags. "You make sure you wear it."

"I'll wear mine if you wear yours."

Rebecca nodded seriously. "Bargain."

They sealed it over a lunch of fish and chips in a nearby pub.

"I love London," Patricia said, rubbing her fried potatoes in vinegar before popping the satisfying concoction in her mouth. "So much history, from the Roman outpost to yesterday."

Rebecca only nodded. "I suppose."

Patricia laughed. "I forgot; you're used to working in 2000 BCE. This must all seem hideously modern to you."

Rebecca smiled. "Somewhat. Why do you think Nico and Andreas let us go off on our own today?"

"You mean why aren't they here protecting us from potential Dyon attacks?"

"Exactly."

Patricia stared at her empty plate, wishing more chips would manifest on it. "They must think we're safe for now. From what I gather, the Dyons are like dogs who have been trained to guard one thing and one thing only. If you get close to that thing, they attack. Otherwise, they ignore you."

"In other words, we're probably not on the right track," Rebecca said glumly. "Or else these Dyon things would be all over us."

"Something like that."

"Why did they insist we come here, then?"

"I don't know. They might have figured something out since we arrived and haven't bothered telling us."

Rebecca sipped her lager, making a face at the taste. "You mean they haven't bothered telling you. Andreas won't tell me anything directly if he can help it."

Patricia peered at her, noting her blush. "Are you falling for Andreas?"

"Seems like it." Rebecca drank more lager. "He . . ." She

heaved a loud sigh. "He teases me, but I don't think he's interested in more."

"Hmm." Patricia waited to feel anger or jealousy that Rebecca confessed her attraction for the tall, sexy Andreas, but none came. She knew she would have burned with hurt if Rebecca's target had been Nico.

"Have you told him?" Patricia asked.

Rebecca suddenly changed from a shy young woman interested in a sexy man to a resigned woman who knew what disappointment was.

"Men like that never want women like me," she said in a dull voice. "I don't know how to talk about anything but my job. He might be interested in having sex with me—getting the nerdy academic to let her hair down—but that's as far as it goes. He won't be moving in and helping me pick out a bathroom rug."

Patricia couldn't answer, because she wasn't sure Rebecca was wrong. Andreas might be compelled to Rebecca by the curse, but that might be as far as it went.

The two women looked for more answers in another helping of chips but drew no conclusions. They walked off lunch by strolling through Green Park and admiring Saint James's Palace, watching people teasing the stiff-faced guards.

They took the tube back to their hotel near the University of London and the British Museum and entered the front room of the two-bedroom suite. There was no sign of Nico or Andreas.

"Where'd they get to, do you think?" Rebecca asked, sounding a little cranky.

"In here." Patricia's voice was hollow as she froze in the doorway of the bedroom. Rebecca came to peer over her shoulder and gasped.

Nico and Andreas lay stretched out across the huge bed, Andreas's head on Nico's shoulder. Nico's wings cushioned both of them, and they were very naked.

Nico smiled at Patricia. "We thought you'd like a little show."

"That is, if you ever got here." Andreas snorted. "What were you doing, buying up the whole town?"

"We stopped for lunch," Rebecca said faintly.

"Hope you're still hungry," Andreas returned.

Patricia felt Rebecca's hand on her shoulder, a faint clutch as the other girl held herself up. Patricia swallowed on her dry throat as Andreas rolled over and gave Nico a full-tongued kiss.

"Oh, my," Rebecca breathed.

Patricia could say nothing. They were enjoying themselves, laughing together at Patricia and Rebecca standing stunned in the doorway. They didn't expect Rebecca or Patricia to *do* anything; this was a show for their benefit.

The two men tangled on the bed were so beautiful, Nico's wings providing a black, feathery background to their tanned bodies. Andreas's white black hair mingled with Nico's dark hair as they kissed, Andreas's strong hand on Nico's chest.

Patricia's quim grew hot as she watched the male sexual play before her. Cocks were rampant, not touching, Nico's lying against the curve of his thigh, Andreas's straight out. It was the most erotic thing she'd ever seen.

"I can't look," Rebecca whispered, but when Patricia glanced at the younger woman, Rebecca's gaze was riveted to the pair on the bed.

The two men broke the kiss, and Nico nibbled Andreas's upper lip. They turned together to the women in the doorway, smiles wide. The identical chains around their necks winked in the sunlight that streamed through the window.

"What would you like us to do?" Nico asked.

Patricia opened her mouth, but nothing would come out. Rebecca was breathing fast, hot against Patricia's shoulder. Patricia at least had grown somewhat used to the pair's blatant sexuality, but Rebecca must have been floored by it.

"Anything you want," Nico continued. "We're yours for the afternoon."

"Command us, ladies," Andreas said in a hard voice. "I'm getting bored."

Nico was laughing quietly; probably she and Rebecca were pop-eyed, their mouths hanging open to their chests.

Patricia cleared her throat, trying to dislodge the shock that had clumped in it. Her knees were shaking, but her nipples had pinched into tiny, hard buds. "Play with each other," she choked out.

Behind her, she heard Rebecca gulp.

"Play how?" Nico asked. His gaze riveted to Patricia, and in it she saw joy that she'd accepted this gift he offered.

"Bring each other off," she said. "Please."

"That's easy," Andreas said in his growling voice. "He's so hard he'll go as soon as I touch him."

"Speak for yourself," Nico answered.

He reached for Andreas's cock, closing his hand around the hard and heavy staff. Andreas arched his back, his eyes closing in pleasure. He swiped his tongue through Nico's mouth, then he grasped Nico's cock in his huge hand.

Patricia longed to go to them, to climb on the bed among all those soft feathers and be with them, but she also wanted to stay right where she was. Rolling around with them, she'd miss watching the ecstasy that made Nico give her a heavy-eyed smile.

They each knew exactly what the other liked. They stroked and tickled, dipped hands down to palm each other's balls. Andreas moved closer to nestle against Nico, and Nico stroked Andreas's back with his feathers.

Rebecca made a strangled noise behind Patricia. She saw the younger woman's eyes go soft, her lips parted and moist. Rebecca's hair had come down, and her cheeks were flushed, mirroring the heat on Patricia's own face.

"Are you glad you came?" Patricia asked her.

"Hell, yes."

Nico's talented fingers stroked Andreas from base to tip, while Andreas wrapped his hand around Nico's cock. Both men started to sink into the feeling, to forget everything around them but the touch of hands on each other.

Nico cupped Andreas's ass, strong fingers indenting his flesh. Andreas kissed him, tongue working against Nico's lips.

Patricia put her hand to her mouth, letting herself suckle her fingertip. Rebecca leaned against Patricia's back, not a sexual move, but for support.

"I can't take much more of this."

"You can if I can," Patricia said.

Of course, Patricia had the advantage of having participated in sexual play with both of them, of already having watched Nico suck Andreas for her. Even so, the waves of excitement that rolled over her were almost overwhelming.

Andreas swore as his seed spilled into Nico's hand, and he sped up his assault on Nico.

"Come on," he said hoarsely. "Come for me, damn it."

Nico held it in for a while longer. He drew Andreas's head against his chest, stroking his friend's hair, kissing it. Andreas squeezed Nico's cock and flicked his thumb smoothly over his tip.

Both men were incredibly sexy, but it was Nico's face Patricia watched, Nico's gaze she wanted to catch. Patricia swiftly unbuttoned her blouse and pulled up her bra, lifting her breasts in her hands.

"Nico," she said.

He looked up at her, watched her flicking her thumbs over her nipples the same way Andreas played with his cock.

Nico's gaze riveted to her a moment, then his body jerked, and he came, groaning hard.

"Fucking finally," Andreas growled.

"Shut up." Nico ground his hips, forcing his cock through Andreas's grip. Andreas held him down on the bed, Nico's wings moving restlessly with his ecstasy.

When both men finally wound down, Nico blew out his breath. "Damn," he said to Patricia.

She pulled her bra down again, the fabric catching painfully on her hard nipples. Andreas laughed at her and at Rebecca, whose forehead now rested on Patricia's shoulder.

"Enjoy the show?" he asked.

"Yes," Patricia answered, heartfelt. "Yes, I did."

"What about you, Becky?" Andreas asked her.

Rebecca looked up. Her face flooded with color, her eyes with panic. She squeaked, put her hand over her mouth, turned on her heel, and fled.

12

REBECCA refused to come out of her room the rest of the night, much to Andreas's annoyance. He decided to take out his feelings by helping Nico pleasure Patricia. Two tongues, four hands, and the delicious memory of Nico and Andreas kissing each other on the bed made Patricia fall asleep very happy.

The next morning, the four of them went to the British Museum, and Patricia accompanied Rebecca to the basement to talk to the assistant in charge of the fragments. He was a small, fussy man who didn't like female academics and told her that the two limestone fragments in question had been purchased last year by a smaller museum in Chelsea.

"So I'm afraid I can't help you, dear," he said, giving her a cool look. "Nothing much to interest you, anyway. Greco-Roman, nothing about King Tut."

Rebecca stomped away with Patricia and joined Nico and Andreas, who were waiting by the stairs.

Andreas's cold blue eyes flickered when Rebecca related what had happened, and Patricia saw a hint of claw in his fingers. "Maybe I should have a talk with him," he said.

"No." Rebecca sighed. "Let's just find the damn fragments."

Andreas nodded but walked protectively beside her as they left the museum. Another tube ride followed by a short walk brought them to a tiny, privately owned antiquities museum in Chelsea near the river.

In contrast to the snobby assistant at the British Museum, this curator was a weedy young man excited about the collection and its owner.

"Mr. Greeley truly *cares* about the past," he gushed. "He's not just trying to show off how much we managed to loot from the Near East a hundred years ago. Mug of tea, anyone?"

Rebecca relaxed and engaged the young man in conversation, while Patricia joined Nico and Andreas, who were wandering restlessly about the gallery.

Nico was quiet and subdued, Andreas boiling over with impatience. Nico slid his arm around Patricia's waist, drawing her close.

"Can we get this over with?" Andreas growled. "What the hell are they talking about?"

"Leave her alone," Patricia said. "She's worked her butt off to get us this far, and this isn't even her fight. She should be back at Cornell grading papers."

Andreas rumbled something else but subsided. Nico leaned and brushed his lips over Patricia's cheek. "This isn't your fight, either."

"It is, in a way."

"No, you could have handed me the information and turned

your back. Or called the police when you found me in your store. Or kicked me out without doing a damn thing."

Patricia knew she couldn't have. She'd been drawn to Nico the moment she'd seen him lying on the floor of her antiques store, spell or no spell. All she knew was that she wanted to take the slave chain from around his neck and see if what he felt for her was real or not. If it wasn't . . .

She'd cross that heartbreak when she got to it.

On the other side of the room, Rebecca's voice rose in distress. "You've got to be kidding me."

Andreas was next to her before she finished the sentence. The curator only grinned. "I adore how Americans talk. I hear it on the telly, but it's not the same, is it?"

"What's wrong?" Patricia asked.

Rebecca's eyes sparkled, the young woman angry enough to forget her shyness. "He says the owner returned the fragments to the Egyptian Museum. You know, the one in *Cairo*. In Egypt."

"Well, they weren't ours, were they?" the curator said, his grin still in place. "The stones were looted early in the nineteenth century by treasure hunters. One thing Mr. Greeley intends to do is send stolen artifacts back where they belong. He's all for returning the Rosetta Stone."

Rebecca made a frustrated noise. "I just wish he'd waited a little longer to be so gracious. Are you certain the fragments went back to Cairo?"

"Have the receipt and everything. I helped pack them."

"Why would they want them back, when they sold the third one to dealers?" Rebecca demanded.

"Who knows, love? Things go back and forth, round and round, or go missing like so many things did in the war. Had a good chat with the Egyptian archaeologist who came to retrieve it. Nice fellow."

"Do you happen to have the nice fellow's name and phone number?" Patricia asked.

"I do. And his e-mail. Hang on, I'll get them both."

The young man was so helpful, Patricia didn't have the heart to be angry at him, though both Andreas and Nico waited in stony silence.

They took the phone number of the archaeologist and the museum in Cairo from the curator, declined several more offers of tea, and left him alone with his treasures.

~ ~ ~

"Now what?"

Rebecca asked the question from the middle of the suite's sitting room, her hands clenched. She wore her shapeless pants and shirt and sneakers, as dowdy as the first day they'd met her.

Andreas was angry and restless as well, but strangely, Nico only leaned quietly on the windowsill.

"We go to Cairo," Patricia said. "We've come this far. Why not?"

"I can't go to Cairo. I have classes to teach. I'm not supposed to go to Egypt until December."

"Think of it as a jump start on your research," Patricia suggested.

Rebecca frowned at her but stopped snarling. She knew, as Patricia knew, that they'd go, and that was that. Arguing was a formality.

"Neither of you are going," Nico said quietly. He remained where he was, but his night-dark eyes glittered. "You'll return home. You've done enough."

Patricia expected Andreas to snap something at him, but surprisingly, he kept silent.

"You two talked about this," Patricia said, suddenly understanding the signals.

"We did," Nico answered. "And we decided that if things didn't work out here, you two were out of it. You have your own lives, and we're not part of them."

"You are now," Patricia said.

Nico shook his head. She sensed troubled emotion deep inside him. "We dragged you into this and didn't try to stop ourselves. We discovered the inscription in the first place. We'll take it from here."

"And who's going to translate it for you?" Rebecca demanded, hands on hips.

"I'm sure we can find someone in Cairo. They have experts, too."

"And leave us behind?" Patricia asked.

"The Dyons will follow us, not you. They haven't attacked us here, because they sensed London had no answers for us. But if the answer is in Cairo, they'll be there. You've given us enough to help; it's time to back off."

"Screw that," Rebecca said vehemently. "You can't seriously think I'd get this close to an answer and abandon it before I know what it is? I'd go crazy."

Andreas's lip curled. "I thought you had classes to teach."

"I do, but I can take a week off. Tell them I'm on a hot lead on a lost artifact; people like that."

"I have to agree with her," Patricia said. "I want to know, too."

"No." Nico rose, rage blazing. The dangerous spark in his eyes gave Patricia a glimpse of the demigod inside, the immortal being with plenty of power. "It's too damn dangerous. The Dyons could kill you. I'm not about to let you die because you wanted to satisfy your curiosity. Go the hell home, Patricia."

"Like a good little girl?" Patricia asked, wide-eyed. "If Rebecca and I want to go to Cairo together, we can. We have passports and money, and we're grown women."

Andreas's eyes flared with heat. "Why don't we show them how we deal with disobedience?"

Patricia saw Nico's arousal expand inside his jeans even when his eyes still held anger. "Spankings, you mean? I don't know. It might be too much fun."

Patricia's throat went dry. The easiest way for Nico and Andreas to turn an argument in their favor was with sex. If Nico tied Patricia with the silk scarves he liked to used and spanked her bare ass . . .

She ripped her thoughts from that delightful path. What he'd likely do was subdue her with sexual play, and then when she was sound asleep, he and Andreas could slip away, leaving her and Rebecca high and dry.

No way in hell would she let that happen. She had to keep control here . . . somehow.

She slanted Rebecca a look. "How about *we* show them just how grown-up we are?"

Rebecca gave her a puzzled look. "What? Oh, you mean . . ."

Patricia caught her arm and dragged her into their bedroom before she could blurt out what Patricia had in mind. They hadn't modeled their new clothes yet; Patricia had intended to keep the clothes for a surprise, perhaps a celebratory dinner out, but it looked like celebrations would be a long time coming.

Patricia closed the door on Andreas's outraged expression and locked it. Then she and Rebecca brought out their new clothes and changed into them, ruining her declaration that they were mature, adult women by giggling through the whole procedure.

Patricia admitted to herself that she enjoyed getting pretty for a man. She hadn't for so long that she'd forgotten how good it felt to slip into slinky clothes and put on a little makeup. She made Rebecca wear some, too.

While they admired themselves in the mirror, Rebecca unbent so far as to hug Patricia and plant a kiss on her cheek. "Thank you."

"For the makeup?" Patricia stepped back and rubbed off the lipstick Rebecca left on her cheek. "It wasn't much."

"I mean for making me do this. I never think about what I'm wearing, because my mind is on so many other things. I don't realize." She gave herself a big smile in the mirror. "You've made me pretty."

"You were already pretty. The right clothes bring it out, that's all. Now let's see if we can make their eyes pop."

Nico's and Andreas's eyes stayed intact when Patricia and Rebecca walked back in, but both men went still. Nico's gaze roved over Patricia, and so did Andreas's, then Andreas's gaze was pulled to Rebecca.

"Don't do this to me," he muttered.

Patricia smiled at them both, while Rebecca blushed, unused to the attention.

"So, while we're still in London," Patricia said, "why don't you take two sexy girls out on the town?"

~ ~ ~

IN spite of his frustration and anger, Nico liked the feel of Patricia's waist under his hand as they wandered the London streets, deciding which club they'd try. She was absolutely beautiful and sexy, and if he didn't get free of her, he'd spiral down into mindless slavery until one word from her, no matter what it was, would be enough to sate him, and a kick would be a caress.

He could already feel it happening, the need to please her more and more, no matter what he wanted. And as he mired in desperate need, she'd become more and more indifferent, until she shoved him away in disgust.

He would be left humiliated and broken, in despair and heartbreak, and he'd hear Hera's laughter. He'd recover slowly, painfully, maybe taking years, until he was caught in another woman's net, and the same thing happened again.

With Patricia, he knew, it would hurt more than it ever had before. Something else lay behind the compulsion of the curse, something he'd never felt in his long life. He didn't understand it, but he knew it would devastate him all the more.

They finally found a club that met with Andreas's approval and got themselves inside, immediately hitting the dance floor. Patricia smiled up at Nico and twined her arms around his neck. She thought her tight red skirt and black sweater made her sexy, and it did, but he was dying to tell her that sexiness radiated from her whether she wore a designer dress or sloppy jeans.

He loved that she'd dressed herself up for him, and that the skirt let his hand slide smoothly over her backside as they danced. Nearby, Andreas showed Rebecca how to dance, she rocking awkwardly on her new high heels.

Patricia laughed up at Nico and kissed him, her lips warm and soft. He was in far too deep with her, and he knew it.

The song came to an end, but they danced through another, and then another, then the four broke off and sought the bar. Patricia declared the need to visit the bathroom and grabbed Rebecca to drag her off. Rebecca looked confused and said she didn't need to go.

"No, we're *supposed* to go together." Patricia laughed at her. "So we can talk about them."

"We are?" Rebecca still looked confused but allowed Patricia to tow her across the floor to the crowded doorway of the women's powder room.

Nico and Andreas ordered drinks for themselves and the ladies and slid onto chairs while they waited. It was too loud to talk, but Nico had nothing much to say.

He noted the interested glances other women threw at him and Andreas, but he didn't regret not being able to return them. His bond to Patricia was strong and strengthening every day. Andreas, he could tell, was feeling pulled by Rebecca's interest, despite his three-way play with Nico and Patricia.

He and Andreas never knew what bizarre twists the curse would take, their bed activities dictated by the whims of the women they were locked to. It was tedious—usually. This time Nico was loving it too much.

"They've been in there a long time," Andreas said into Nico's ear. They'd finished their beers, and the ice was melting in the women's drinks.

Nico knew women could linger in restrooms, primping or, as Patricia said, discussing their men, but a feeling of unease went through him.

"Let's find them."

Andreas nodded once. They strode through the crowd, dancers melting out of their path. The crowd around the women's bathroom had gone, leaving the door closed and ominous.

Nico strode in without compunction. The room was empty, silent except for the trickling of water flowing unheeded into one sink.

Nico snapped off the tap, while Andreas checked the stalls,

every one of them empty. He sniffed the air, his nose more sensitive to scent than Nico's. But Nico knew even before Andreas said it, and his blood burned.

"Dyons."

A square window at the back of the room was wide-open. It led to an alley, with a small drop to the pavement, but there was little doubt the Dyons had taken them out that way.

"They're still alive," Nico said. His bond to Patricia had definitely not broken.

"I know," Andreas said grimly.

Nico pushed past him and climbed through the window, and Andreas followed.

13

THE tape around Patricia's wrists was painfully tight, as was the duct tape across her eyes and mouth. She felt Rebecca's warmth near her, heard the young woman's quick breathing.

Her psychic senses told her the Dyons stood around them. Two of them had burst into the bathroom where she and Rebecca had been laughing and renewing their lipstick like the teenage girls they'd both somehow missed being.

Neither had been the one Mrs. Penworth had shot or the one from the B and B in Ithaca, but they had the same white hair, strange snakelike eyes, hissing voices, and hideous strength. They'd overwhelmed the two women and dragged them through the window, through an alley, and into a car, where a third Dyon waited.

Patricia had no idea where they were, thanks to the makeshift blindfolds. Patricia knew London fairly well, having had to locate obscure dealers and galleries in her capacity as an antiques buyer, but lying blindfolded in the back of a car didn't help her get her bearings.

Fortunately, a blindfold meant nothing to her psychic senses. The vibrations from the place they were in were thick, layers upon layers of them. That meant the building was old, which meant the inner city, not a new suburban development. It didn't help much, because they couldn't be too far from the club in High Holborn, and this part of London was hundreds of years old.

Patricia could tell even without her psychic ability that the room was not very big, and it was underground, like a cellar. The air was dank, the walls not sealed against the weather, and the floor was cold, hard stone.

Next to her Rebecca jerked and gave a little cry, and a moment later, the tape was ripped from Patricia's eyes and mouth, taking skin with it. One of the Dyons, shorter than the other two, held up a sheaf of papers. "Where are the rest?"

Rebecca half sat up. "Hey, where did you get that? I left everything in my briefcase, you thieving shit."

"Obviously they went through our rooms," Patricia said, her mouth dry from the tape. "While we were out enjoying ourselves."

"This is not all of it," the Dyon said in his hissing voice. "Where is the rest?"

Rebecca scowled. "Wouldn't you like to know?"

Patricia leaned to her. "Maybe we should pretend to help."

"Oh, please. I've faced archaeology profs and customs officials tougher than him. Remind me to tell you about the dragon lady from hell who was my dissertation advisor."

"Archaeology profs aren't supernatural minions of a vengeful goddess," Patricia pointed out.

"Want to bet?"

"You're giving yourself away, you know," Patricia said to the

Dyon. "If we weren't close to an answer, you wouldn't bother with us."

The Dyon's slitted eyes blinked once, but no emotion emanated from him. "Where is the rest?" he repeated.

"How do you know that isn't everything?" Rebecca asked, sounding innocent.

The Dyon slammed the papers to the floor. One of the others brought out a matchbook from the club Nico and Andreas had taken them to. Silently, the Dyon lit a match, caught the entire matchbook alight, and dropped it onto the papers.

Rebecca wailed, and Patricia's heart sank. "You bastard," Rebecca yelled. "Do you know how many hours I worked on that? How much sleep I lost for it?"

Patricia watched as the photographs of the ostracon burned to blackened curls. The original was back in New York, far from here. She wondered if the Dyons had gone back to Mrs. Penworth's apartment and destroyed it, and if Mrs. Penworth was all right.

The lead Dyon kicked aside the ashes and lifted Rebecca by the shirt. She kicked at him, but the Dyon flung her to the floor again and ripped her top open. He thrust his hand inside, not to grope her, Patricia saw, but to check if she'd hidden any papers there.

Rebecca screamed and bit him. Patricia tried to roll to her to help fight him off, but a second Dyon hauled Patricia to her feet and held her back. She saw then a table laden with various implements for slicing, and realized what the Dyons had in mind. Convenient that London was situated on a large river.

Patricia redoubled her efforts, having no desire to become fish food. The Dyons didn't seem to mind that the two of them screamed their heads off, so this area must be relatively deserted. Not helpful.

Patricia was not a telepath; she couldn't read minds or project her thoughts into other minds, and so she couldn't broadcast a distress signal or anything. All she could do was fight the Dyon who held her and watch as Rebecca was dragged by the other two toward the table, her clothes in shreds.

"How about if we take you to the rest of her translation," Patricia panted.

The lead Dyon turned to her, his snakelike eyes flaring. "Tell me where it is, and we will spare your lives."

"Sure, I believe you. We'll tell you when we get there."

Rebecca glared, but Patricia couldn't convey her plan. Not that she had a plan. But if the Dyons took them out to the street, they might have more of a chance to get away or to attract enough attention to bring help.

The lead Dyon came to Patricia. He grabbed her hair and yanked her head back, bathing her with his foul breath. "Tell me, and I will spare the other one. Don't tell me, and she dies."

Patricia swallowed as the third Dyon held a thick-bladed knife at Rebecca's throat. Her breasts hung exposed, but she glared in fury, more enraged than afraid.

Patricia had no idea where Rebecca had put the rest of her notes, so she'd have to improvise. She wet her lips, but before she could speak, the incredible aura of a demigod brushed her stretched psychic senses.

"Nico!" she screamed.

Half the wall splintered inward as a wooden door flew off its hinges. Nico sailed in on a spread of black wings, his body surrounded by blinding light.

Two Dyons went down with Nico on top of them, the third bowled over by the leopard that came charging in. Patricia sprang out of the way and shielded Rebecca the best she could with her wrists still taped. Rebecca was shaking, tears of anger and fear rolling down her face.

After a brief but nasty fight, the Dyons dissipated into smoke, then the feathered whirlwind that was Nico stopped in front of Patricia. She cringed from the incredible power surrounding him, unable to look directly at the light. She'd snapped her psychic shields into place the instant he and Andreas had burst in, but the light still blinded her.

She watched him deliberately suppress his divinity. Nico's form solidified into the tall and strong man with black, feathery wings that Patricia loved. His face lost its terrible power, returning to the sinful handsomeness of Nico, but his dark eyes retained something grim and hard.

"Nico?" Patricia felt tears start in her own eyes, then Nico's warm wings were surrounding her and Rebecca, protecting and comforting. Patricia rested against the warm strength of Nico's body, feeling safe.

Andreas the leopard stretched, shook himself, and became Andreas the man, stark naked and unashamed. He surveyed the room and Patricia and Rebecca clinging to Nico.

"Don't I get a hug?" he asked.

"No." Rebecca scrubbed tears from her face. "You took too long getting here. They burned my notes!"

"But I saved your life," Andreas argued.

Rebecca was far gone in relief and hysteria. "Never mind my life; these were my *notes*. The only record I had of your damn inscription. I spent so many hours—"

"But you have more," Patricia said from Nico's embrace. "You have what the Dyons were looking for."

"There isn't any more. I wasn't finished writing it all down; the only translation I have is in here." Rebecca jabbed the side of her head.

"Oh." Patricia shivered. "I'm glad I didn't know that."

Andreas reached for Rebecca, but she spun away from him. "Don't touch me," she shrieked. "And for God's sake, find some *clothes*."

~ ~ ~

PATRICIA lay with Nico in their bed in the hotel suite, warm from a bath and relaxed with brandy, but she still couldn't bring herself to sleep. She wasn't sure what had frightened her more: the Dyons ready to snuff out her and Rebecca with as much indifference as they would a bug, or seeing the divine being that was Nico.

She could pretend all she wanted that he was a sexy human male, even one with wings who delighted in giving her pleasure, but she knew she'd never seen the real Nico. Nikolaus, son of Dionysus, Andreas had said. Half god, the other half not even human.

He was a being she couldn't comprehend, bound into his humanlike form and enslaved to Patricia. She couldn't pretend around it anymore. It was all too bizarre.

She'd tucked Rebecca into bed after making her take a sleeping pill fetched from a nearby chemist's shop. Rebecca had been shaking and curled in on herself during their drive to the hotel, the trauma of their ordeal finally taking hold. Andreas had wrapped Rebecca in a blanket, his movements almost tender.

Upon their return, they found that their rooms had been searched, their belongings dumped in a pile in the sitting room, and Rebecca's laptop smashed to pieces. Patricia had gotten Rebecca to bed and helped Nico clean up, Andreas waltzing out with no word of where he was going, probably off to look for more Dyons.

Nico had carried Patricia half asleep into the bathroom and deposited her under a hot shower, then fed her brandy and curled up next to her in bed. He hadn't tried anything sexual, as though knowing that what she needed now was just to be held.

As the window went gray with dawn, Patricia finally spoke. "How did you find us?"

Nico lay with his head on his bent arm, his strong hand on Patricia's abdomen. "Through the scent," he said. "Dyons smell."

"They drove us through a lot of streets. How did you track us?"

Nico's smile didn't reach his eyes. "They really stink."

"I didn't notice any particular stench."

"You wouldn't. They're foul beings, made from the clay of Hades; the smell of death clings to them. It's how Andreas and I knew the Dyon had come to your store in Manhattan."

"Where do they go when they evaporate? Or dissipate, or whatever it is they do."

Nico shrugged. "To tell you the truth, I don't really know. Back to Hera, back to the underworld, I don't know. I don't much care. They die or are at least reduced to the mud from whence they came."

Patricia shivered. "Why couldn't you smell them tonight, at the club?"

He was silent a long time, and when Patricia looked up at him, his eyes held shame and anger. "We weren't paying enough attention. I was distracted by the crowd and smoke and smells of humanity—and your scent."

"Are you saying I stink, too?"

He smiled again, but again without warmth. "Your pheromones were strong, and I couldn't think of anything but you." He stroked her hair. "It wasn't only the Dyons I could track; it was you. I can feel you; I'm bound to you. I'm for your pleasure but also your protection. I won't let anything happen to you."

"Part of the curse?"

"A good part," he whispered against the softness of her hair. "A very good part. I know you're still scared. Let me soothe that from you."

The points of his wing tattoo moved in the shadows of his shoulders, and she traced where the bottom of the tattoo brushed his backside.

"Can we make love?" Patricia whispered against his mouth. She shied away from the word *fuck*, wanting something that sounded intimate and not just a physical act. "Why haven't you done that yet? I crave you."

"To make it all the sweeter," he whispered in his flirtatious voice.

Something flickered in his eyes, but he looked away before she could read it. She took his face between her hands.

"Bull. You told me it hurt you to not take me when I wanted it. You've been holding in the pain, haven't you?"

"Maybe."

"Why would you do that?"

Nico kept stroking her hair, his fingers soothing. "I don't want it to end too soon. I want this part to go on longer, you wanting me, you not having enough of me. I'm dreading the boredom in your eyes."

"I could never be bored with you."

His gaze was neutral. "You won't be able to help it. All I can do is savor you while I have the chance."

"Andreas doesn't seem to worry about it much."

"Andreas isn't pulled to you as I am; he hasn't bonded to you, because you didn't want him as much as you wanted me. I'm flattered."

"Of course I wanted you. How could I help it?"

He shrugged. "You happened to see me first."

"I met Andreas not long after that. I remember you protected me from him. I liked that."

"I consider you mine. I'm tied to you, but I get very protective, very possessive. I can't help it."

Patricia kissed him, loving how warm his lips were. "I don't mind."

"You might mind later."

She framed his face in her hands again. "Nico. This is now, not later. I want to make love to you. I've been dying to have you inside me. Please."

His eyes darkened, pools of night. "Do you want it rough?" he asked. "Or sweet?"

Her pulse fluttered. "Can I have a little of both?"

"You can have whatever you want. Do you want me to find Andreas?"

"No," she said quickly.

He studied her, his eyes hinting at the power she'd spied earlier that night. "I know what you truly want, Patricia. I can feel it."

He slid his hand between her legs, his fingers finding wetness. She swallowed a groan, not wanting to come too fast. She wanted him to be inside her when she did.

"You want two cocks, don't you?" he whispered. "Both of us in you at once?"

"I couldn't . . ."

"You could if you wanted it. With me, you can have anything you want. I'm a demigod; I'm good at granting wishes."

"I just want you."

"For now." He slanted his mouth across hers, his tongue wet and hot. "For now it will just be me. Spread your legs."

She obediently parted them, expecting him to climb on top of her and slide right inside. Instead, he stroked her, thumbs playing over her opening.

"I love your hair," he said, fingers circling in the curls. "Blond all over. I like that you don't shave."

"I don't want to itch."

"My sweet, practical Patricia."

"Do you think it would be sexier if I did?"

He kissed her softly. "No. I like to rub my tongue in it. I like feeling it against my fingers."

"Good."

His fingers were certainly doing delightful things. He knew how to easily bring her to readiness, how to soften her for anything he wanted. Her body responded quickly to him, already knowing to trust him.

When the tip of his hard staff nudged her opening, she tensed. She'd had his fingers and tongue inside her, but his cock was huge and thick, and she wasn't sure if she could take it.

"Shh." He soothed her with lips and fingers, his wings sliding out to caress her to quietness. Her limbs felt heavy but excited at the same time, and her hips began to lift.

"That's it, love," he murmured, and then he slid halfway inside her.

The feeling was explosive. She wanted to spread her legs, wider, wider, wanting him squeezing inside her.

He went maddeningly slowly, a small inch at a time, though she was so wet and slick she wondered that he didn't slide right in.

"There is a lot of me," he said, as though reading her mind.

"I want you," she begged. "I want it all."

He took his weight on his hands, his big body between her spread legs, his feathers warm and silky. "Close your eyes," he whispered.

"No, I want to see you."

He kissed her eyelids, closing each one. She felt a warmth, then a brief burning, and then he was inside her, filling her so full.

He was huge and stretching her, and it felt so damn good. She hadn't had sex in a long time, and she knew why he wanted to take it slow. He was bigger than anything she'd ever felt.

She opened her eyes to find him staring at her, his dark eyes fathomless. He'd offered to make it sweet or rough, and she wondered which one this was. His hardness was opening her wider than she'd ever been, but at the same time, the dark heat filled her tenderly.

That was nothing to the sensation when he slid partway out and all the way back in again.

"Did you do your spell to muffle the sound again?" she gasped.

"Yes."

"Good, because I am going to scream so loud."

"Do it." His voice throbbed with longing. "Scream for me, Patricia."

He pumped her again, a hard in and out. She opened her mouth in a long moan.

"Yes, love," he said. "Feel me fucking you."

"I feel it. You fucking me. I love it."

He closed his mouth over more words, and he shifted his hips back and forth, sliding his enormous cock in and out of her. He sped up, the friction in her quim getting faster and faster, the warmth turning to unbearable heat.

Nico snaked a few feathers between them, letting them tickle her clit as his loving went on and on.

"Come with me," she gasped.

"Yes."

His whisper was like the night, her dark god-man who made

her feel crazy and happy. She knew she loved him, and she wanted that love to be real, no matter how many Dyons she had to fight off to make it so.

She felt herself building, the black surge coming toward her. Nico kept pumping, hard and strong.

She tried to shout *I love you*, but her climax grabbed her and took her over the top, and her words trailed off incoherently. Nico kept on driving into her, his big body sweating, his muscles working in silence.

Just as she hit the top of her climax, Nico groaned out loud, and his seed filled her. It scalded every inch inside her, a demigod's semen in her body. She wondered for a giddy instant if she could conceive from him, and a wild hope blossomed inside her.

His thrusts became frantically fast, his control snapping, then he wound down until he was resting on her, panting, his cock still inside her.

She stroked his hair, soothing him, feeling cleansed and beautiful. She kissed his temple and said into his skin, "I love you."

She regretted the words in the next instant, because he lifted his head and gave her a look so anguished it was as though all the pain in the world had come to settle in his eyes.

14

PATRICIA swam to wakefulness, smiling when she felt Nico's feathers cradling her body. His eyes were closed, his dark hair falling over his face. They'd made love twice more after the first time, and Nico had brought out some lube to make things even slicker and hotter.

She remembered stupidly telling him she loved him after the first time, but she did not want to take the words back. Even if the feelings didn't turn out to be real, they were real enough now.

She touched Nico's face, loving the strength of him. He didn't wake, didn't even stir in his sleep. His body was relaxed, wings still, feathers warm.

She heard a growl. "Nice."

Patricia looked up to see Andreas standing over them, gazing at the pair of them in approval. He was dressed in jeans, his hair wet as though he'd just finished a shower. He smelled of soap and shampoo, and his feet were bare.

Nico's eyes slid open, but he said nothing and didn't move. Andreas laid his hand on Patricia's ankle, then smoothed his way up her leg to her thigh.

"What are you doing?" she croaked.

Andreas's grin widened. "What you want me to do."

"I don't want you to do anything. I thought you were out looking for Dyons."

Andreas parked himself on the edge of the bed and rested his hand on her sheet-covered hip. "Patricia, I wouldn't be here if you didn't want it." He touched the chain around his neck. "You start wanting me, I respond. That's the way it works."

Patricia remembered Nico's look as he wove his fingers together. "Tangled," he'd said.

Nico lay quietly beside her, his arm heavy on her abdomen, waiting to see what she'd do.

"The solution is simple," she said to Andreas. "I'll tell you to go away. If you have to be my slave, then this is what I'll ask for: you in another room."

"It doesn't work *quite* that way. You crave the greatest pleasure. Now I crave to give it to you. You can't tell me you haven't been looking at me and wanting me inside you."

Patricia wanted to deny his accusation, to tell him to get out, but she fell silent. She knew she'd been fantasizing, in the back of her mind, about him doing more to her. Nico had told her that last night.

"I don't know what I really want." She propped herself up on her elbow and looked at Andreas. "I don't know."

"Go ahead, Patricia." Nico said from beside her. "This is what we're here for. To indulge your fantasies." His eyes were warm.

"I meant what I said before. That I—"

Nico's finger on her lips stopped the words. "This isn't about what you said before. This is what I am here for, why I'm bound to you." He smiled a little. "I'm not worried you're going to run off with him or anything."

"He likes to insult me," Andreas said. "He thinks he's so subtle I don't understand."

Nico ignored him. He stroked Patricia's hair, waiting for her to make her decision. Something stirred in her belly, a dark excitement she'd never experienced.

"Damn," she whispered.

She lowered the sheet from her body. Andreas grinned, his smile hot and wide. He stood up and shoved off his pants, revealing his tall, naked body and very needy cock.

Nico's expression remained controlled, but she sensed his growing excitement.

"Let me see you, too," she begged.

Without changing expression, Nico shoved the rest of the covers from the bed, revealing his strong, thick cock standing up from a thatch of black hair.

Andreas's was a little longer and a little less thick, his hair dark. He held himself, lifting to her, showing off for her.

He caught up the lube Nico had left on the nightstand and squeezed a bit into his hand. He rubbed it on his erection, stroking up and down until he glistened and gleamed.

He poured more on his fingers and gently rolled Patricia onto her stomach. She hugged the pillow, her face in the warmth of the blankets. Air hissed through her teeth when she felt the cool of the lube against her anal star.

"You ever done this before?" Andreas asked.

"Not *that*."

Nico chuckled. "Well, there's a first time for everything."

Andreas's skilled fingers smeared the lube over her star, then began to press her gently, relaxing her. Patricia had never had any-one touch her there before, and she had no idea what to do.

Nico got out of bed and came around to stand beside her. "Look at me," he told her. "Enjoy looking at me and let him get you ready."

She did enjoy looking at Nico, and this view was particularly nice. His hair curled crisply at the base of his penis, the organ jut-ting out dark and dull red. She loved it.

She felt herself relax and open, then Andreas slowly slid a fin-ger inside.

She gasped and tensed, but as he worked his finger around, she suddenly grew warm all over. She found herself relaxing, feeling herself opening to him.

Andreas didn't rush her. She kept gazing at Nico, taking in not only his penis but all of him, a tall, powerful man. His hips were narrow, his thighs strong, his hands large and sinewy, fingers brushed with wiry black hair.

"Why not feathers?" she asked in a dreamy voice as Andreas filled her with a second finger.

Nico looked bemused. "What?"

"You have wings. Why do you have hair instead of feathers?"

"Because I'm only half a winged creature. I don't even look like this when I'm with the gods at Olympus. But I can exist in the hu-man world like this, with part of my otherworld self that I can hide if I need to."

She remembered the incredible light that surrounded him when he'd rescued her from the Dyons, the divine power shining from him. Would she be able to see his true form at all, and would she understand that it was Nico? She wasn't sure. She liked him as he was, a gorgeous man with wings.

Andreas's hands warmed her buttocks, squeezing them gently,

then parting them. She'd taken two of his fingers, and now she felt the soft bluntness of his cock.

She moaned, sure she couldn't do this. Fingers were one thing, but Andreas was huge.

"It's all right," Nico whispered. He brushed back her hair, his fingers warm and gentle.

Behind her Andreas pushed the slightest bit in. His hot weight covered her back, his cock so big and pulsing that she cried out.

"Shh," they both said at the same time. Nico stroked her hair, and Andreas pressed quiet kisses to her spine.

"I want you." Patricia reached for Nico and pulled him to her by his cock. He came willingly, bumping his tip against her mouth.

"That's it, sweetheart," Nico breathed. "Suck me while you let Andreas in."

She resisted one last instant, then suddenly her body relaxed. Nico slid into her mouth while Andreas entered her ass.

She gasped with joy and found her mouth full of Nico. She suckled him, reveling in the unique taste of him, the feeling of his pulse beating under her tongue.

Andreas filled her. His cock was just as huge as Nico's, and she imagined her ass welcoming him as much as her quim had welcomed Nico last night. Andreas stretched and warmed her, her hips moving of their own accord to accommodate him.

Andreas leaned to her, his arms coming down on either side of her to enclose her against his body. His chest was damp with sweat and his shower, his hair dripping to her back.

It felt so . . . different. She shivered but was hot, wanted to scream and yet wanted to enjoy in silence.

She nearly did scream when Andreas pumped once.

It felt as good as regular sex, and then again, better—no, not better, different. It was warm and loving, hot and exciting. She wanted to thrust her hips back at Andreas, have him ride her fast and hard, and at the same time she loved the feel of him simply inside her.

Nico groaned softly, and she realized she was suckling him with all her might. His hands curled, one coming up to play with her hair.

"She's tight," Andreas said. "She's so fucking damn tight."

"Do her," Nico urged. "Pump her."

Patricia didn't know whether to cry *yes* or *no.* Andreas laughed, a feral sound, and suddenly he was riding her as she longed him to, his cock sliding in and out of her, the lube and her eagerness smoothing the way.

She realized a long time later how much he could have hurt her. He was a strong man, and he could have taken what he liked no matter what she felt.

But Andreas didn't. He slid in and out, going hard and fast, but never so hard that he caused pain. It was delight, not hurt, a feeling of fulfillment she'd never had in her life.

Nico pumped a little into her mouth. She used her lips and tongue on him, wanting to give him as much pleasure as she was getting. She loved him for letting Andreas do this; she loved him for getting excited with her.

I'm in a threesome, she thought, suddenly wanting to laugh. She wanted to shout her sheer joy and delight that she, Patricia Lake, had two beautiful men making love to her at the same time.

Andreas slid his hand between her legs and pressed his fingertip to her clit. Hot liquid poured out of her, wetting her thighs and Andreas's hand. Almost at the same time, Nico squeezed his hands shut and groaned his release, filling her mouth.

And then Andreas. He shuddered against her, his seed scalding, filling her and trickling from her to mix with her own juices.

"Oh, damn, that was good," Andreas moaned. He bit Patricia's neck, not hard, then licked it.

"Did you like it?" Nico asked Patricia. He'd withdrawn from her mouth and wiped her lips clean with the sheet.

She tried to say, *Oh, yes. Let's do it again, please. Please?* but she could only make a noise of exhaustion. She dropped onto the bed as Andreas slid very slowly and carefully out of her.

Nico laughed. "I'll take that as a yes."

Behind her, Andreas stretched, letting out a groan of satisfaction. He bounced off the bed, still full of energy, and patted her lightly on the behind.

"I told you, you have a great ass, Patricia."

He scooped up his pants, slid them on, then, whistling, waltzed out of the room.

"Is he always like that?" Patricia asked sleepily.

"Afraid so." Nico stroked her hair once, then came around the bed and climbed back in.

His wings slid across her, and she leaned back into him, so in love with him that tears flowed from her eyes and wet her cheeks.

~ ~ ~

REBECCA woke to hear someone running the shower in her bathroom. Weak sunlight trickled through the windows, London cloudy and foggy, which went with her mood. She hated taking sleeping pills, because she always woke up groggy, and this morning was no exception.

She shoved her hair from her eyes and sat up, memories of the night before floating to her. She and Patricia had survived being kidnapped and nearly killed, but that was not what made her heart sink to her toes.

She'd lost every bit of the translation she'd done on the ostracon and the photographs of the thing itself. Not to mention her expensive laptop and all her notes on it.

She supposed they could call this woman Mrs. Penworth and have her take more photos, but she hesitated, not wanting the Dyons to harm anyone else over this.

She remembered enough of the strange inscription that perhaps when she saw the other two fragments of the text, everything would make sense. They could take photos of the pieces and then visit Mrs. Penworth again when they went back to Manhattan and take another look at the third. Nico and Andreas could protect them all from Dyons while Rebecca worked.

She threw back the covers, noting she was in her underwear and nothing else. She vaguely remembered peeling off the tattered remains of the gorgeous clothes Patricia had made her wear, and felt momentary grief. She'd been sexy and pretty, if only for a few hours. Now she felt fusty and needed a shower.

The shower was running full blast when she entered the room, filling the room with steam that filmed the mirrors. She'd expected to find Patricia, but Andreas stood behind the opaque glass door to the shower, his large body naked, his head thrown back in enjoyment, as hot water poured all over him.

~ ~ ~

ANDREAS felt someone looking at him. He turned his head, wiping water from his eyes, and saw Rebecca, her flyaway hair a mess, her half-nude body still.

He smiled at the same time he felt the bond between them snap into place. Good thing he'd had so much fun with Patricia this morning, because he wouldn't be going back to her now. She'd never fully engaged him; her longing was for Nico.

But Rebecca's longing had touched him more and more, and

now it was certain. He felt the lock around his heart and felt a mixture of dismay and excitement.

He opened the shower door, letting water rivulets run all over the floor. "Come in."

She stared at him, her eyes dull with induced sleep, her face creased by the pillow. Andreas reached out and dragged her into the shower, underwear and all.

Rebecca made a muffled shriek. She blinked up at him as the shower got her panties sodden.

Andreas hooked a finger on the waistband and dragged them down over her ankles. He threw the panties over the top of the shower stall, and they landed with a wet splat somewhere on the floor.

Rebecca's mouth was still open, so Andreas slanted a kiss across it. She tried to step back, but the shower was too small.

"Don't kiss me, I'll taste nasty," she said.

Andreas laughed. She'd never taste bad to him, his shy academic. Not shy, really; she'd had the balls to work her way up to what she was now, and she'd go further still. But she was hesitant with men who noticed her sexuality.

"I'll just lick your skin instead," he said, and proceeded to lap his tongue along her neck and shoulders, working down to her breasts.

She held on to him, raking her fingers through his hair as he suckled first one nipple, then the other. He had to bend his knees and push her breasts to his mouth, but the awkwardness made it more exciting.

Andreas lifted her in his arms and wrapped her legs around his hips. His cock still hung outside her, but it was nudging her sweet quim.

Eons ago, before Andreas had been caught in Hera's revenge, he would have simply slid into Rebecca and pumped until he was satisfied. Now he had to make sure she was the one pleasured, not himself, but somehow he didn't mind having to. It was something he would have chosen anyway if he'd come upon her.

Rebecca tried to look so dowdy, but the reality of her body was lush and lovely. He slid his hand between them to massage her clit, liking the way she jumped.

"Feel good?" he asked.

"Why are you doing this?"

"Why not?" He continued to stroke her, moving his fingers around her quim. She was wet from her come and shower water, a fine combination.

"Patricia is prettier than me."

"That's what you think."

She moved her hips, her body loosening and liking what he did. "I had the feeling you were being pulled to her, you know, because of your curse."

"A little bit. But you pulled me harder, Becky." He grinned. "So here I am."

"Why do you call me that? Everyone calls me Rebecca."

"That's why. I want something special, so you're Becky to me."

She smiled shyly but with apprehension in her eyes. "I don't want you to be here because of some compulsion by some goddess. If it isn't real, then please go away."

Andreas slid a finger inside her, and she broke off with a gasp. "This is real," he said. "You don't want me to go."

"No," she whispered.

"You believe the story, then? About Hera and the curse and our enslavement? Patricia said you were skeptical."

She shook her head, her hair plastered to her face. "Stories can be powerful. I know all about stories as an Egyp—*oh*—tologist."

He'd slid a second finger into her. Her quim gripped him, pulsing, and he knew she hadn't released in a very long time.

"That's all right, Becky. I'll take you over the top."

Rebecca tried to answer, but her excitement was getting the better of her. Her head rocked back, right in the stream of the shower, water sliding over her face.

He rubbed and tickled, smiling at how very wet she was. Her legs clamped hard over his buttocks, and he held her with one hand planted on her sweet ass, the other fingering inside her. She was light in his arms, like she was made to be there.

"Oh, God, I love it," she moaned.

"You should do this every day," he murmured. "Every day let me release you. You'll be so relaxed."

Her fingers furrowed his hair. "No, I'd never want to do anything else."

"And that would be bad because . . . ?"

"So many reasons." She gasped and moaned as he slid in a third finger. "I can't remember any of them."

She squeezed him hard, harder, and suddenly she came beautifully, her body jerking, her cries incoherent. She was warm and lovely, and his cock wanted her so badly.

Slow. Don't scare her.

"Do you love it, Becky?"

"Yes. *Yes.*"

She was laughing and shaking her hair in the water, splashing it all over everything. Andreas kissed her, drawing her hot excitement into him.

He felt his anger at the curse and Hera and the Dyons receding as he got lost in her kiss. Something inside him tried to fight it, knowing that pain was going to hit him hard.

But that something was far away now, and his heart warmed as Rebecca kissed him sloppily back, humming in satisfaction. He liked that he'd made her happy, and he wanted to do it again.

Andreas snapped off the water and carried her out of the shower, with her still wrapped around him. She laid her wet head on his shoulder and gave a little sigh of contentment.

He took her out to the bedroom and set her gently on the bed. She unwound her arms and legs from him with reluctance, then yawned and stretched. He liked that the look of stark fear she'd had last night had vanished. When he'd found her with her clothes all torn, he'd burned with rage and enjoyed snapping the Dyon's neck.

"I didn't find any more Dyons last night," he assured her. "I hunted them, but they are gone. They did what they came to do."

"Destroy my research," she said mournfully. "They broke my laptop, the stupid bastards." Her eyes filled with tears.

He stretched out beside her, bringing the blanket around her to keep her warm. "I won't let them near you again, sweetheart. I'll stay a leopard, so I can scent them better and protect you better. I won't leave your side."

She blinked brown eyes at him, then her red lips curved into a smile. "I think everyone would stare if a leopard followed me around. I don't think they'd let you on the bus with me. We'd have to get you a leash."

"Very funny."

She giggled, drunk with pleasure. "You need to think of these things if you plan to stay a leopard. What about feeding? We'd have to set up an account at a butcher shop. If you have to chase and kill your meat yourself, I don't want to know about it."

"Stop." He kissed her to halt her words. She turned readily into the kiss, and his heart squeezed. Maybe if he pleasured her sense-less, she'd get tired of him quickly, and then it wouldn't hurt so much when she broke it off.

Sure.

Andreas rolled on top of her. "Do you want to fuck?"

She smiled sleepily. "Direct, aren't you?"

"I can make you feel so good you won't remember the Dyons or even your own name. Want me to?"

"That sure of your sexual prowess, are you?"

He shrugged. "Why be modest?"

She started laughing, shaking his body in a delightful way. "You are such a shit."

"You haven't answered my question. Do you want to fuck until we pop the bedsprings?"

"It's a platform bed; there aren't any springs. Besides . . ." She put her hand on his lips as he started to growl a smart-ass answer. "I don't want to jump into this without thought or protection. What about STDs?"

He gave her an incredulous look. "I can't give you STDs. That's a human thing. I don't carry any kind of disease. I'm part god; it doesn't stick to me."

"What about fleas?"

"What?"

"You're a leopard. Can you give me fleas? I couldn't put up with that . . . or the cat hair."

Andreas growled and nipped the side of her neck. "Think you're smart, don't you, sweetheart?"

"And then there's pregnancy." Her eyes were serious.

"You don't want kids?"

"I didn't say that. I want them someday. I'm just not picturing you sticking around to raise the cubs. You and Nico will get what you want and go."

"Is that so?"

She shrugged. "Whatever it is you want from the inscription, you'll be finished with me once you have it. Nico seems pretty attached to Patricia, so he'll try to stay with her, but you wouldn't stay with me. You're not the stay-with-one-woman kind of man."

"You sound pretty sure of that," he said.

"I work with lots of men, Andreas. I've seen what they do, and I make sure they never do it to me."

Her stubborn expression told him a lot. "Is that why you hide your beauty? Why you conceal your body under ugly clothes?"

"I mostly don't think about my clothes."

He nuzzled her. "You looked absolutely gorgeous last night."

She blushed, but her stubborn look remained. "Is that why you are suddenly interested in me? Because I wore a tight skirt?"

"It's the curse, sweetheart. It's called me to you, so here I am. Your love slave."

"I don't like the *it's the curse* line. If you don't want me just because you do, no way am I doing anything with you."

"You already let me make you come in the shower. You seemed perfectly happy with that."

"I was half asleep and still scared. That's all. You're not doing it again."

He laughed low in his throat. "I'll do it again. And again, and again. We're connected now, you and I, until this spell wears through. You surrender to me, and I make everything very, very good."

"But you're the one under the curse."

"So are you. You want the pleasure I can give you. You need it."

Rebecca's brown eyes darkened as his words sank in. Her pulse beat in her throat, her desires making her body flush with warmth.

Her scent grew stronger, her pheromones pouring over his animal senses. She was hungry, the pleasuring in the shower only partly sating her.

She snaked her arms around his neck and pulled him down to her. He licked her, loving running his tongue all over her face.

"Andreas," she said, her voice low. "My answer is yes. I do want to make love."

He shook his head, water dripping onto her as he pulled away. "Not yet."

She made a noise of exasperation. "But you just said—"

"I said I would give you what you need. You need to work up to it, to be so excited that when we finally mate it is the best you've ever known."

Her eyes darkened again, her excitement building despite her frustration. "Then why did you ask me if I wanted to? That's the first thing you said when we got on the bed."

"I know. I changed my mind."

Her hungry look turned to a glare. "I was right; you are a shit."

"Better get up and get dressed. The other two lovebirds are going to want breakfast." He kissed her nose, then lifted himself away.

It was physical pain to do it, but he knew that what Rebecca needed right now was not mindless screwing. She needed to savor it, to enjoy every moment with her full attention. His body screamed at him to take her now, but he held himself back. It had to be her utmost pleasure, not his.

Rebecca smacked him with a pillow, glaring at him in rage. She was beautiful lying there naked with her brown eyes glowing.

Andreas deflected the pillow with one arm, still grinning at her. His cock was rampant and moving with his pulse, aching for him to fall on her and fuck her.

But the pain was worth it, he thought as he walked away from her. He'd achieved what he'd needed to this morning: he'd erased the terrible fear in her eyes that had been there the night before. He'd eased her and made her forget.

He sent her a hot smile, then went off to find some clothes.

15

Nico booked tickets to Cairo the next day, the first flight available that he could get four seats on, which would leave a few days later. Patricia decided to enjoy the extra time in London and took Rebecca shopping again to replace the clothes ruined by the Dyons.

Patricia also indulged in casual clothes that were sexier than she usually let herself wear. She was a businesswoman, not someone who wore cute cropped tops and tight skirts or pants that bared her hips. But her real life seemed far away, and she wanted Nico to find her sexy. He did, nuzzling her belly when she modeled the clothes for him, dipping his tongue into her conveniently bared belly button.

Rebecca bought sexier clothes, too, though she blushed a lot when she wore them. She spent most of her time trying to re-create her translation from memory, but her frustrated swearing told Patricia she wasn't having much luck.

Rebecca seemed awkward with the attention Andreas now paid her, although she flushed with pleasure under it. Andreas had moved his rough charm firmly to Rebecca, and Patricia was glad.

Not that she hadn't loved what he'd done with her and Nico, but something had changed in her relationship with Nico, and Andreas wasn't part of it. Nico never said a word about their three-way sex play, but he made love to Patricia with increasing fervor, replacing what Andreas had done with his own dark seduction.

They flew out of London to Cairo, entering a country Patricia had never visited before. She was excited; she'd dreamed of going to Egypt since her teen years, ever since she'd read Agatha Christie's *Death on the Nile*. She wanted to see chaotic Cairo and the pyramids at Giza, sail down the Nile, and visit Karnak and the Valley of Kings.

Rebecca, on the other hand, was comfortable almost to the point of being blasé as they went through customs and stood in line to obtain the tourist visas they needed. How Nico and Andreas had obtained passports, Patricia didn't know, but she supposed that, like the endless quantity of money they seemed to have, they'd solved the problem of identification a long time ago.

It was warm, the temperature far higher than late September in New York or London. Patricia and Rebecca had bought more concealing clothes to wear in a country that didn't like bare flesh, and Patricia found that the layers helped keep the baking sun off her body.

They left the airport to take a hired car Nico had arranged to a small hotel. Nico and Andreas stood out in the crowds, two tall, broad-shouldered men, especially Andreas with his strange, mottled hair. Rebecca spoke to the driver in hurried Arabic as soon as they got in, and the car jerked forward to dive into the hideous snarl that was Cairo traffic.

The hotel they reached was a small luxury hotel on the banks of the Nile near the Egyptian Museum.

"How did you find this?" Rebecca asked, as she looked wide-eyed around the suite of rooms obviously meant for the ultra-wealthy. "When I come for the digs, we're lucky we find someplace acceptable to fall into bed."

"I know the owner," Nico said but wouldn't elaborate.

The suite was an elegantly tiled apartment with a fountain in the antechamber and four bedrooms, so there was no ambiguity about who would sleep where or with whom.

Nico and Andreas had also decided to become abnormally protective. They wouldn't let Patricia and Rebecca leave the hotel, and both women loudly protested.

"You can be right next to us," Rebecca insisted. "We won't get lost; I know my way around Cairo."

"And it's an antiquer's dream," Patricia put in. "I could get so much for my store, as long as the import fees don't kill me." She was almost salivating, the antique lover in her wanting to dive into the back streets and browse.

"I'll take you shopping when all this is over," Nico said. "The Dyons are much closer to home here, and they'll be more powerful."

"I thought you said they come from Hades."

"They do. But Greece is where Hera made them, and the closer they are, the stronger."

Patricia had to concede that it would not be smart to invite the Dyons to follow them, even though she was dying to explore. The hotel had a screened balcony that overlooked the river, the flowing Nile looking so peaceful compared to the craziness of Cairo streets.

"You mean I have to stay cooped up here?" Rebecca wailed. "I wanted to take Patricia to Giza."

Patricia smiled. They were hardly "cooped" in a huge, arched living room that boasted seven Egyptian-style couches and satellite television, and four enormous bathrooms with deep whirlpool tubs. There was a maid and concierge for this room only, who said they'd serve supper to them here as well.

The furniture was true antiques, Patricia could tell from their psychic residue. One of the screens on the patio was an old carved seraglio screen. Patricia ran her hand along it, feeling centuries of women, some frustrated with their confinement, some who felt safe and protected. The vibrations of their love, anger, happiness, hope, despair, and grief came to Patricia loud and clear, and she stood for a long time, her hands on the screen, absorbing the energies.

"Did you hear me?" Rebecca's voice cut through the din in her head. "They're being way too quiet."

Patricia opened her eyes, letting her shields slide back into place. "You mean Nico and Andreas? Yes, I noticed."

"Andreas is driving my crazy."

Patricia hid a smile. "I see the way he looks at you."

"Like a cat waiting to pounce on his next meal? Do you know he said he'd insist on staying a leopard to protect me if he had to?"

Andreas's pull to Rebecca had become very obvious, but Patricia could tell the two of them hadn't had full sex yet. Rebecca was too irritable: a woman craving a man, not a woman satisfied by him.

"I think they're worried," Patricia said, glancing inside where Nico and Andreas lounged, the male attendant having brought in coffee.

"I think they're anxious to get this over with," Rebecca said. "And be rid of us."

"Maybe." Patricia looked at Nico again, who was blowing on his coffee to cool it. Her heart squeezed. He was a beautiful man, at her side protecting her during the day, warming her at night. She'd never had it so good. "I'm not ready to be rid of Nico, though."

"You make a great couple. I'll bet you stay together a long time."

"Nico says their curse doesn't work that way. I still think he's wrong. I can't imagine me pushing him away."

"Andreas—" Rebecca broke off and tugged her loose hair with one hand. "I don't want to push him away, either. But he says he has to make me wait until I really, really want him. He doesn't believe me when I say I do."

Patricia thought of Andreas's sinful smile whenever he'd stolen into Patricia's bed and helped Nico pleasure her. He was a taunting, calculating lover, like a cat stalking its prey, while Nico was playful, teasing, and maddening. His silken wings made her entire body sing.

When they ducked back inside, Patricia started to laugh. The cat she'd seen down in the hotel lobby had managed to get into the room and now stood on Andreas's lap, having his chin scratched by Andreas's broad finger.

"Fleas," Rebecca said. "Like I said."

Andreas growled at her but continued to scratch the cat.

They ate in the suite, the hotel staff bringing them a huge meal of koshari, a pasta and rice dish with spicy sauce, a fish stew, chicken kebabs, and plenty of bread and baba ghanoush. It was tasty, and between the four of them and the cat, they reduced it to crumbs.

After dinner, to Patricia's and Rebecca's exasperation, Nico and Andreas told the two young women to stay put in the hotel room and vanished into the night.

~ ~ ~

"WHY do you think he's following us?" Nico asked, glancing behind them.

"Hell if I know."

"Want to make any guesses who it is?"

Andreas shook his head, his gaze on the pavement. "No."

They rounded a corner into Cairo's busy streets, where mostly men roamed. "You'd think Hera could leave us alone to be miserable."

"You like to dream."

Nico glanced at him. "And you don't?"

"No point in it." Andreas hunched his shoulders, his hands in his pockets. "Forget about it, Nico. It's not real, and you know it isn't. Doesn't matter how many times you fuck her. It will turn out the same in the end."

"This inscription might help break the curse," Nico said.

"Wishful thinking. I doubt it."

Nico doubted it, too, but he didn't like hearing Andreas say it plainly. "You were the one who first pointed out the inscription," he reminded Andreas.

"I changed my mind. We shouldn't have pursued it; we wouldn't be here chasing a wild goose."

"We wouldn't have met Patricia and Rebecca."

Andreas's ice blue eyes flashed. "Like I said. We wouldn't have met them and been spared what will happen when they are ready to dump us. It's going to hurt like hell, worse than it ever did before."

Nico stopped. Two men who'd been walking behind them nearly

ran into them, and Nico said a gruff apology. "You're saying that meeting them is part of the curse, that you spotting that inscription in the magazine was one more step in Hera's idiotic game."

Andreas nodded. "I wouldn't have been so long-winded, but yes. That's what I think."

"Shit," Nico said.

"She's a pissed-off goddess," Andreas growled. "She'll grind us under her heel for eternity; that's what vindictive goddesses do."

"Shit," Nico repeated.

"You said it. Still interested in catching our stalker?"

Nico nodded, though every muscle in his body hurt. "We'd better. Doesn't smell like a Dyon, though."

Andreas agreed. They strolled along like nothing more than friends walking off their dinners. Nico had sensed someone behind them all day, but every ruse they tried to make their follower reveal him- or herself didn't work. Nico also felt a ripple of something he didn't understand, something he *should* understand, but he couldn't quite place it.

They didn't speak much on their way back to the hotel. The night was warm and overlaid with the smell of exhaust, food, and many people living in close quarters. The lobby of the hotel was airy, with pointed arches and polished screens, open to the first three floors. It had a hushed elegance, a hotel for the wealthy who didn't want too much flash. Their friend Demitri had done well for himself.

Andreas entered the suite upstairs and then swore. Nico barreled in behind him, heart hammering, to find Andreas standing with his hands on hips in the middle of the empty living area. "They're not here."

A check of the bedrooms and bathrooms proved Andreas right. Rebecca and Patricia were gone.

"Damn Demitri," he snarled. "I told him to look after them, not to let them out."

Shutters were still fastened at the windows, with no sign of disturbance. The two women, probably pissed at being told to stay put, had gone.

Nico's heart jumped when he heard laughter from the corridor, and a moment later, Rebecca and Patricia entered the room together.

"There you are," Patricia said, looking happy.

Nico wanted to grab her and hold on so tight she couldn't slip away again. "Where the hell were you?"

Andreas glared at both women and Rebecca glared right back.

"Downstairs talking to an Egyptian antiques dealer," Patricia said. "He was harmless—not a Dyon in disguise or anything."

"And how did you get downstairs to meet him?" Andreas demanded. "You were supposed to stay here."

"We weren't planning to leave the hotel," Rebecca said. "We're not stupid. We went downstairs to look at the gift shop and got to talking to this man. He deals antiques all over the world, and he and Patricia knew a lot of the same people. We were downstairs an hour, no big deal."

"The big deal is we told you to stay put," Nico said.

Andreas looked at him. "I liked women better in the old days: obedient."

"I agree," Nico said.

Patricia's glare was palpable. "Well, welcome to the twenty-first century. If we think men are idiots, we're not afraid to tell them so."

"The point is, it was damn dangerous to leave the room." Nico loved how Patricia's green blue eyes flashed in rage, making her more beautiful than ever. He knew Demitri wouldn't have allowed Patricia to sit and talk with anyone who wasn't safe, but he was enjoying the argument. He enjoyed every aspect of being with Patricia.

"Not really," Patricia countered. "There are two big men on the door, courtesy of your friend the hotel owner. We noticed them. They wouldn't have let us out if we'd tried."

Nico tugged her into his arms. "You scared me. I don't like worrying that I've lost you."

She looked up at him in surprise. "You don't need to worry about that."

He did, and he knew he did. He kissed her hair, pulled her close.

"Anyway," Rebecca said, still fuming. "We won't be here long. We'll visit the museum tomorrow, take photos of the other fragments, and be done."

It sounded so easy. Nico remembered the strange feeling he'd had on the street and knew it would not be as easy as Patricia and Rebecca supposed.

He also thought of Andreas's conviction that chasing after the inscription was yet another twist of the knife in their long torture.

He held Patricia even closer, need sparking as it always did when he was near her. He had to have her, had to pleasure her. She was annoyed with him, but it didn't matter; he would break through that and please her, or the pain would flare to make him crazy.

When she looked up at him, she seemed to understand. Her compassion for him broke his heart, but he growled in animal-like madness as he swept her into his arms and carried her from the room.

Rebecca and Andreas watched them go, but the distance between the two of them remained wide.

16

THE Egyptian Museum was crowded and dense, tourists pouring off buses to tramp through the five thousand years of history packed inside. Patricia tingled with excitement despite Nico's bad mood, and she couldn't wait to feel the vibrations of some of the most exquisite objects in the world.

Rebecca confidently bypassed the long line to the Tutankhamun gallery, saying she'd show them even better artifacts stashed away in the basement. Patricia was eager to see the fragments, which a phone call yesterday had assured them were here.

As they made their way into the administrative offices, people began to stop and greet Rebecca. She waved at men and hugged women, her shyness gone.

One of the men offered to take them downstairs so they could see the ostracons. Patricia had brought her digital camera, complete with fresh batteries.

The basement was even more densely packed than upstairs,

with storage rooms and huge spaces crowded with shelves and boxes. Patricia wondered how anyone found anything down here, but their guide seemed to know his way around. A larger museum would be opening soon in Giza to take the load off this one, their guide said, then added, *"Inshallah."*

Their guide, whose name was Ali, stopped at a door and opened it with a key. Inside were shelves covered with grills, all locked. He led them unerringly to a grill whose lock looked newly cleaned and oiled, and opened it.

"Two fragments found near Alexandria," he said.

He pulled out one piece of limestone, about two feet square. Andreas reached for it, but Rebecca beat him to it. She gazed down at the stone in reverence.

The second fragment was larger, about two by four feet. Nico lifted that one, and Rebecca touched it, her eyes shining. Ali moved boxes from a rickety table, and Rebecca positioned both pieces on it.

"This one first, I think," she said, tracing the hieroglyphs on the smaller piece. "And the other one fit in between. Yes, that's just lovely."

She gazed happily at them, unable to stop touching them. Patricia pulled out her camera and turned it on, waiting for the light to tell her all was ready.

A shout from Nico startled her. She looked up to see Ali heft a sledgehammer and bring it straight down on the fragments.

Rebecca screamed and dodged out of the way. The smaller piece shattered, and then Nico and Andreas were on him. Ali, a small, slim Egyptian man in his twenties, fought them off, suddenly having the strength of ten.

Nico wrestled with him, while Rebecca tried to grab the pieces of fragments. Ali threw Andreas and Nico off like they weighed nothing and brought the sledgehammer up again. Andreas dragged Rebecca out of the way as the sledgehammer came down.

Patricia watched in sickened horror as Ali pounded the fragments to dust. Nico tried to catch his arms and stop him, but Ali threw him backward across the room.

Nico pushed himself up, his rage bringing out the divine light inside him. Andreas had already morphed to his leopard form, kicking out of his clothes and snarling like crazy.

Ali brought the sledgehammer down one more time, then he wilted. The sledgehammer slid from his grip, and he crumpled to the floor, his eyes rolling back in his head.

Andreas leapt on him, but Patricia rushed to them. "Wait. I don't think—"

Andreas flashed sharp teeth at her, but he backed off and sat on his haunches. Rebecca was crying, hugging pieces of limestone rubble to her chest.

Nico retrieved the sledgehammer and stood above Ali. Ali opened his eyes and blinked up at them, then went pale with fright and started babbling in Arabic.

Andreas growled again, lips curling back from his teeth. Rebecca wiped her eyes and dragged in a deep breath. "Leave him alone, Andreas. He doesn't know what happened."

Rebecca spoke to him in fluent Arabic for a few moments, then Ali switched back to English. "I do not know why I did that. I could never do such a thing. A demon must have got me."

He climbed shakily to his feet, his face almost green with fear. He looked at Nico and Andreas, who surrounded him menacingly, and held up his hands. "I truly do not know. I would never destroy an artifact. Never." Tears leaked from his eyes.

"I believe him," Patricia said. She quietly clicked off her camera, not needing it now. "But I don't think it was a demon that possessed you, Ali. I think it was a goddess."

~ ~ ~

PATRICIA left the museum in fury, but Andreas and Nico seemed strangely subdued. "Dyons don't have the brains to track down the fragments," she said as they walked back to the hotel. "They can only follow us. But getting into the museum in broad daylight to attack would have been too hard for them. So she takes over the mind of an innocent to destroy the fragments once she knows where they are. We do all the work tracking them down; she walks in and takes over." She raked a hand through her hair, wanting to scream in frustration. "What a bitch."

Rebecca nodded, her eyes glinting with the same anger. "Remember what I told you about my dissertation advisor? Same thing. I did the grunt work; she walked in and used every bit of it. But this is worse. Destroying an artifact is unforgivable. Unforgivable." She stabbed the air for emphasis.

"It doesn't matter," Nico said.

"Of course it matters." Patricia rounded on him in the crowded street. "It must have been the key to getting you free. Why else would she destroy it?"

"He means it wasn't meant to be," Andreas said. "We weren't meant to be free. It's not going to happen."

"You can't give up now," Rebecca said, her face set in determination. "What we find on ostracons are mostly copies of other inscriptions, for practice learning hieroglyphs or to allow people far from a monument to read what was on it. All we have to do is find the original inscription. I remember some of what was on the first fragment. If we can find inscriptions with the same kind of theme, we can look until we find a match. We can—"

She broke off as Andreas seized her hand. "Peace, Becky. We're finished. The inscription is destroyed. It was a nice try. Why don't we just enjoy what time we have left?"

Rebecca jerked away. "Forget it. I didn't win all those research awards for stopping the minute it got hard. It's just another challenge."

"Exactly," Patricia said. "I'm good at tracking down elusive antiques, and Rebecca is good at tracking down elusive information. Between the two of us, you can't lose."

Nico and Andreas exchanged a look. Patricia recognized the look for what it was, and her rage mounted. They'd given up, tired from struggling to free themselves. They didn't want to hope.

She folded her arms, not letting Nico go anywhere. "I refuse to run back home with my tail between my legs. I will keep searching and helping Rebecca. Besides, I'm in Egypt for the first time in my life, and I want to see a pyramid."

Nico gazed down at her from his height, his eyes dark as sin. She knew she'd never find a man like him again.

"All right," he said quietly.

Patricia had drawn a breath to fling more arguments at him, and she stopped in surprise. Nico gave her a nod and turned her to walk next to him again. "Keep looking," he said as they went. "I won't stop you."

He wouldn't explain what he meant and was quiet all the way back to the hotel.

~ ~ ~

THE pyramids of Giza, across the river from Cairo, were every tourist's destination. Nico, Patricia, and Rebecca found people from every corner of Europe, North America, and Asia waiting in lines to ride camels or be ushered across the rocks by tour guides to the base of the ancient pyramids.

Andreas had refused to come, much to Rebecca's annoyance. She pretended she didn't care as she walked with Patricia, but Nico sensed her hurt.

Nico knew exactly why Andreas had remained behind. The feeling of being watched hadn't left either of them, and Andreas had faded into the shadows to see if he could flush out their mysterious follower. It hadn't been Hera or a Dyon; they were far more direct and gave off different vibrations.

Patricia's face lit up as they came to the base of the Great Pyramid, a structure built before Nico was born. Even the famous Tutankhamun had considered the pyramids of Giza to be ancient.

He looked up the great blocks of stone, while Patricia and Rebecca took pictures of each other with it in the background. Climbing the pyramids was now forbidden, but that didn't keep them from scrambling around the base, looking in wonder at the giant blocks of stone. Rebecca knew much about it and kept up a babbling commentary to Patricia.

Nico scanned the crowd with caution, on the lookout for Dyons. Now that the fragments were destroyed, perhaps the Dyons would back off, but then, with Rebecca's and Patricia's determination to keep looking, Hera might well decide the best way to stop them was with their deaths.

He looked back at Patricia and Rebecca in time to see them disappear around a rock. Cursing under his breath, he leapt lightly to the top of the slab he had been leaning against, to see them descending to the temple behind the pyramid.

Nico could move fast when he wanted to and skimmed over the

stones on their trail. He saw them stop and greet an Egyptian in a Western business suit, odd attire for this dusty venture.

Nico moved toward them, wondering if this was the antiquities dealer they'd spoken to before at the hotel. Patricia was certainly chattering with him without fear, Rebecca nodding at points. Nico slowed a little but continued his descent.

Then he felt it, the whisper of *wrongness* that had bothered him ever since they'd walked out of the Cairo airport. The whisper touched him, and the Egyptian man looked up at him.

He saw a sudden flash of light, blinding power that seared his eyes, and when he blinked them clear, the Egyptian man, Rebecca, and Patricia were gone.

~ ~ ~

ANDREAS reached him within half an hour of Nico's call. "What the fuck?" he panted, drawn and gray with the effort of getting there.

"The man following us was a god," Nico said, his throat tight. "I don't know what god, but that explains why we couldn't track him down. If they don't want to be seen, they're not seen. Patricia wouldn't have seen his aura, either, unless he let her; it doesn't matter how psychic she is."

"Damn it." Andreas looked around the crowds of tourists and camels, Egyptians in caftans and Western clothes, colors amid the dusty white. None of them seemed to have noticed the flash of white or the three vanishing. "What the hell did he take them for?"

"With a god it could be anything."

Andreas growled agreement. Gods were capricious. He might want to share a good wine with Patricia and Rebecca because he liked them, or he might want to father a new race with them. It depended on who he was and what agenda he had. And if he was friend of Hera's . . .

"You didn't recognize him?" Andreas demanded.

"No. He was hiding his true form and hiding it well."

"So what do we do? Tear apart Egypt, or toddle quietly back to our rooms and wait for him to return them, if he ever does?"

"They might be far from Egypt by now," Nico said.

"I know that." Andreas flashed a scowl around the crowds. "You know, it would be great if I could say this is the best thing, the easiest way to get ourselves away from them, but you know I can't."

"No." Nico knew he didn't have to say anything else.

Andreas had his hands on his hips, still scanning the crowd. "Now that we know we're looking for a god, we might be able to spot him."

Nico wasn't so sure. Gods were experts at keeping themselves hidden. They'd become especially adept in the last millennia or two as belief in the old gods was all but destroyed.

Nico had already searched the spot from which the three had vanished and found nothing, not even a disturbance in the dust. He and Andreas looked again, then walked around the pyramid and gazed into the shadows of the entrance.

Patricia suddenly stepped out into the bright sunlight and smiled at him.

"Patricia, damn it," he said, starting toward her. "Where did you go? I thought—"

She didn't seem to hear him. She laughed and beckoned to him. "Well, come on."

Nico turned to call to Andreas, and when he looked back at the entrance, Patricia was gone again.

With Andreas right behind him, Nico dove past the line of tourists and into the dark hole of the pyramid.

~ ~ ~

PATRICIA had no idea where she was, but the vibrations of the ancient tomb were spectacular. The place was lit with generator lights, showing all four walls and ceiling painted with beautiful, bright scenes of Egyptian life. The tomb must be thousands upon thousands of years old, the vibrations so strong she had to raise an extra shield to protect herself.

Rebecca, who didn't have to worry about psychic residue, simply gazed at the walls with the hunger of an avid archaeologist.

"I've never seen these before," she said in wonder. "I can't believe how well preserved it is. No one's tried to chisel off the panels, the paint hasn't faded, the colors are as fresh as the day they went on. Of course, the Egyptians knew how to make things last. It's amazing how smart and practical they were and how romantic at the same time."

The woman was nearly salivating.

"They are coming, yes?" their Egyptian friend, Mr. Ajeed, said.

Patricia couldn't quite remember how she'd gotten here, into this deep tomb that Ajeed promised held wonderful artifacts. The best in Egypt, he'd said, but a well-kept secret. They would have to traverse many secret passages to find it.

Patricia had no memory of walking down here, though her legs were tired enough. She'd gone back outside, to see Nico staring at her in amazement, though she didn't quite remember that journey, either. She'd told Nico to follow, but he was taking his time.

"Why *don't* I know about these wall paintings?" Rebecca was asking. "This is my field: reading and translating inscriptions.

When one is uncovered, someone calls me or at least sends me an e-mail. I've never heard about these."

Ajeed smiled, showing white, even teeth. "That is because, my dear young woman, it has not yet been discovered."

"Huh?" Rebecca stared at him. "If it hasn't been discovered, how did you know the way down here? Giza's been gone over pretty thoroughly. I'd be surprised if *someone* doesn't know about it."

"It is not in Giza."

"What the hell are you talking about?" Rebecca demanded. "We didn't walk that far; we should be just behind the Great Pyramid, in one of the temples."

Ajeed smiled. "You must trust me. You need answers, and I have found them for you."

Patricia frowned at him. When they'd met him in the lobby of the hotel, Ajeed had seemed an ordinary antiques dealer, the same kind she'd met in her business travels before. He dealt in antique furniture, mostly from the Ottoman period, and sold to dealers throughout Europe, the U.S., and the Arab world.

Patricia had tried to read his aura, on the lookout for Dyons in disguise—not that they seemed bright enough to use disguises—but she'd found the aura of an ordinary person. Nothing supernatural about him.

Without changing expression, Patricia let her shields down again, touching Ajeed with her psychic senses.

She nearly screamed. The power that emanated from him was brighter and fiercer than any she'd ever seen. Even Andreas's and Nico's auras weren't as strong, and Andreas and Nico had knocked her to her knees.

Ajeed lifted his hand, and abruptly the white-hot light vanished. Patricia gasped, finding herself flat on the floor, her head pounding.

"I am so sorry, Miss Lake," he said, reaching down to help her. "I should have anticipated you would try that again."

"What are you?" She refused his offered hand and climbed painfully to her feet herself. "No, wait, maybe I don't want to know."

Rebecca was looking on in shock. "What do you mean, what is he? What did he do to you?"

"He isn't human." Patricia's headache began to recede, but the muscles in the back of her neck still pulsed.

"No," Ajeed agreed. "Your friends, they are demigods, half god, half mortal. I am like them, only nothing about me is mortal."

Before meeting Nico and Andreas, Patricia would have assumed the man was crazy, but now she was not so sure. "A god, then. Which god?"

"There are so many," he smiled. "Gods, gods everywhere. It's likely you wouldn't have heard of me."

"Try me," Rebecca said, hands on hips. "I've studied most of the ancient Egyptian religious texts."

"Very well, then you can call me Bes if you want. But I prefer Mr. Ajeed. I like having a human name."

Rebecca looked him up and down. "Bes was a dwarf god. You're pretty tall."

"Ah, but human forms can be so deceiving." Ajeed cocked his head toward the entrance, looking for all the world like a harmless, friendly Egyptian man. "I believe your friends have arrived."

He turned as Nico strode from the stone stairs into the tomb. Andreas came behind him in his leopard form. Patricia wondered why they had taken so long, but maybe they'd had to look for a private spot where Andreas could change into his leopard shape.

But then, Mr. Ajeed—Bes—had claimed that they were no longer in Giza. Frowning, she marched out past Nico, taking the stairs up. Nico turned and followed, and she heard Rebecca clattering behind them.

Patricia emerged in a shallow room that looked out over a place of bright emptiness, a land she'd never seen before.

17

"WHERE are we?"

Patricia felt Nico behind her, his tall, strong body protectively at her back. The shallow, square-cut cave opened out to a steep, rocky cliff. Below them empty desert rolled away under a blue sky to the gray green smudge of cultivation around the Nile. Dry air burned through her lungs.

Rebecca stopped beside them. "I'd swear this is Amarna, a cliff tomb on the north side. But that's like two hundred miles south of Cairo."

"Mr. Ajeed claims to be a god," Patricia said, staring at the stark beauty of the landscape. "Why couldn't we follow him into the Great Pyramid in Giza and emerge a couple hundred miles south?"

"I never would have believed it before I met you people," Rebecca muttered. She shook her head, turned around, and marched back down into the tomb.

Nico slid his arm around Patricia's waist. "I'm not sure what's going on, but I'm happy I haven't lost you."

"I wouldn't have left you behind."

He didn't answer. His arms tightened around her waist, and she turned around and kissed him.

Their mouths took each other's in slow warmth, with only a taste of the incredible hunger of the sex they'd been having. Right now she was just a woman loving a man.

Nico smoothed her hair back from her face and touched his forehead to hers. "Patricia."

His dark eyes held so much sadness. She kissed him again, trying to wipe away the loneliness that made her heart ache. He'd spent so many years alone, and she wanted to assure him that he never would again.

"We should go see what this is all about," she whispered.

Nico nodded, still holding her. She would have loved to stay there forever, the two of them against the barren and beautiful landscape, the sun warming them as they held each other.

Nico took her hand and led her back down the passage.

At the bottom, Mr. Ajeed stood smiling at Rebecca, while the leopard Andreas sat protectively in front of her.

"So, now we know where we are?" Ajeed asked, still affable.

"I was right; it's Amarna," Rebecca said stiffly. "I'll gloss over how we got here, because I have the feeling I don't really want to know. But why?"

"I will show you."

Ajeed started to go around her, but Andreas rose, hackles up, teeth drawn in a snarl.

"Let him, Andreas," Patricia said. "I want to see why we've been tricked here."

Andreas subsided, still pressing tight to Rebecca, his blue eyes ice-cold.

Ajeed led them through a small doorway built of precisely chiseled thick blocks and down another passage. It, too, was lit by a string of generator lights, which made Patricia wonder about the power source. If this was an undiscovered tomb, who had put in a generator?

Ajeed led them down a ramp and down again. The air was cooler here than outdoors, the sun a long way outside these giant blocks of stone. It was also not stale, which meant there was another source of air, some shafts far above, perhaps.

When they reached what must be the very base of the tomb,. Ajeed stopped. They stood in a burial chamber, a stone sarcophagus prominent in the middle of the room.

The walls and ceiling were covered with more paintings, the colors vivid white, green, red, black, orange. The human figures were the expected half-turned surreal forms. The animals were more lifelike: birds in flight, wild cats hunting among reeds, the curved prow of a boat on a lake, looking remarkably like the feluccas that sailed the Nile now.

Rebecca stared around in great delight. "An untouched Amarna tomb? No way."

Ajeed flashed his smile. "It is. It was put into my care, I a lesser god, so honored by this task. I have protected it all this time, kept away robbers old and new. The lord, he rests in peace, enjoying his afterlife."

Patricia glanced at the sarcophagus, suddenly imagining the mummified body that must lie inside it. She stepped back into the curve of Nico's arm. This place was indeed peaceful, the psychic vibrations soothing and almost still. No one had been into this room since the grave tenders had sealed it up more than three thousand years ago.

Rebecca frowned at Ajeed. "The entire city of Amarna was built by Akhenaten to worship one god, the Aten," she said. "Other gods weren't welcome, in a big way, so why should you have been asked to guard this tomb?"

Ajeed looked modest. "The lord who lies here, he secretly disagreed with the pharaoh. But one couldn't say that, oh, no. He remembered Amun and Osiris and the old gods, and asked me personally to look after him."

"Hmm." Rebecca looked around again, the gleam of the true historian entering her eye. The past was alive to her, Patricia realized, more alive than shopping in London boutiques or going to clubs with a gorgeous man. Her eye saw more than Patricia's could, even with her psychic vision.

Nico turned to look at the wall behind them and went still. "Andreas."

Andreas padded to him. He stretched his leopard limbs, then he elongated into his human form and stood up, naked and casual.

Rebecca joined them, her gaze lingering on Andreas before she looked at the wall. Patricia looked, too, and realized what she was seeing.

"The inscription," she gasped.

"All of it." Rebecca nearly jumped up and down in excitement. "There's the bit I translated," she said, pointing to a patch near the ceiling. "There's so much of it. No wonder it didn't make much sense; whoever copied it out on the ostracons only used part of it. This is terrific." She spun in a little circle, prettier than Patricia had ever see her. "I've just made my career. I'm the first one to ever see this; I'll be the first one to translate it. I'll have journal articles out the butt, interviews, job offers. Woo!"

She danced around until Andreas caught her, his grin wide. "Take it easy, sweetheart. Don't pass out from happiness."

Rebecca flung her arms around his neck. "I don't care." She kissed him on the mouth, then smiled at Ajeed. "Thank you, Mr. Ajeed, or Bes, or whatever you want to be called. You've made me the happiest girl on the planet."

~ ~ ~

PATRICIA had not said much about the discovery, but Nico didn't have time to ask her why until later. The upper rooms of the tomb provided dry accommodations out of the heat and wind, and Ajeed had furnished them with cots and camp chairs, and plenty of food and water. He'd also somehow transported all their bags from the hotel.

Nico stood in the entrance, looking out from the cliff face to the empty valley below. No one stirred there, not tourists nor archaeologists.

"He was prepared for us, wasn't he?" Patricia stood next to him, fanning herself in the heat, a bottle of water in her hand. "There's enough stuff here for us to stay for weeks. But if anyone saw him setting up, or sees us now, this won't be an undiscovered tomb for long."

"I think he did something," Nico mused. "Suspended time or drew a curtain across this area or something. There's nothing out there."

She joined him to look over the ruins of the kingdom of Akhenaten and his famous queen, Nefertiti. There was nothing left except a few faint ruins covered over by dust. A green smudge in the distance showed a line of cultivation and then the sparkling waters of the Nile.

"I was advised that this area was dangerous to visit," Patricia commented.

"He's protecting us."

"I have to wonder why. Bes wants Rebecca to translate that wall. Is he for or against Hera?"

"Come here."

Patricia went to him as Nico stripped off his T-shirt. He unfolded his black wings, enjoying stretching them out. "You asked me once if these worked, if I could truly fly. Want to see?"

Patricia's eyes began to glow, the blue green light of the sea. "I'd love to."

Nico pulled Patricia to stand in front of him and wrapped his arms around her waist. She gasped. "You mean with me?"

Instead of answering, Nico jumped off the cliff. Patricia shrieked once, and then Nico's huge, feathery wings caught them in outstretched black glory.

He glided on the hot wind from the valley floor, then pumped his wings to take them higher. He loved the feel of the wind in his feathers, the strength of his wings holding them easily aloft.

After Patricia's initial fright, she went very quiet. When he looked at her, Nico saw that she was grinning.

"Like it?" he asked.

"Like it?" She laughed. "Nico, I love you!"

The words smote his heart. She'd said them before, when he'd first made love to her, and he still couldn't be certain if they came from her heart or from the joy of the moment.

He soared over the valley and to the barren stretch to the east, not wanting to chance being seen by farmers near the river, not sure how far Bes's power stretched. He wheeled over the cliffs, again catching the updraft to glide across the valley and its ruins.

The sun was sliding westward, streaking the sky with red as it hit the dust in the air. Twilight descended, quickly followed by dusk. The stars were silver pinpricks in the sky as Nico landed at the cliff-top entrance to the cave again.

He turned Patricia in his arms and kissed her. She tasted like the wild joy of flying and the honey sweetness of herself. He wrapped his arms around her and lowered her to the clean-cut floor, letting his wings cushion her.

"Let me pleasure you," he whispered.

"Now? Right here?"

He swept his tongue through her mouth, feeling her respond like he'd taught her.

"Right here."

Patricia's pulse sped under his touch. "What if the others come looking for us?"

"What if they do?"

Her eyes burned bright. "That would be bad."

"You like it bad, Patricia."

"Do I?"

"You've had it sweet, now let me show you rough."

She smiled, a glint in her eye. "You've tied me up before. And I remember a gag once."

"That was nice playing." He bit her cheek. "I mean bad, Patricia. Do you trust me?"

Her pheromones were pouring from her, her excitement increasing. "Yes."

"Are you sure about that?"

For answer, she licked him across the lips. His cock tingled and lifted. She certainly wanted to play.

He could tell the difference in their kiss. Things had changed between them, no longer she being uncertain and he teaching her.

She'd learned to give in to her naughty self, the one that loved two men in her bed, liked playing with the silk scarves around her wrists.

Now she wanted more, the most he could give her. Their relationship would peak; after this, she'd start losing interest in him, and her affection would drift away, maybe even manifesting itself as disgust. She wouldn't be able to believe she'd let him do what he did—if their lovemaking even lingered in her mind.

"Strip," he said.

She started, then smiled again, glancing over her shoulder to see if anyone was on their way up the passage.

Nico growled. "I mean now." He ripped open her blouse from neck to waist. Her hands came up to stop him, but he let his god strength and magic manifest to have her clothes in shreds and her naked in seconds.

"That isn't fair—"

"I don't care about fair," Nico said. He snatched her up in his arms, got himself to the edge of the cliff, and flew off into the night with her.

~ ~ ~

PATRICIA had seen movies like this. The savage man dragged the woman off with him, and the others went wild with worry, but the woman discovered that beneath the beast lay a heart of gold. She'd already found Nico's gentle heart, but she hadn't experienced his savage strength.

In silence he carried her through the desert night, her naked body against his for warmth. Something seemed to jar the entire world, then he landed in a strange place that was nothing like where they just were.

She seemed to be on a balcony overlooking a lush, green world, perhaps an oasis in the desert. It was night, everything in hues of silver, black, and gray. The room behind her had a marble floor and cushions everywhere, no other furniture except two low tables heaped with food and drink.

She started to open her psychic senses to discover where she was, but Nico clamped his hand on her arm. "No. Let it be."

"Why? Where am I?"

"In a world of my making. Enjoy it for what it is."

She looked perplexed. "But where are we really?"

For answer he seized her wrists and pushed her down into the cushions. He kissed her, his mouth masterful, and she stopped squirming.

Nico was heavy on top of her, no longer playful and laughing. He was strong, pinning her wrists to the floor. Before she could ask what he intended to do here, he'd shoved her legs open and thrust himself inside.

What he did to her—what she let him do to her—in that room amazed her. She never thought she'd like what he wanted, to surrender entirely to him and let him do as he pleased.

He pumped into her until they both were ready to climax, then he withdrew, flipped her onto her hands and knees, and entered her from behind. They both came not long after that. Then he made her stay in that position while he worked lube into her ass and then slid inside there.

Andreas had done this, but with him it had been tingling, experimental, daring fun. Nico meant business. He filled her and pinned her, his strength letting her know that he could do whatever he wanted, and she couldn't stop him.

But he never hurt her. As hard as he drove, as firmly as he held her down, it was nothing but pure pleasure.

Afterward, he carried her to a bathroom like the one in their Cairo hotel and laid her in a huge fountain with warm water running from its spigots. He washed her and himself, then he made love to her against the tile.

He tied her to one of the spigots and made her promise him all kinds of sexual favors to secure her release. Then he made her do them. They used the fruit and wine that loaded the two candlelit tables, he feeding her or eating from her as he liked.

When she was exhausted from this play, he carried her to the balcony and let her rest, watching the wind in the trees and the moonlight on the lake there.

Nico laid himself on top of her to warm her. "I never want you to forget me."

She gave him a sleepy smile. "How could I ever?"

"You could. But I don't want you to, even if you hate me. I know I never will forget you."

"Because of the curse?"

"Because of you."

The emptiness in his eyes hurt her. She knew she could never reassure him, and she also knew she didn't really understand the curse of the goddess. Both he and Andreas had decided that whatever Rebecca or Patricia did couldn't help them.

"If you're *my* slave," she asked, "why can't I order you around? You've been pretty masterful all night."

An interested light entered his eyes. "What would you do?"

"Oh . . ." She let her imagination go and began to smile with where it went.

He took her hand and wrapped her finger around his gold chain. "What would you do?" he repeated. "Command me."

Excitement shot through Patricia. What would she dare? But

they were in a place of magic, a place that didn't really exist, and maybe anything she did here wouldn't be quite real. It was a fantasy, and Nico was letting her live it.

"All right," she whispered, then pushed him away. "Get your butt back in that fountain. *Now.*"

Nico suppressed a smile as he rocked to his feet and sauntered back inside, his beautiful ass moving as he walked. Laughing at her, was he?

Patricia stalked after him, and when she entered the chamber, she found a whip in her hand. She snapped it.

It flew around and hit her own bare skin, stinging like crazy. Nico started for her, concerned, but Patricia waved him off, her face flaming.

She practiced with the whip until she mastered it better, and Nico watched, unable to hide his grin.

"You asked for it, buster," she said.

She cracked the whip again, loving that she had her own beautiful, naked, willing slave at her beck and call.

"You're not in the fountain," she said. "Stand in it, against the wall."

Nico stepped into the fountain tub, putting his back against the blue-and-green-tiled wall. Water trickled from vents in the top, coating his body with a sheen of it.

She wanted to stop and salivate, but she kept up her persona. "Hands above your head."

Nico lazily raised his arms, crossing his wrists. She wondered what she could use to bind him, or bind him to, when manacles suddenly appeared around them.

"You do a convenient fantasy," she said. "I want your wings, too."

They peeled out from behind his back, splashing water droplets all over her. He fluttered them, then settled them along his body.

There he was, a winged god, sleek and wet, his arms stretched above him and crossed at the wrists. Every muscle gleamed with water, his body tight and dark.

"You are so beautiful," she said.

He only smiled at her, his eyes sin-dark.

He was giving her an incredible gift. She'd known Nico long enough to know he hated giving up control, that his bond to the curse chafed him. He turned it around by assuming mastery over the one who enslaved him, pleasuring her so well that she surrendered to him.

And here he was, surrendering to her.

His cock was already hard and tight, taunting her to do her worst. She sashayed forward, aware that his hungry gaze roved every inch of her body.

Patricia had never considered herself a knockout—pleasant in a subdued way was as far as she'd go—but Nico looked at her like she was the sexiest, most delectable woman in the world. She felt her power as he looked at her. He wanted her, and she could play with that.

First she came close enough to almost touch him, body to body; then, when his gaze blazed with need, she stepped back a few inches. Something dangerous flickered in his eyes, and she laughed.

Next, she slid the leather of the whip behind him and wrapped it around his hips, further pinning him. His cock poked through a crisscross of the leather.

She tied it off and stepped back, surveying her creation. Delectable.

Patricia sensed Nico's god powers rumbling through his body, and him keeping them in check. If she dared lower her psychic shields, his aura would no doubt throw her across the room.

He was calming himself for her, letting her enjoy her illusion that she controlled him.

Patricia eased herself to her knees in front of him. Leaning carefully so that she didn't touch him, she blew on his stiff, smooth tip.

He moved slightly, a groan escaping his mouth. Patricia licked where she'd blown, rewarded by a louder groan and a shift of body.

"You're killing me," he said hoarsely.

"You're a demigod," Patricia said brightly. "You'll get over it."

He said something under his breath she didn't understand, but she recognized swearing when she heard it. She felt a little glow of satisfaction.

Patricia got up and fetched the lube they'd used, then returned to smear it all over his cock. She rubbed it in, letting her fingers dance, sliding under his balls and playing with them.

He moved and groaned, straining against his bonds. She caught up a slim candlestick from one of the tables, sans candle, and slid it between his legs. He parted them, and she rubbed it over his thighs and balls and buttocks.

He was sweating, the water still trickling over him, his wings fluttering and flattening against the wall. He rocked his hips, helping her please him with the candlestick.

"I'm going to come," he moaned. "Let me be in your mouth."

"Not until I say." She unwound the whip from him and cracked it in the air, pleased with her newfound skill.

"Please," he begged.

"No."

He glared at her, a divine being who didn't want his wishes denied.

"When I'm ready," Patricia said.

Nico growled, his wings slapping the wall. She knelt again and opened her mouth wide, taking his whole cock inside.

His groan rang through the room. She slid her lubed fingers between his buttocks and warmed his anal star before sliding one gently inside.

Her mouth never let up its play while she carefully caressed his ass. Beautiful Nico stood still and let her, even though he could at any time smash away the chains and take her to the floor.

She sucked him a little longer, then withdrew and looked up.

His hair was wet and plastered to his face, his eyes heavy, cheekbones flushed. His wings moved restlessly.

"Now," she whispered. "Now you can come."

She closed her mouth over him again, just as he cried his release and shot his seed over her lips.

She smiled up at him around his cock, her heart full. *I love you, Nico,* she wanted to say.

As though he heard the silent words, he roared. He ripped his hands apart, the manacles breaking and falling before they dissipated into mist.

He scooped Patricia from the floor and ran with her to the cushions of the bedroom. Still hard, he pushed into her, making love to her until her laughter turned to screams.

Then, when he'd come a second time, he held her against him, his heart thudding beneath his hot skin. The beautiful and strange room dissolved, and they were lying in the dusty tomb at Amarna, snug on their cot.

"Was it a dream?" she whispered as she slid into sleep.

"No," he said.

18

REBECCA closeted herself with the inscription for the next five days straight. She slept down there, barely remembering to eat or drink.

It made Andreas crazy. He hovered over her, growling at her to take water or she'd dehydrate. Rebecca would drink, but absently, staring up at the hieroglyphs and jotting notes like crazy.

"She'll kill herself," Andreas said to Nico and Patricia where they liked to sit on the cliff side. Rebecca had told him pointedly to leave the tomb and stop interrupting her. Andreas hadn't wanted to leave her alone, but her frazzled look told him he should give her some time to calm down. "She'll kill herself for nothing," he continued.

"She's a trained archaeologist," Patricia said. "She's probably like this with all her finds. It excites her—like me with antiques."

Andreas only growled back, "This is crazy."

Of course Patricia would take Rebecca's side, and Nico was so twisted around Patricia, he wouldn't try to help. Andreas knew why he was crabby. He was worried about Rebecca, worried that the inscription meant nothing, worried he was about to lose her.

Also, Rebecca worked on the inscription until she fell asleep in exhaustion, and Andreas hadn't had the chance to be with her. He snuggled down with her at night, but she was too far gone for sexual games, and he was too bound to her to return to Patricia for relief. He had to release himself before he boiled over.

Sometimes, when Nico and Patricia weren't having sex, he'd go with them down to the ruins, and Patricia would tell them about the special kingdom that had been built there. Akhenaten had designed and built Amarna to give reverence to Aten, the god of the sun disc. He'd moved the capital here from Thebes, to the consternation of the powerful priests of Amun. Archaeologists still weren't sure what to make of Akhenaten, and many conflicting theories abounded. He'd been married to the beautiful Nefertiti and possibly sired the famous Tutankhamun.

The ruins weren't as romantic as the pyramids at Giza or the Temple of Karnak, far to the south, but Patricia seemed fascinated by the mosaics on the floor of Nefertiti's palace.

During this time, they saw no one. No tourists, no farmers, no police. No one. Bes was protecting them well.

Andreas wasn't quite as interested in the ruins as Patricia was, not caring much about how people worshiped long-ago gods. Most of the gods he'd known had been powerful, arrogant, obnoxious shits. Bes betrayed his lesser status by being nice. Gods of Andreas's pantheon were only generous when they wanted something.

At night, after Rebecca fell asleep, Andreas would become too restless to stay put. He'd change to his leopard form and enjoy himself racing across the rocks, basking in the cool of the night. The stars were unobstructed by pollution here and stretched thick and white across the horizon. He longed to show Rebecca this beauty, but the damn woman wouldn't come out of her tomb.

One night he returned from his nocturnal exploration and pulled on his pants, in case Bes, who turned out to be extremely modest, saw him. He wandered barefoot back down inside the tomb, annoyed that the lights were still on. Rebecca was still at work.

Andreas entered the lower room and stopped. Rebecca had fallen asleep over the inscription, her face childlike in slumber.

Andreas smiled, then went to her and smoothed back her hair. She made a soft sigh at his touch, then as her awareness returned, she jumped and woke.

Andreas knelt next to her, still stroking her hair. He kissed her cheek, trying to keep his impatience and raging lust in check. She smelled nice, warm and damp from sleep, her mussed hair exactly like it would be when she left his bed.

"Did you finish?"

Rebecca looked momentarily confused, then her face cleared. "I think so," she said heavily. She threw her arms around him and buried her face in his shoulder. "All that work, and it doesn't help you at all."

Andreas gently pried the papers from her fingers. "Come to bed."

"I want to check a few more things."

"No, you don't."

Andreas swept her into his arms and carried her up to the antechamber where she and Patricia had their cots. Patricia was with Nico, he knew. Nico had taken her somewhere to be alone with her as he had done of late.

Rebecca, on the other hand, had kept on working. He carried her to her cot and laid her on it, wiping the tears from her eyes.

He knew in his heart that their mission was a failure. Whatever Bes was trying to do—infuriate Hera, or prove he was more powerful than other gods gave him credit for—he didn't know. It didn't matter. He had known from the start that it was a long shot, and he'd kept going because he hadn't wanted to give up the chance to be with Rebecca.

He stripped off her clothes without her either resisting or helping him, then he opened his jeans to show her how hard he was for her. Rebecca looked, her pheromones starting to stir.

She reached up and grasped his swollen cock, her light touch making him want to fuck her then and there. He resisted, letting her touch to her enjoyment.

"Are you sure you wouldn't rather be with Patricia?" she asked.

He'd wondered how much she'd known about the threesome. "That was just playtime, sweetheart. Now it's all you."

Her strokes on him grew bolder, and then she sat up and kissed the tip of his cock. "That's it, baby. Do whatever you want with it."

A hungry look entered her eyes. She studied his length, touching lightly as though learning him. She swiped him with her tongue a few times, and he held still and let her.

When she'd played a little longer, he eased her down to the bed.

"I want to suck on you some more," she whispered.

He knew she did, and he craved it, too. He pulled his jeans and underwear off and got on his knees on the bed. He straddled her, then leaned forward so he could put his mouth on her pussy.

Lovely little blond curls met his tongue, and he flicked them until her legs opened for him. He breathed her scent, all female musk wanting him.

"Suck on me, Becky," he said.

He felt her move his cock with her fingers, and then her sweet, hot mouth closed over it. She suckled softly, and he groaned.

He lowered to her quim again and licked it. He started to lap it, loving the taste of her.

She kept working on his cock, and he fit his mouth to her clit, sucking her at the same time she sucked him. Her hips shifted, excitement taking over.

He needed so much to fuck her. Her mouth was fantastic, but he wanted to dip into this pretty little pussy and feel it squeeze him hard.

He held back. Like Nico, he didn't want to rush things and have them over too soon. He wanted to savor her, every minute of her, and then have an amazing climax with her before it was all over.

Andreas couldn't imagine not having this pixie of a woman in his life anymore, but he knew it would happen. Sooner rather than later.

The despair made him growl. "Come on, baby, suck me."

Rebecca doubled her efforts, her mouth and tongue doing wonderful things to him. In return, he kissed and licked and suckled her until her hips lifted from the bed, and she began to come.

Her sweet cream filled his mouth, hot and wet, and she writhed all over the place, her teeth closing around his cock. She sucked hard, too far gone in ecstasy to be gentle.

Andreas didn't mind. He moved his hips, fucking her mouth, while he petted her pussy to bring her back down again. Soon he was coming, too, shouting his release as she pulled it into her throat.

Everything went black for a moment, his coming was so hard;

then he found himself collapsed on the bed, with her smiling and snuggling up to him.

"Can we fuck?" she asked sleepily. "I mean, for real?"

He touched her face, her come still all over his lips. "An amazing climax isn't good enough for you?"

"It was wonderful—better than wonderful, but . . ." She gave him a wistful smile. "I want you inside me. Then I'll believe that you're really mine."

Andreas fingered the gold chain around his neck. "I am really yours."

"I don't mean that." Tears filled her eyes. "I mean that you might like to be with me, not just responding to the whim of some goddess."

Andreas tried to keep his heart cold, but pretty Rebecca was tearing a hole in it. "I do want to be with you, sweetheart. That's why I want to save it." He hesitated. "The inscription has nothing on it that will free us, does it?"

She looked mournful and shook her head.

"That's all right, darling," he said. He pulled her against him, resting his cheek on her hair. "I didn't really think it would. So I'm going to savor you as long as I can, all right? And keep on savoring you, until the end is the best both of us will ever have."

~ ~ ~

NICO cradled Patricia against him as they listened to the disappointing news. Bes had made them all coffee, looking proud that he'd mastered the art. It was thick, syrupy Egyptian coffee, but Patricia and Rebecca drank it without comment.

"It's a story," Rebecca said. "A homily, if you will. I don't think anyone's seen this wall except Bes until we got here, but I'm betting this story was known in other places, and the Greeks copied it onto what became our ostracon because it's a moral tale. Egypt's power had waned; even the tales of their gods were starting to be forgotten. Some of the names got changed or superimposed on Egyptian ones or hybridized to make entirely new god names, which is why it was hard to figure out."

"Never mind the history lesson," Andreas began. Nico shared his impatience, but Patricia stopped him.

"Leave her alone. She worked her ass off on this."

Rebecca scrubbed her hand over her tired face, distracted instead of angry. "What I'm trying to explain is that the priests started to use Egyptian stories, but this story came from even more ancient times than Amarna—before there was much civilization in Greece at all, back when legend says the gods walked the earth without restriction. What this wall shows is the story of Nico and Andreas. Or Nikolaus and Andrei, as they were then."

Patricia sat forward, while Nico tried to hide the bite of disappointment. Rebecca's face was drawn, and he knew they'd reached a dead end.

"What does it say?" Patricia prompted.

Rebecca looked over what she had written. "It's long and flowery, but to summarize, the sons of the gods, Nikolaus and Andrei, were wild and untamed. Nikolaus had wings of softest sable; Andrei took the form of a beautiful leopard, and together they pursued and seduced as they liked.

"One day they abducted a priestess of Hera. She fell in love with them and did whatever they wanted, then they abandoned her for their next conquest. The priestess, spurned and angry, prayed to Hera for vengeance. Hera devised a potion for her, which the priestess sprinkled on Andreas and Nico as they slept.

"When they awoke, they again pursued the next maiden they saw, but suddenly, instead of wishing only to fulfill their lust, they became her slaves and found chains around their necks. When the maiden was finished enjoying them, she banished them from her, and they had to leave with broken hearts. When they spied another maiden, they sought to regain their lustful ways, but the same thing happened. As it will to eternity."

Rebecca sighed and pushed aside her scribbling. "The point of the story is that pursuing lust for its own sake will only return to punish the lustful, while true love will be rewarded with happiness. It uses the tale of Nico and Andreas, our Nico and Andreas, to drive the point home. That's all."

They were all silent for a moment. Far outside in the night, a bird cried, but except for that, all was quiet.

"That's it?" Andreas asked.

"Afraid so," Rebecca answered.

Andreas got abruptly to his feet and stalked to the entrance, looking sightlessly through the dark opening. Nico slid his hand into Patricia's.

"It's a story to teach the evils of lust," Rebecca said glumly. "Nothing about how to free yourself from the curse. I'm sorry."

Patricia was frowning, not in disappointment but in confusion. "If the inscription means nothing, why were the Dyons so adamant about us not finding it? They didn't need to pursue us so hard if it doesn't help us."

Nico shrugged. "Hera is tricky. She could have sent them to keep us on the path, to drive us this way when the answer—if one exists—lay somewhere else. Or as Andreas suggested to me, it's just another way to twist the knife."

"Torturing us, you mean," Andreas said without turning.

"Something like that."

Rebecca stood up. "Well, I'd like to talk to her. Ask her right now what she hoped to obtain by keeping you trapped for centuries. Sure, I'd have been pissed, too, if you'd made love to me and dumped me, but I mean, keeping you trapped for eons is insane. I think you learned your lesson."

Nico tried to keep his voice neutral. "Maybe the spell is the only thing that's keeping us nice. Perhaps if the spell is broken, Andreas and I go back to what we were, learning nothing."

Andreas snorted. "Our slavery is based on the idea that we never fell in love—didn't understand what it was like. She thinks we never did anything but satisfy our lust, so she had to teach us what the pain of love was. But that isn't true. I fell in love, and lost, and hurt, long before all this started."

"Me, too," Nico said. "And because of Hera, I lost everything I could have had."

Rebecca and Patricia exchanged a look, both stubborn, both so sure they could solve any problem if they picked at it long enough. He squeezed Patricia's hand, a dull ache in his heart as he realized that he was going to lose everything that could have been.

"It's over, Patricia," he said. "You and Rebecca should go soon. We're going to lose you anyway—might as well get it over with."

"If we did that, what would you do?" Patricia asked.

Andreas turned around again, his face hard. "What we always do. Exist."

Existence, not life. Nico felt the familiar burn in his heart, the pain that never quite went away.

Bes scanned the wall, his friendly face distressed. "There must be something in this you can use."

"I don't know what," Rebecca snapped.

Bes turned hopefully to Patricia. "Maybe it says something to you, as you call it, psychically?"

Patricia studied the wall as she had many times since their arrival. "I've tried that, but it's just an ordinary wall. I mean, ordinary for an intact tomb painting from three thousand years ago."

"I was so certain."

Andreas smoothly stepped to Bes, grabbed his lapels, and lifted him from his feet. "What is your interest in all this, Bes? Did Hera send you to watch us? Are you going to report how upset we are so she can gloat?"

Bes squeaked as he hung from Andreas's grip. "No, no. I promise."

"Why, then? Why should you care whether two Greek demigods got free of a curse?"

"Because it is unjust." Bes looked indignant, his dark eyes flashing. "When I heard you were trying to break the curse, and I found out what kind of curse it was, I was so angry. She is a great goddess, such as our own Isis, but she is too arrogant. How dare she punish you like this?"

"And if you can get us free, you can rub her face in it?"

Bes wet his lips. "Something like that. She cannot have it her own way all the time."

"Thwarting Hera is dangerous," Nico observed.

"Yes, but it needs to be done," Bes said. "Perhaps I am the only one brave enough to do it."

Andreas shook him. "What you mean is you think you have the weight of your pantheon behind you, that Isis and Osiris will protect you."

Bes shrugged the best he could. "If that is the only way. Isis would not openly defy a head goddess of another pantheon, but she would not let Hera hurt me."

"And it would give you so much more clout with the other gods," Andreas suggested. "They might even have to take you seriously."

Patricia advanced on Andreas. "Oh, leave the poor man alone. He tried to help us. If it had worked, you'd be praising him to the skies and buying him beer."

Andreas returned the man to his feet and stepped back, scowling but knowing Patricia was right.

Nico came to Patricia and slid his arms around her from behind. She leaned back into him, but she was angry; he could feel it thrumming through her.

"You tried," he whispered. "I'll always remember that you tried. Thank you."

Patricia gave him a glare. "I'm not giving up yet. If we do this together, Nico, we'll—"

She broke off, staring at something behind Nico. At the same time, Andreas snarled and shifted into his leopard form, shaking off the clothes that ripped from him.

Nico turned. The room had filled with Dyons.

Bes drew himself up. "How dare she? This is *my* domain."

The Dyons stood in a row, about a dozen of them, shoulder to shoulder, a wall of muscle. Bes crackled with light and threw it at them with his hands.

The Dyons flinched, but the light deflected from them. They were being protected. But that meant . . .

Nico felt it first. He dragged Patricia to the floor, shielding her with his body as the air rent and everything inside the tomb exploded.

The wall paintings cracked and burst into a million pieces. The stone sarcophagus, which Rebecca had been using as a desk, splintered, the dry mummy inside crumbling instantly to dust. Pieces of limestone and alabaster, and chips of paint showered down on them in a needlelike rain.

Patricia coughed as the tomb filled with dust and crumbling, ancient paint. The tomb itself didn't fall, the stone blocks strong and enduring, but everything else was gone.

As the air cleared, he heard Rebecca wailing. "No, not the wall painting!"

Nico sat up. Bes was coughing, his black hair coated with yellow dust.

Rebecca huddled in a ball by the remains of the sarcophagus. Andreas, still a leopard, paced at her feet, stopping to shake the dust from his fur.

Patricia gasped. "The Dyons."

They were melting, collapsing in on themselves. Their bodies spun down into dust, returning to the clay from which they'd been shaped.

A tall woman rose from the middle of them, a large, stout matron wrapped in Grecian robes. She had very black hair, large dark eyes, and a cold hauteur that froze the molecules in the air.

Bes ran at her, enraged. "This tomb is under my protection. You don't belong here."

"Oh, please," the matron responded. She waved her hand, and Bes tumbled back across the room. Andreas snarled, fur rising.

"So you almost found the secret," the woman said to Nico. "But you didn't know what to do with it."

Nico raised his brows. "It is here, then."

"Yes, but gone now. Some stupid priest in this backward land liked the story, and he wrote in the solution. If you had been smarter, you would have understood immediately."

Andreas's growls grew loud and long. Nico hoped he wouldn't do anything stupid like leap on her, because Hera could kill him.

They were demigods, not gods. Their tainted half blood meant that the gods could kill them if they saw fit.

"But I am compassionate," Hera went on. She adjusted the cloth over her ample bosom, her eyes narrowing. "I have come to end your suffering."

"How?" Patricia demanded. "You'll break the curse?"

"No, my dear. I will end their long, miserable lives. That will free you as well, to get back to your little store."

"No." Patricia broke from Nico's hold. "You can't; I won't let you."

Nico seized her. "Patricia, don't." Hera in this form looked like a harmless woman out to do her shopping, but she was the most powerful goddess in the pantheon, bad-tempered and unpredictable.

Hera looked at her in pity. "You poor thing. Bow to me and thank me for relieving you of this pathetic fixation."

Patricia's knees bent, though she obviously tried to hold back. She stiffly sank to the floor, and her body folded over until her face touched the dust.

Nico gave in to anger. His wings split the shirt from his back, and he sailed across the floor and bowled into the goddess.

Hera threw Nico across the room. He landed hard on his back and felt the snap of bones, both wing and body.

He heard Andreas growling his leopard growl and rolled over in time to see Hera slam him to the ground in another burst of power. Rebecca screamed. Andreas's paws scrabbled on the stone floor, then suddenly he went limp and still, his eyes clouding over.

Rebecca crawled to him, crying. She flung herself on him, stroking his dust-choked fur.

Hera fixed her attention on Nico again, and through his pain, he sensed her power draw to a point. She was going to release it at him, and then Nico would die.

"Patricia," he croaked. "I love you."

Hera let fly. Her power was too mighty to look at, a huge golden light that was a deadly missile. Through his blurred vision, Nico saw Bes step quickly in front of him and take the entire brunt of the blast.

19

Bes's body absorbed Hera's power, expanding hideously, then he exploded with light. The whiteness of it filled the tomb, burning fire on Nico's retinas. He wanted to reach Patricia, to protect her, but he couldn't move.

When the light died, Bes stood upright in front of Hera. He no longer looked like an Egyptian but a short man with a lionlike face with horns in his dark hair.

"This is *my* jurisdiction," he said. "I told you."

Hera regarded Bes in fury, her matronly form elongating to something powerful and huge. "And those two lascivious demigods are my creatures. Guard your mummified man and give those two to me."

"No," Bes said. "I read the story on the wall, too, a long time ago, and I know what it means."

Hera's face went white. "It has nothing to do with you."

"It's all about love being stronger than lust."

She drew herself up, thrumming with power. "What of it, little god?"

"What are you going to do with that one?" Bes asked, pointing at Andreas's still body.

Nico's grief hit him hard. The one constant in his life had been Andreas, his snarling, snarky, smart-ass companion in hell. Andreas lay lifeless on the tomb floor, his eyes staring sightlessly.

Rebecca had draped herself over him, moaning incoherently. Patricia sat against a wall, her knees drawn to her chest, crying, dust smeared on her cheeks.

"He's nothing to me," Hera said. "A bastard fathered by my promiscuous husband."

"If you don't want him," Bes asked her, "will you give him to me?"

Hera's eyes narrowed. "Why?"

"As a treat. To compensate me for destroying my tomb."

Hera regarded him wearily. "Do as you like with him. I resign all claim. Will you mummify him?"

"No." Bes grinned at her, his low stature and the horns making him look cocky. "Do you give up all claim on him?"

"If you insist. Not much more vengeance I can take on a dead leopard."

"Excellent." Bes beamed.

Nico could only watch, broken and in pain, as Bes went to Andreas and put a kind hand on Rebecca's shoulder.

"My dear, I think you should go sit with your friend."

Rebecca clung to Andreas's body. "Leave him alone."

Patricia staggered to her feet. She went to Rebecca and pulled her up, letting the smaller girl cry on her shoulder. She led Rebecca away and they both sank down next to Nico. Nico watched Patricia, unable to reach for her.

Bes straightened Andreas's limbs, which were already stiff. He shook his head in pity.

"He didn't deserve to die."

"He is a male creature who gave female creatures much misery."

"And yet, this little one weeps for him." Bes pointed to Rebecca, being soothed by Patricia.

Hera shrugged. "She was caught in my curse."

"But she is free of it now, yes?"

"She should be."

"And yet, she still grieves."

Hera did not look impressed. "She will recover soon."

"I must think how to ease her pain." Bes rubbed his hands together. "I've always wanted to try this."

"Try what?"

"Reanimation."

Hera snorted. "You need much power to do that. Get it wrong, and he's a zombie leopard—not pretty."

Bes gave her a *Well, maybe* look and continued to position Andreas's body.

Patricia looked up in horror. "Can't you just leave him alone?" She glared at Hera. "There's a difference between taking vengeance and torturing someone because you enjoy it."

"Patricia," Nico whispered.

She didn't hear him, or at least she pretended not to. She cradled Rebecca against her and bravely faced the most powerful goddess in the Greek pantheon.

Hera got a gleam in her eye Nico didn't like. "I see." She turned back to Bes. "Well, get on with it."

The room dimmed. Nico wondered if the generator power was

tied to Bes, and now that he needed to use more of his magic, the lights were going. Or maybe it was Nico's vision. He was in so much pain he couldn't tell if he was dying or not.

Things had definitely gotten darker. White light concentrated around Bes, and the small god closed his eyes, lips moving silently.

Hera watched, a smirk on her face. The light coalesced around Bes, touching Andreas softly and making his open eyes shine.

Bes's power burst out from him in an incredible wave, ripples sending the rubble bouncing around the floor. Patricia drew protectively closer to both Nico and Rebecca, and Rebecca lifted her head to watch with dull eyes.

Andreas's body leapt as though electricity had licked through it. The leopard jerked, limbs stiff, and then slowly came upright, as though dragged by puppet strings.

Rebecca started to crawl forward. "No, please, leave him alone."

Patricia dragged her back again, urging her to keep still.

Hera laughed. "There is a difference between reanimation and resurrection. You obviously have them confused, Bes."

The leopard was on its feet, not alive, but standing on its own. Nico felt sick to his stomach.

"You are correct." Bes smiled. "I can't do a resurrection, but my friends can."

He pointed to something high up on one wall. A painting still clung there, having miraculously escaped the explosion. There were two figures: a woman with long, thin horns on her head in a transparent dress, and a man facing her. Isis and Osiris, Nico realized, the goddess and the husband she'd brought back from the dead.

"Isis and Osiris," Bes shouted. "Lend me your strength."

The painting began to crack. Before it crumbled into nothing, a shaft of light lit up Bes, which he transferred to the leopard.

Nico held his breath. Sudden animation sprang into Andreas's eyes, and the big cat yawned. The new life rippled down his body from ears to tail—Nico could follow the wave all the way down. At last Andreas did a full cat stretch and shook himself.

Still bathed in light, Andreas rose on his hind legs and took on his human form, stretching tall. Rebecca's eyes lit with joy.

The thin gold chain around Andreas's neck broke with an audible snap, and the pieces clinked to the floor. Andreas put his hand to his throat in wonder, then he laughed.

"Ha!" Rebecca shouted to Hera. "You said you resigned all claim to him, which means he's no longer under your curse."

Hera's eyes blazed, and she raised her hand, power gathering in her palm.

"No," Bes said quickly. "You gave him to me. He is my creature now, protected by the power of Isis."

Hera stared at him, then folded her hand, and the light faded. "I suppose it doesn't matter. He is nothing. An unimportant demigod."

Andreas laughed again. He closed his hands around his throat, his blue eyes dancing with mirth.

"In that case," Andreas said to Hera, his voice strong and powerful, "I have something to tell you."

He grew taller, his demigod divinity filling the chamber. He changed again into a leopard—his true leopard form, huge and powerful and painfully bright.

"*Fuck you.*" Andreas ended on a very leopard snarl, then he leapt straight upward and vanished.

Rebecca was on her feet. "What did you do to him?"

"She didn't do anything," Nico said. His heart lightened, joy that Andreas was beyond her reach mitigating some of the pain inside him. "He's free."

"But where did he go?"

"Who knows?" Nico wanted to laugh. "It doesn't matter."

Hera's outrage faded, replaced by a knowing smile. "How does it feel, Nikolaus? Your friend, bound to you for millennia, deserting you when you most need him?" She switched her gaze to Rebecca. "How does it feel for you, dear? You see, he never loved you, never even liked you. He used you with absolutely no thought of caring for you. Does that make you angry? Would you like me to punish him?"

She watched Rebecca hopefully, but Rebecca only looked back at her.

"No. I'm happy he's free of you. Let him run wild if that's what he wants."

"How disappointing." Her look hardened, and Nico understood that Rebecca had changed in Hera's eyes from Andreas's victim to Hera's enemy.

"How does it feel?" Hera asked her again. "To know that the only man who found you beautiful was a liar? He didn't think you beautiful at all. He only wanted you to translate the inscription for him, and he'd have done anything to make you do it."

Rebecca watched her expressionlessly. Nico wanted to smile his encouragement.

What Hera couldn't see in Rebecca was her courage and strength, her fortitude. She was not a woman who would crumple and fall because another woman told her she couldn't catch a man.

"You know," Rebecca said mildly, "my dissertation advisor was much better with insults than you. And still I got my PhD with honors."

Hera's brows rose. "You are quite amusing, my dear. Andreas has just deserted you. It doesn't matter whether you care about the truths I tell you. He's left you."

"If he would only come to me because he was compelled, then I don't want him," Rebecca said.

"How brave you are."

She sounded like she was losing interest. Hera glanced over at Nico, who couldn't move for pain. "The question now is not Andreas, it is what I will do with you."

"You'll do nothing." Patricia said. She'd gone to stand with Rebecca. "Nico is still under the power of your curse. Isn't that good enough?"

"Not really. Someone has to pay for Andreas escaping me, and Bes is beyond my reach."

"He's already hurt. He can't even move."

Hera smiled sadly. "I see that. Poor little demigod. I will have to repair him."

She raised her hand and sent a ball of light to Nico. He gasped as the shock of it hit him.

Mending his bones hurt worse than the breaking of them. He clenched his teeth, holding in his agony. His bones cracked and snapped as they melded together, his wings spreading. Nausea kicked his gut.

Patricia made a noise of anguish. He heard her footsteps, then felt her slim arms around him, her tears falling on his cheek. He tried to lift his hand to touch her, to soothe her, but the pain was too great.

He heard Hera walk to them, felt the goddess stop and look down. "I could hurt you far worse than that, you know."

Nico did know. The punishments the gods devised could be cruel beyond imagining, such as Prometheus, chained forever to a rock while an eagle plucked out his liver every day. He wondered what endless horror Hera would bind him to.

Right now, he enjoyed Patricia's lips in his hair, her cool hands on his skin. *I love you,* he wanted to whisper.

Bes came to them, the half-sized god's body thick and strong. "I read the inscription. You know what you have to do."

"Tell me," Patricia demanded. "What does the damn inscription have to do with all this?"

"It's a test," Bes said, ignoring Hera's splutters. "Nikolaus and Andrei are tortured for centuries, but if they pass Hera's test, they will get free." He shrugged. "Andreas is already free, of course. Death did that."

"The test?" Hera shrieked in an awful voice. "You dare challenge me?"

Bes looked hesitant, his gaze straying to where the painting of Isis had been. "Yes," he said.

Hera smiled, looking suddenly happy. "Good."

Her smile widened as she gazed down at Patricia and Nico, and a dry, hot wind blasted through the tomb. Patricia screamed suddenly, and then she and Rebecca vanished.

Nico started up, no longer caring about the pain. "Where did you send her? What did you do?"

"The test has begun," Hera said. Her fussy draperies fluttered in the wind. "Your bond to her is broken. How much do you care about her—really?"

"Enough to want to save her from you."

"Truly? Well, then, you'd better get on with it."

She smiled, leaning closer and closer to him. Then she vanished, along with Bes and the rubble-strewn tomb. Nico found himself facedown in the hotel room in Cairo, cool tile pressing his face.

A man stood next to him, neat shoes and crisp pant legs dust-free. "Nico, what the hell?"

He lifted his head to find Demitri, his demigod friend who owned the hotel, staring down at him in great surprise.

~ ~ ~

DEMITRI had dark hair that he wore pulled into a sleek, businesslike ponytail, which went with his well-tailored suit. He'd always been meticulous in his dress, no matter what the century.

He was a son of Apollo and a longtime friend of Nico and Andreas, but when the slave chains were being handed out, he'd luckily been elsewhere.

Demitri had become a good friend over the centuries, a help when they needed it. Nico felt a brother's closeness with him, though they weren't brothers by blood. When Patricia and Rebecca had decided they needed to come to Cairo, he'd known there would be no safer place to stash them than at Demitri's.

Now Demitri listened with shock in his brown eyes as Nico related the story.

"Holy shit," Demitri said. "What test was she talking about?"

"I have no idea." Nico rose to look for a shirt. Their luggage had mysteriously reappeared, as though it had never left the suite. "I have no clue what danger Patricia is in, or where she is. She could be anywhere in this world or maybe not here anymore. Hera could have magicked her to Hades. Who knows?"

"I can check on that," Demitri said. "Hera doesn't rule there, as much as she thinks she does." He sat in thoughtful silence a moment. "Andreas just took off?"

"Yes, and I don't blame him. He was dead, right in front of me, my best friend, and she just laughed. I thank all the gods he's all right."

"Me, too. But I wonder what he's up to. You never know with him."

That was true enough. "And Rebecca," Nico said. "I don't know if Hera sent her off with Patricia or killed her, or what. Both of them stood up to her. I've never seen anything so brave, but I wish they'd cowered in a corner and begged her to help them against us. Then they'd be all right."

"I can see that." Demitri sat up, his pristine suit a sharp contrast to Nico's T-shirt and jeans. "I'll help you look, Nico. We'll find her."

Nico wished he could be so confident. He stood looking out of the window over the Nile and the city beyond, so many houses and buildings and people, millions of them. Patricia was out there somewhere—maybe.

He loved her with every part of himself. Whether it was the curse or not, he didn't care; he loved Patricia, and that was all there was to it. He loved the way she groaned when he pleasured her, how she'd laugh and bite the tips of his feathers.

He loved her riot of blond curls, the pucker she'd get in her forehead when puzzled about something, the aquamarine sparkle of her eyes. Even if she never returned his love, if it was only magic, he didn't care. His love for her would never die.

"That bad?" Demitri stopped beside him, looking out over his adopted city.

Nico nodded grimly. "That bad."

Demitri clasped Nico's shoulder. He didn't have to say anything; his friendship and support radiated from him.

The door of the suite banged open. Nico and Demitri whirled, poised to fight, then Nico stopped, heart beating in relief as Andreas slammed his way in.

He'd dressed in a ragged caftan he must have picked up along the way. His hair was sandy, his face creased with dirt.

"Where the hell is she?" he demanded of the two of them. "Where's Becky?"

~ ~ ~

It was dark where Patricia was, and she had the horrible feeling of aloneness. Not alone as she might be in her apartment above her store at night; there she was aware of the churning, teeming city around her, people above her and down in the street. Now she felt utterly alone, as though she'd been buried alive.

She hadn't been. She could move and sit up and even stand, and there was air here, cool and fresh, as though the place was ventilated.

Patricia explored what she could, walking around with arms outstretched, and found that her prison was six paces by six. The ceiling was beyond her reach, even when she jumped.

When she stretched out her psychic senses, the walls began to glow and pulsate with the auras of people long past, hundreds and hundreds of them. She was someplace very old, but not a tomb, which would be quiet with the passing of ages.

This place had seen much activity, and the people here had been excited, bored, hopeful, worried, and happy. She could feel no powerful godlike aura, so she thought perhaps it hadn't been a temple.

"Not that this is helpful," Patricia muttered to herself. "I'll still starve to death. Or perhaps die of thirst."

Very cheerful.

She rose again and paced the confined space. *One, two, three, four, five, six . . . seven, eight?*

Patricia stopped, confused. It had been six paces before, she'd sworn that.

"Now I'm losing my mind," she said out loud. "This just gets better."

No doubt about it, her prison was now eight paces by eight. Moving walls? Patricia pushed at the stone blocks, but they were solid. She banged on them once with her closed fists, then slid to the floor again.

She sat quietly, frustrated, but not in panic or despair. One thought came to her over and over again: *Nico will find me.*

She knew this deep down inside. This was the test Hera and Bes had argued about: whether Nico and Patricia would love each other enough to find each other again. She knew the answer was yes.

She did hope that the test of her and Nico's love wouldn't be like some of the weird myths she'd read in which the beloved object was turned into a rock or tree or something, in order to make a point. She had mixed feelings about spending eternity as a symbol of true love.

"I'd rather have the reality," she said, grinding her teeth. "Hurry up, Nico."

~ ~ ~

"WE need Bes," Nico concluded.

The other two had dragged him out to a coffeehouse in a back alley, feeding him potent Egyptian coffee. The streets were teeming as usual, men filling coffeehouses or strolling, enjoying the cool darkness. Two men shared a water pipe in one corner, and at any other time, Nico would have found the pungent scent of spiced tobacco and the slow bubbling of the pipe soothing.

He'd wanted to fly away and search every corner of the world for Patricia, but Demitri convinced him they had to do this logically.

"Bes knew the story on the wall," Nico continued. "What this test was. What I'm supposed to do."

Demitri turned to Andreas. The leopard-man had lost his habitual bitter look, his throat free of the gold chain he'd worn for millennia. But he was still angry and desperately worried about Rebecca.

"Andreas," Demitri began. "If you spent all your time with Rebecca, you saw the inscription the most. You were with her when she finished her rough translation. Do you remember anything about it, especially at the end?"

Andreas ran thick fingers through his hair. "I wasn't paying attention to the damn wall, if you know what I mean."

Demitri nodded. "You, a woman—I know what you were paying attention to. But do you have anything, remember *anything*?"

"Nothing helpful," he growled. "It was the sad story of Nico and me getting caught by Hera's spell, and how we were eternally punished for our lust. After that it was stuff about how lust dwindled and love was stronger, how love could shine through where lust failed."

"All right, that's good." Demitri tried to sound reassuring. "What does that mean to you?"

"That love is stronger and more important than lust," Nico said. "Love has great power, where lust fades. I already knew that."

Demitri agreed. "What I think it means is that if you truly love Patricia, not just want her, you'll prevail."

"That's helpful," Nico said in an ironic voice. "Wasn't there anything on the wall that said, *Start looking here*?"

"No," Andreas said glumly. "It didn't say anything about whether Patricia and Rebecca would be together, either." He sighed. "I have to find Rebecca. She doesn't know how to handle goddesses. She's too blunt. She'll get herself killed."

Demitri looked at them both and raised his brows. "I think you've both gone way beyond the lust part. Now it's just legwork."

Nico shook his head. "This is Hera we're talking about. Nothing will be that easy."

"I know. But I have some ideas and friends who might know things."

"It's good of you to help," Nico said.

Demitri looked offended. "How long have we been friends?"

"Four thousand years. Give or take."

"Exactly." He clapped Nico on the shoulder. "I won't leave you in the lurch when things get tough. I say we draw up a battle plan."

20

NICO insisted that they try to summon Bes. In ancient Egypt, the god Bes had defended homes against evil spirits and other dangers like snakes and wild animals. He was a protector of hearth and home, a handy god to have around.

Modern-day Egypt had thoroughly embraced Islam, but statues of the old gods, copies of those found on archaeological digs, were plentiful. Demitri had one.

The statue was squat and square, Bes's legs stubby. His face was almost lionlike, his horns two tiny bumps on his head.

"He looks better in person," Andreas growled. "Barely."

Demitri studied the statue as it reposed on the table in the middle of the suite's living room. "If anyone hears I've been conjuring pagan gods in my best guest suite, I'll be run out of business."

"We'll keep it down," Andreas assured him.

He was as restless as Nico, pacing and growling all morning.

His movements were jerky as they surrounded the statue with greenery and candles. Gods liked offerings, but Nico wasn't sure what Bes would enjoy. Wine? Fruit?

"Coffee," Andreas said. "Remember, he was so proud of his coffee machine."

Nico decided it had as good a shot as anything, so Demitri sent for a tray of hot, fresh coffee with four cups. The waiter who brought it tried to look into the room to see what they were doing, but Demitri grabbed the tray and slammed the door.

"He probably thinks we're having an orgy," Demitri said as he set down the tray.

"An orgy with coffee?" Andreas asked.

"He has a vivid imagination."

"I wonder what he'd think if we asked for some DVDs?"

Nico looked up irritably from where he was arranging the altar. "Can anyone who's not still a slave please shut up?"

"Sorry," Demitri said at once.

"Just relieving the tension," Andreas added.

Nico finished and sat back on his heels, still wondering how to do this. He'd never actually conjured a god before, mostly wanting them to leave him the hell alone.

He started to chant in an ancient tongue that was not Greek or Egyptian but the language that had existed before those civilizations rose. It was a language of the gods, when they walked the earth, before leaving humankind to have contact with them only through worship, through rituals like these.

"God of hearth and home, I summon thee," Nico said. "Proud god who faced down the queen of my pantheon, hear my plea."

Nothing happened. Andreas moved restlessly. "Where is he? It's not working."

"Shh," Demitri admonished. "Let Nico finish."

Nico tried to block out their words and focus on the statue. Bes looked back at him blankly, the stone remaining immobile.

"Maybe he's not positioned right." Andreas grabbed the little god and turned him to face the window. As he lifted his hand away, he knocked against the small cup of coffee, which overturned an spattered all over Bes.

"Damn it," Nico muttered.

Swearing, Andreas reached for a towel, but Demitri stopped him. "Wait."

As the coffee dripped from the statue, the stone flushed with warmth. Life trickled into it, inch by inch, until at last a tiny figure stood amid the garlands. The three men leaned forward to look at him.

"No, no, no," the small Bes said, waving his arms. "I can't give hints. It's against the rules."

"I don't give a damn about your hints or your rules," Nico said. "Where's Patricia?"

"I can't tell you. If I do, I'll void the test."

"Screw the test. I'll be a slave for eternity if Hera releases her. I don't care. I just want her to be all right."

"That isn't the answer," Bes said.

"I told you, I don't care . . ."

"Staying a slave isn't the solution to the test," Bes said. "You have to find it on your own."

Nico clenched his hands. "What is the test? What did the wall painting say?"

Bes looked pained. "I can't tell you."

Andreas leaned forward and poked the little god. "Listen, you. I've had enough of games with gods and goddesses. Give back our ladies and stay the hell out of our lives."

Bes's expression turned mournful. "I can't. I wish I could help you. I have no desire to see Patricia hurt."

Nico's heart felt like lead. "Are you saying that if I don't pass the test, Patricia *will* be hurt?"

"Yes, unfortunately. I can make things better for her if you do the right things, but if not . . ." He trailed off with a gesture of helplessness.

"What about Rebecca?" Andreas interrupted. "She's not part of Nico's test, is she? Where is Rebecca?"

Bes jumped back a foot, nearly tripping over the garlands. "She's safe. She's safe, I swear it. In Greece."

"Greece?" Andreas stood up. "What the hell is she doing in Greece?"

"She's in the land of Odysseus and Penelope," Bes said, perplexed. "In Ithaca."

Andreas let out a long growl, his claws emerging. "Not Greece, you little stone idiot. New York. She works at Cornell—in *New York*."

"Oh," Bes said. "I just heard Ithaca. I hope I sent her to the right one."

"You'd damn well better have sent her to the right one." Andreas reached down and grabbed Bes in his big fist.

The little god shuddered and froze into hard stone. Andreas started and dropped the statue, which shattered on the tile floor into three large pieces.

"Damn it," Andreas said. "Nico, I'm sorry."

Nico shrugged, his heart aching. "It doesn't matter. He wasn't going to give us much more than that."

Demitri retrieved his broken statue and tried to fit the pieces together. "What did he mean, he could make things better for Patricia if you did the right things?"

"Who knows? I don't know what the right thing is." Nico stared at the tangled garlands and spilled coffee, the statue Demitri was trying to repair. "I have to find her."

"What's the phone number for Cornell?" Andreas broke in.

Nico looked up. "I don't know. Patricia's cell phone is in her room. She might have it from when she first called Rebecca."

Andreas was out of the room before Nico had finished speaking.

Nico rose to pace. His back itched, his wings wanting to break free of their confinement. He wanted to soar over the city, blast open every building with his half-god magic, and find Patricia.

He couldn't; he knew that. He sensed that if he resorted to brute force, he'd never see her again, or he'd kill her in the process.

Where could they hide her that a normal search wouldn't find her? A living woman couldn't be taken to Hades and survive, the legend of Persephone notwithstanding. He'd met Persephone, and he had no doubt she had the god of the underworld wrapped around her little finger.

It had to be somewhere magical, mysterious, but someplace she could exist and he could find. That let out any of the god realms; she must still be on the tangible earth.

I'll find you, Patricia, he thought, hoping that somehow she could hear him. *I love you. I'll find you and break this test and prove my love is real.*

He pictured her standing in front of him, her riot of blond curls snaking over her shoulders, her smile, her laughter. He lifted his hand as though to touch her hair, his heart breaking when his fingers brushed only empty air.

~ ~ ~

THE room had definitely gotten bigger. Patricia could walk twelve paces each way now, and on her next circuit, her foot bumped something hard.

Wincing, she leaned down to see what it was and found a square shape that felt smooth and cool, like tile. She also felt droplets of water, and reaching forward, she encountered the unmistakable silken feel of water.

Her heart lurched, her parched throat pinching. She hesitated, fearful of drinking water that hadn't been purified, but her dry mouth urged her to at least taste it.

She scooped some in her hands and let droplets dribble across her tongue. They tasted as clear and pure as the best bottled water.

Well water? If she was out in the middle of nowhere, well water might be all right to drink. It was cold and good, and she couldn't resist scooping more into her mouth.

"Now, if I could just have a sandwich to go with it," she said hopefully.

She waited, but no smell of roast beef and mustard assailed her, and she sighed. "Oh, well, it was worth a try."

Patricia started to walk back to her corner, then had the sudden fearful thought that the basin might vanish if she turned her back on it. She whirled around and banged her foot on it again.

She scooped more water into her mouth, then found a dry place to sit next to it. She hung her fingers into the water, its touch comforting.

"Come on, Nico. You're supposed to find me. I know you are."

She wished for the hundredth time that her psychic ability included projecting her thoughts to others. Even if she closed her eyes and concentrated, she could feel nothing more than the auras of this room, nothing outside of it.

"Nico, if you can hear me . . ."

She sighed. She knew Nico couldn't, and she could not hear him, as much as she projected.

"They could have left me a cell phone," she muttered. "But, oh, no."

Not that it would have worked in this thick-walled building out in the middle of nowhere. Cell phones were only as good as their ability to pick up a signal.

Patricia sighed, hoping that whoever found her phone put it to good use.

~ ~ ~

"I'm in Egypt; where do you think I am?" Andreas yelled into Patricia's phone. At the other end, Rebecca's shrill, tinny voice came back to him.

Andreas's heart beat thick and hard. Rebecca's number at Cornell had indeed been stored on Patricia's phone's recent call list, and one touch had it ringing far off in New York. Rebecca's breathless "Hello" reached him after the second ring.

She was safe. She was all right. Hera hadn't killed her.

"How should I know where you are?" Rebecca said back to him. Her voice sounded shaky, like she'd been crying. "You magicked yourself out of the tomb, leaving the rest of us stranded."

"No, I didn't, sweetheart. I'd never leave you stranded."

Rebecca huffed. "I saw you."

"I had to get out before she could think of some way to trap me again. I knew that was the only way I could help Nico. When I came back for you, everyone was gone. I thought Hera had done something with you. Nico and Demitri didn't know where you were."

"I blacked out and woke up here, in my office, with my clothes all dirty from the tomb. The department chair walked in thirty seconds later."

Andreas imagined it, Rebecca filthy from the rain of rubble and wall painting, tears tracking through the dust on her face.

"And do you know what?" Rebecca's laugh sounded strained. "He didn't even notice anything was wrong. He just asked me how my research trip to Cairo had been." She kept laughing, hysteria edging her voice.

"It's all right, Becky," Andreas said. "You'll be safe enough there. Go back to the B and B and tell the cats we'll be coming soon."

"What about Nico and Patricia? Are they all right?"

Andreas hesitated, not sure what to tell her.

"What is it?" she squeaked as his hesitation went on too long. "What happened to Patricia and Nico?"

Andreas told her. He clenched the phone, not liking to hear her cries of dismay. He hated being half the world away from her.

"Damn it," Rebecca said. "I'm coming out there."

"No, you bloody well are not. You're safe there. The Dyons will stop tracking you now."

"Screw that. I have my passport, and my visa's still good for another three weeks. I can get a British Airways out of JFK and change in London. What else am I going to spend my postdoc stipend on?"

"Becky, no."

"Stop calling me Becky like it means something. You aren't under the curse anymore."

"I know that," he shouted. "Don't you get it?"

"I'm coming out there," she said firmly and hung up.

Andreas slapped the phone closed and stalked out to the living room.

Demitri watched him with an amused look on his face. "Trouble with the little woman?"

Andreas had the sudden urge to go to the man and jerk his tie crooked. Demitri always had to look perfect. "I thought once the curse was gone, I wouldn't care what she thought of me. But I do. Damn it."

"I think Nico is having the same problem. What he's feeling is more than just the curse."

They both looked at Nico, who had spread maps all over the table, marking places to look. Andreas's heart burned for him. Andreas at least had the satisfaction of knowing Rebecca was all right, even if the headstrong woman wasn't about to stay quietly safe at home. Nico was hurting.

Andreas sat down next to him, looking over the places Nico had marked: the pyramids at Giza and the ones farther south at Dashur, the valley of Amarna, the remote areas of the Valley of Kings.

"Why these?" he asked.

Nico looked up, a fanatic light in his dark eyes. "They're places god magic would have built up over the centuries. If Hera wanted to confine Patricia magically, these would be good. I can't imagine Patricia staying long in a place that wasn't magical. She's resourceful and would figure a way out."

He spoke proudly, and at the same time, his face was stark with grief and worry.

"There are magical places like this all over the world," Demitri said, his voice gentle. "Stone circles in England, the Mayan temples, caves in India."

"I know." Nico looked up with a frown. "But we have to start somewhere."

"Good point," Demitri said, trying to sound cheerful.

Andreas shook his head at Demitri, and rested his hand lightly on Nico's shoulder. "We'll find her," he said. "Demitri and I will do everything we can. Promise."

~ ~ ~

LATER that night, Andreas found Nico out on the balcony, looking over the Nile. The river was a black streak in the city of light and noise, the boats on it strings of brightness.

Nico had agreed to rest and start searching for Patricia at first light. Demitri was putting together tickets and passes for them to get around the country.

Andreas leaned next to Nico on the balcony. "You all right?"

"No." Nico wouldn't look at him. "She's out there, in danger, and I don't know what to do."

"Yes, you do. You look for her. You keep looking for her."

Nico sighed. "I'm in love with her, Andreas. I feel it, even beyond the curse."

"I know."

"I should have made her stay in New York. I let her argue her way to coming out here because I wanted to be with her. I wanted to have her as long as I could."

"I know. What do you think I did with Rebecca?"

"I thought my feelings were physical, part of the curse," Nico continued. "But they go so far beyond."

Andreas didn't answer. He didn't have to. He saw the tears glisten on Nico's face and moved closer to him.

Sometimes words weren't enough. Andreas snaked his arm around Nico's shoulders and turned Nico's face to him so he could kiss his mouth. This wasn't about sex but about comfort.

Nico kissed him back, shakily, his lips cold. The world had changed in so many ways, Andreas thought. But once upon a time, in their ancient world, a man could kiss his best friend without condemnation.

He heard Demitri stop in the doorway. "Don't do that out here," he said, exasperated. "I have a hotel to run."

"Piss off," Andreas rumbled.

Nico stepped away from Andreas, his stance a little stronger. "I'm all right now."

"No, he isn't." Nico was bowed with grief and fear, and Andreas knew it.

"Come on inside," Demitri said. "If Nico needs comfort, we can both give it to him."

Nico nodded. He passed Andreas, and Demitri moved aside so that Nico could enter.

Nico took Demitri's hand and pulled the other man inside with him. He kissed Demitri's mouth, then started with him for the bedroom, Andreas following.

~ ~ ~

NICO woke a few hours later, snug in a nest of his two snoring friends. He was grateful to them for their comfort, lying with bare bodies touching for warmth and reassurance, like littermates.

Both Demitri and Andreas advised caution and waiting, but Nico knew he could do neither. They also advised against using his demigod magic to search, but Nico knew he had to use everything in his power to find her.

Nico rose and left the bed, pulling on his pants. Still sleeping, Andreas and Demitri moved closer together, Andreas draping one arm over Demitri's bare torso.

Nico walked through the dark suite and out onto the balcony. The night businesses had closed, and it would be several hours before shops opened to take advantage of the cool of the morning.

Nico unfurled his wings, letting the breeze from the river ruffle his black feathers. He stepped up on the balcony rail.

I will find you, Patricia, if I have to search for the rest of eternity.

Eternity sounded like a long time for her to wait, but he hardened his resolve. *Hold on, my love.*

He leapt out into empty air, his wings catching the cool draft rising from the river. He stretched out his powers to *see*, and the world changed.

Solid shapes receded into irrelevant details. What he saw was humanity, the teeming brightness of it, families gathered for warmth and love against the night.

He soared over the city of Cairo, seeing the spread of domes and minarets of the Islamic city, faith clinging to them like warmth.

Across the river, the cities of Heliopolis and Giza spread before him, densely packed with humanity. The river itself gleamed with boats.

He found no sign of Patricia. He hadn't expected to, thinking Hera would have put her somewhere far more dire. He turned to swoop out over open desert, the chill of the night catching in his feathers.

Soon that chill would change to unbearable heat, and Patricia would be out in it—somewhere.

He circled south, following the life-giving Nile, and out across the desert cliffs.

~ ~ ~

Patricia jumped awake, her limbs cramped from the hard floor and her folded position.

Her hand had fallen to her side, and she quickly reached for the basin again, sighing in relief to find the water still there. She didn't feel any ill effects from it, and her thirsty body didn't stop her from leaning over the tile and scooping handful after handful of water into her mouth.

She felt a little better after she drank and bathed her face in the cool liquid. Her frustration mounted after that. She had to get out of here.

Another exploration of the room showed that it had expanded in size even more. One wall jutted out a little now, and around the corner, still in the dark, she bumped into a table.

Sinking to her knees, she cautiously touched it, thoughts of snakes and scorpions prominent in her mind. Her hand found something ball-shaped, with the unmistakable feel of orange skin.

Laughing, Patricia lifted the orange to her nose and inhaled the citrus goodness of it.

Then she peeled it and devoured it. While savoring its tangy sweetness, she felt the table again, finding a whole pile of oranges and a plate of what smelled like figs. She ate a little of those, too, saving the rest.

Now that her hunger and thirst were somewhat assuaged, she began to want light. She had to figure out where she was and figure out how to get out of there and find Nico.

She hoped Nico was all right. Hera had killed Andreas by barely lifting a finger, and she might think it fun to murder Nico and keep Patricia imprisoned and wondering for the rest of her life.

Best not to think about things like that.

She also wished she knew where Andreas had gone. Had he deserted Nico and Rebecca as Hera claimed? Or was he biding his time? She'd seen Rebecca disappear the split second before Patricia had been teleported out herself, and she wondered if Rebecca, too, was confined somewhere.

She had faith in Nico and Andreas, even if Hera didn't. Nico would come.

Patricia wasn't certain how she knew—she'd met Nico only a couple of weeks ago—but she did. She and Nico shared a bond, even if it first started as a curse.

He would come for her.

~ ~ ~

Halfway down the Nile, a man with a rifle aimed into the dawn sky and brought down the largest black-winged bird he'd ever seen.

21

Andreas wasn't surprised to wake up and find Nico gone. Demitri was already up, showered, and immaculately dressed by the time Andreas wandered out to look for coffee.

"Are you going to just let him go?" Andreas asked. He stretched, letting the morning sunlight warm his body through the windows.

"Do you have any suggestions as to where to start looking for him?"

"Not really."

"That's what I thought."

Andreas gulped the coffee Demitri handed him and scowled at the smoggy morning. "I'm not going to sit here while Nico gets obliterated by Hera."

"I don't suggest we do." Demitri set his cup down with economical movements. Demitri's hair was pulled into his neat, short ponytail, his expensive Italian suit precisely tailored for his frame. Andreas felt scruffy in jeans with bare torso, his hair a mess, and he didn't care.

"What do you suggest then?" he grumbled.

"Nico's running on adrenaline and emotion. If you and I use our brains, we can figure this out and help him."

"You're optimistic."

"He's hurting." Demitri arranged the empty coffee cups carefully on a tray. "And I saw you both with Patricia even if I didn't meet her. She wasn't looking at you or any other man; she only had eyes for Nico. He needs someone like that."

"Nico's a demigod. Patricia's a mortal. How is that going to work?"

"We'll make it work. And even if they can have only a fleeting time together, don't you think it's worth it?"

Andreas thought about Rebecca, how she could move from shy smile to steely determination back to shy smile in seconds. She was two women: the brainy scholar who'd made her name as one of the top archaeologists of the day and the hesitant young woman who'd never realized she was sexy.

"Yes," Andreas said slowly. "I think it would be worth it." He studied Demitri a moment, taking in the man's dark eyes and tanned skin, remembering when Demitri had been a wild hellion running all over the world beside Andreas and Nico. "When did you become the matchmaker?"

Demitri shrugged. "When I realized Nico had a chance to be free and happy."

"I'm free, if you noticed. Are you happy for me?"

"Well, of course." Demitri straightened his tie a fraction. "But do you know what to do with the happiness you've been handed?"

Andreas thought about Rebecca again, how his longing for her hadn't abated, even though his slave chain was gone. This was real.

"I'll figure it out," he promised.

~ ~ ~

NICO lay facedown with his wings over him, trying to be as still as he possibly could.

The shot had taken off a chunk of wing feathers, enough to knock him out of the sky. He'd spiraled down to this clump of rocks and crawled behind them, hurt and out of breath. Out in the desert, he heard men shouting to one another, searching for him.

He wished he had the power to make himself invisible, but he was only a half god, with limited magic. He couldn't retract his wings with part of one damaged, even though it would be almost as awkward to explain to whoever hunted him why he was lying in the middle of nowhere without a shirt. His full-back tattoo would cause comment as well.

All he could do was huddle in stillness in the middle of the rocks and hope they didn't see him.

To quiet himself, he thought about Patricia. He imagined himself carefully licking her leg all the way up to her quim, then kneeling back and slowly spreading her legs.

She'd laugh down at him, her blue green eyes shining in anticipation, her hair a riot of curls on the pillow. She'd touch her clit like he'd taught her to and spread the lips of her quim. She'd be glistening with moisture and wanting his mouth. And his cock.

That organ inflated as soon as his thoughts spun. His heart throbbed with worry for Patricia, and his cock throbbed with need for her.

The men spoke in Arabic, coming closer. Nico lay utterly still, the warmth that flooded him thinking of sex with Patricia relaxing his limbs.

"I'm telling you, it was the biggest bird I ever saw. A black swan, maybe."

"Sure, little brother. Like the huge fish you caught last month that none of us ever saw."

"I told you, some cats ate it."

"You tell good tales, Ahmed. Very entertaining."

The first man, Ahmed, trailed off into disgruntled murmuring. They were three feet from his hiding place, their pace not slowing. With any luck they'd tramp on by, unable to see Nico in the early light.

The two men walked past, the second one admonishing the first to hurry up so they could go home and have their coffee. Their footsteps had almost faded, when suddenly the younger man cried out.

"There. You see?"

Nico hid a groan as they dashed back to where he lay, wings spread over his body. He raised his head to see a rifle barrel pointed right in his eyes, and behind the rifle, an astonished Egyptian face.

"Hello," he said in careful Arabic. "Do you think you'd have enough coffee for me, too?"

~ ~ ~

PATRICIA wondered if she imagined the light. She waved her hand in front of her face and saw nothing, so she decided it was her imagination.

When she saw Nico again, what would she tell him? That she loved him, first. If the test was finding her, and he did and got free, would he still want her? Andreas had been quick enough to disappear, leaving Rebecca heartbroken. She was a resilient young woman, but Patricia had seen her pain.

Would Nico be a carefree demigod again, happy to be rid of Patricia?

She thought of his upright body, broad shoulders, fine torso, the black spread of his wings. She thought of him naked, with his cock standing straight out from a thatch of black hair, his own feathers caressing himself.

He was a beautiful man—no, demigod—and she was in love with him.

The light was definitely there. It was a faint flicker on the edge of her vision, back where she'd found the tiled basin of water. She rose from the dirt and moved toward it, going slowly in case it was Hera waiting for her with a sword of doom or something.

But her psychic senses still told her she was completely alone. However these things were appearing, no person brought them in.

The light had the dim quality of phosphorescence. She knew that some fungi could glow like that, but she had no idea if such a fungus could be found in Egypt—if she was still in Egypt.

She rounded the corner. The tiled basin glowed as though from within, lighting it up in luminescent blues and greens and reds.

"Great," she said. "And I drank it."

She peered into the basin, which, she now saw, was beautifully decorated with mosaic tile. The light was fixed at the bottom, an electric light, not glowing plant life. The water bubbled up from inside the basin, as though from a spring.

The strangeness of all this, which might have frightened Patricia weeks ago, now bounced off her. She had no idea how the room had expanded or how normal-looking things had appeared out of nowhere, but it seemed to go with the situation.

She drank more water, wondering if the light would stay. It was nice to be able to see a little bit. Patricia walked back around the corner to the food table, figuring she might as well have another orange.

The table had grown. She could see its faint outlines in the light, a low, oriental table like what had been in their hotel rooms. It was now covered with brass plates heaped with fruit, not just warm-climate fruit, like oranges and figs, but strawberries, grapes, apples, and dates.

Patricia sat down and made a nice fruit meal, not surprised that everything tasted so good. These were the juiciest oranges, the sweetest grapes, the crispest apples she'd ever had.

This is very weird, she thought. *Or maybe it's Hera's way of driving me insane. Are these really apples I'm eating, or am I dreaming all this?*

The juice running down her chin was real enough. What she wanted most in the world, though, was Nico there to lick it clean.

~ ~ ~

STRANGELY enough, it didn't take Nico much effort to get his hunters to accept that he was a divine being. The two brothers, Ahmed and Faisal, lived in a small house in a village of the Dakhla oasis out in the western desert. They were farmers and lived there with their older brother, Mahmud, his wife and children, and their aging mother.

Nico was welcomed into the house and given food and drink, although it was obvious they didn't have much to give. The brothers were convinced that Nico was an angel sent to bring them luck and divine guidance, and Ahmed took much ribbing for shooting at him.

Fortunately, except for the wing feathers, he'd missed. Human bullets couldn't kill Nico, but he'd still bleed and hurt. Once Nico's wings had healed enough, he drew them in, to the family's delight, and he accepted their offer of a caftan to cover himself.

Nico spread a little magic over the house and the rest of the village to help keep the people here healthy and bring them a good crop yield. He decided to tell them about his quest, which the brothers listened to with interest.

"The divine Nico searches for his beloved lady," Ahmed said. "I've never heard that story."

"That's because it's still being told," Nico said, cradling the tiny cup of Egyptian coffee they'd given him. "I don't know what the ending is. Can you think of somewhere around here a goddess might hide a lady?"

They seemed happy to help and speculate, and the oldest brother's three sons chimed in. The wife, mother, and daughters had taken themselves into another room on Nico's arrival, but the wife called to her husband, and she and her mother-in-law loudly told him their opinion on the matter.

It took a long time and a lot of argument and then another meal for the family to reach a conclusion.

"There is a place," Ahmed said. "It is out in the desert where there are no roads. The foreign archaeologists search here, there, and everywhere for sites to dig, but they always miss that."

"Why don't you tell them about it?" Nico asked.

Ahmed looked innocent. "It's fun to watch them look. And it might be nothing, just some square stones in the desert."

"I'm willing to see them," Nico said.

Their mother and Mahmud's wife related that they approved, and preparations were made for a journey into the desert.

Nico waited outside while they prepared, enjoying the cool breeze under the palm trees. The brothers farmed here where life-giving water bubbled from the surface of the desert. They liked it here, Ahmed said, far from the bustling crowds of Cairo and the tourist spots of Luxor and Thebes.

"A man can be his own person here," Ahmed told Nico. "He can walk with a long stride, and he knows all his neighbors, good and bad. When I go to Cairo . . ." He shook his head. "So many people, so much noise, and I can't breathe the air."

Tourists did travel out here to look at the tombs and Roman temple, but for the most part, Ahmed's village was quiet.

Mahmud had an ancient jeep, which they supplied with gas and water, and the two younger brothers and Nico piled in for their trek into the desert. It took several tries to get the jeep going, and then they were off.

Ahmed and his family were of Bedouin descent, and Ahmed drove the jeep with the same fond restlessness with which his ancestors must have ridden their horses. The sun blazed full and high, but the autumn morning was crisp, the air fresh.

The jeep shot down roads Nico could barely tell were there, Ahmed steering with reckless abandon. Gravel and sand shot up from the tires, and the vehicle tipped with each turn.

From what Nico could tell, Ahmed was driving them straight into the desert, toward the Great Sand Sea. Nico held on to the roll bar as the jeep rocketed onward, Ahmed promising Nico would thank him when they reached their destination.

Nico held out hope that the journey would prove fruitful, because before he'd left the brothers' house, he'd seen something that startled him. In a shadowy corner, on a forgotten table, he'd seen a stone statue that looked exactly like Demitri's statue of the stumpy-legged, lion-faced old god, Bes.

~ ~ ~

ANDREAS and Demitri spent much of the day trying to figure out where Nico had gone, and couldn't.

"He marked places everywhere," Andreas said. "Eastern Egypt, the western deserts, the south by Aswan. Why couldn't he tell us what he was thinking?"

"Because he knew he had to go alone," Demitri said.

Andreas heaved a sigh. "I'm no longer a slave, and I feel just as helpless as before. I'm supposed to be there with him, my friend, a man closer to me than a brother, and here I sit in your cushy hotel."

"I feel the same," Demitri said glumly. "We could have sex to pass the time. Maybe something will come to us."

Sex with Demitri and Nico had helped Andreas get through many years of the curse. Andreas could sate his immediate need with his friends until the curse caught him again, and he had appreciated that.

But now that he was free, he knew he wanted Rebecca, not his two friends. She called to him, and he wanted to go to her. At the same time, he didn't want to abandon Nico in his hour of need.

"This sucks," Andreas said.

"I know." Demitri came to him and put his hands on his waist. "It's a poor substitute."

Andreas looked at his friend's handsome face and coffee-colored eyes, feeling the leopard in him respond. Andreas was half an animal, with animal instincts that kicked in at the worst times.

Demitri was half an animal, too, and their animal selves called out to each other. Mesmerized by Demitri's eyes, Andreas tilted his head and slanted a kiss across Demitri's mouth.

"Oh, goodness," Rebecca's light voice cut across the living room. "I came at the right time."

Andreas abandoned Demitri to charge to Rebecca and catch her in a crushing hug. "What the hell are you doing here? I told you to stay in New York."

"I'm happy to see you, too, Andreas."

Rebecca kissed him on the mouth, then pushed and squirmed to get out of his arms. She looked Demitri up and down with great interest. "You look nice," she said. "What do you turn into?"

"A tiger," Demitri said.

~ ~ ~

THINGS were improving in Patricia's prison. The food table now boasted candles that threw a light on her surroundings. By the candlelight, she saw that an oval, tiled bath had appeared on the far wall, enticing steam rising from it.

She didn't hesitate long before she stripped off her clothes and immersed herself in hot, scented water.

"This is all good," she said to the air. "But what I'd really like is a door, or a cell phone that works, or even better, to be back at Nico's friend's hotel."

She held her breath, wondering if the magic room would provide any of it, but nothing happened. The things that appeared hadn't appeared in response to her direct wishes but as though someone else were thinking what next she'd need.

"Some DVDs? To pass the time?" She glanced around at the bright mosaic tile and the gleaming brass of the dishes. "Or is that too modern for you? How about someone to tell me stories, then? Like Scheherazade."

Nothing.

She sighed, leaning back to at least enjoy the bath.

Here she was, so far from home, waiting to be rescued like a princess in a fairy tale. And all she could think about was the memory of meeting Nico for the first time, liking how he looked with his wings covering his half-naked body.

Then meeting Andreas with his wild cat's eyes, and Nico becoming all protective of her. Then the incredible way Nico had taught her to feel. It hadn't been just sex, but learning to appreciate her own body and the beauty of it.

Patricia slid her hands down her wet body and cupped her breasts, feeling them warm and heavy in the water. She pinched her nipples between thumb and forefinger, liking the tingle as she rolled the nubs back and forth.

She wished for Nico to lean down and suck on her, but she had to be content with her imagination.

It wasn't enough. Patricia rose in the tub, water cascading from her body. The tub was large enough to let her kneel in it, her legs apart, the water lapping her thighs.

She parted the lips of her quim as Nico had taught her, fingers on either side of it. She dipped her finger to touch her clit, closing her eyes at the feeling that spread through her.

Her skin tingled and warmed, her quim going soft. She was wet, not just with bathwater but also with her own juices, and the slickness lapped her fingers as she rubbed herself.

Her head went back, the feel of her long curls brushing her skin, soft and erotic. She imagined Nico trailing his fingers down her spine, his touch gentle, while she played with herself.

Patricia rocked a little against her hand, spreading herself wider. She pretended Nico's tongue wet her, the tip of it tickling her clit.

She moved her finger faster with the fantasy, a groan dragging from her throat.

Patricia slid fingers inside herself, wishing she had something bigger and thicker. Visions of Nico's cock played through her mind, the feeling of it long and hot and hard in her hand. She envisioned the dark hair at its base, the heavy balls warm against her palm.

She liked what came with his cock: his tall, muscular body, his sinful smile, his black-dark eyes.

Come for me, Patricia, he'd say in his sexy voice. *Show me what you feel.*

Patricia rose, her body hot and shaking. She straddled the side of the tub, the tile cool on her backside, and thrust her hand between her legs, pulling up tight.

"Nico," she said out loud. "Watch me play with myself for you. Watch me want you."

She worked her clit, thrusting against the cold tile, until her world spun around, and she shouted her release to the echoing ceiling.

She slid bonelessly back into the tub, a smile on her face. "Did you like that, Nico?" She sighed, then she laughed. "What? You want more?"

She pictured Andreas joining Nico, as he had before he'd become bound to Rebecca. His mottled hair tangled down his neck, his ice blue eyes focused on her. His cock, too, would be stiff and hard, ready to find her.

She remembered his cock filling her ass, the lubrication sliding him right in. It had been so good, so . . . satisfying, in a way she'd never been satisfied before. Not the same as Nico inside her, loving her, but in a bone-jarring, dirty fantasy kind of way.

She'd *loved* it.

Patricia draped herself over the edge of the tub again, smiling at the memories. Nico's huge cock in her mouth, filling her while Andreas fucked her.

And then Nico inside her, letting her ride him on the bed while he clasped her breasts. His feathers warm and cushioning, tickling her back while he made love to her.

They'd done some naughty things, and she'd loved every second of them. She'd never believed that she, Patricia Lake, could have let herself do them.

Patricia was still hot and needy. She slid two fingers inside herself, pushing like Nico did, trying to stem the ache. She cried out, then her body took over. She fucked herself with her fingers while she shouted Nico's name, she writhed against the blunt hardness and imagined Andreas in her ass at the same time.

"I love you, Nico," she cried out as she came, waves of pleasure undulating her body.

"I love you," she repeated softly as she sank back into the warm water, her eyes closing. "Love you so much."

Out in the hot desert in back of the rocking jeep, Nico jerked awake, hearing her.

22

So, why do you like to kiss men?" Rebecca asked Andreas. She sat with him at the table in their hotel suite, eating a much-needed meal.

Andreas looked puzzled. "I don't."

"You did with Nico in the hotel in London." She slid a piece of spiced chicken from a kebab and savored the taste. "And when I walked in, you were kissing Demitri."

"Oh. They don't count."

"Thanks, old friend," Demitri said. He was still poring over the maps, a worried look on his handsome face. Demitri was just as tall and muscular as Nico and Andreas, but he dressed in finely tailored suits instead of sloppy jeans and shirts.

Rebecca thought she preferred sloppy jeans, at least on Andreas. He had a raw sensuality that she liked; Rebecca, who'd never done anything raw in her life.

"We're like old comrades," Andreas said. "Closer than brothers. And we're not human; the same rules don't apply to us."

"Convenient."

"I think so."

Rebecca's gaze strayed to his throat, where the chain he'd worn was gone. She wondered what that meant to what was between them—if there ever had been anything between them.

She made herself walk away from him to the maps spread across the table. Demitri gave her a little smile, unembarrassed, as comfortable with himself as Andreas was.

They'd told her about summoning Bes and what he'd said, and Nico taking off before dawn. She looked at the places Nico had marked, rough circles on the neat layout of the map.

"Here," she said, running her finger along the line of oases in the deserts west of Cairo. "Somewhere along this road."

"How do you know that?" Andreas looked over her shoulder. "We've got the whole country to search—the whole world, actually."

"Because I read the wall in the tomb," Rebecca said.

"Which said what?"

"The ending wound off into gibberish—at least, I couldn't read much of it. But it talked about secluding the lady in the hidden palace and the lover searching adamantly until he found her."

"What has that got to do with the western oases?" Demitri asked in a more polite tone than Andreas had used.

"It was talking about gardens in the desert," she told them. "Ancient, beautiful palaces that have died and wait to live again. Places where forgotten kings will rise from the sands and things like that. That might mean ruins in or near one of the oases. I've been out there—lots of fascinating stuff."

"I've been out there, too," Demitri said, pained. "Lots of sand."

"Why only in the west?" Andreas asked. "There are oases in the eastern part of the country, too. All over the deserts out here, in fact."

"The forgotten kings." Andreas and Demitri looked blank, and she shook her head in exasperation. "The mummies that were found near Bahariyya about ten years ago. About a hundred of them, and they think there are hundreds more. Don't you read the archaeological news?"

"Sorry," Andreas said. "Been busy."

"I heard about it," Demitri put in. "But ten years ago."

Rebecca couldn't imagine anyone not knowing everything about an exciting find, but she let it go. "Anyway, that's what the inscription could have been referring to. The forgotten kings rising from the sands might be the mummies. There are plenty of ruins out there. It hasn't all been explored, because most people want to do the Valley of Kings."

"You know that," Demitri said. "Does Nico?"

"Doesn't matter. If we can find Patricia, then we'll find Nico."

"But it's Nico who has to find her to break the spell," Andreas reminded her. He traced his fingers down her spine, which had her instantly flushing.

"It may be that only Nico *will* be able to find her. But nowhere on the wall did it say his friends couldn't help him along the way. In fact, there was a picture of friends around the winged god, including a leopard." She looked straight at Demitri. "And a tiger."

"Are you sure?" Demitri asked in surprise.

"Why not? The ancient Egyptians could know about tigers. The caravan routes went a long way east. Pharaohs had all kinds of exotic animals in their menageries. It was a very cosmopolitan society."

"I meant, how could the person who made the inscription in the first place have known that we'd all be there to help him?"

"Well, I don't know." Rebecca tried to step away from Andreas and his intriguing warmth, but she couldn't. "I only know what I read and translated."

"It's good enough for me," Demitri said, folding the maps. "Better than sitting around here worrying. I'll go with you. I can arrange for transportation." He looked down at his exquisite suit and winced. "I'll have to find something to wear."

"That's settled, then." Rebecca yawned and rubbed a hand through her tangled hair, but her adrenaline was kicking in. "Let me clean up and change. I wish Bes hadn't sent me all the way back to New York. I'll never get over my jet lag at this rate."

She walked out of the room, feeling Andreas's gaze on her every step of the way. She hoped as she showered that he'd enter the room and try to join her, but he never did.

~ ~ ~

PATRICIA got up before she faded too far into the bath. The air was warm enough so she didn't shiver, but she appreciated the pile of fluffy towels she found on a stand next to the tub.

She couldn't bring herself to dress in her filthy clothes again, so she kept the towel wrapped around her. She went around the corner again, to find her prison had expanded yet more.

Now a bed stood in the corner, an exotic bed with a canopy of pointed arches and plenty of silk hangings and cushions. Exhausted, Patricia had no compunction about climbing onto the bed and letting the softness take her weary limbs.

She didn't mean to sleep, but she woke abruptly several hours later to see that she wasn't alone. A man stood about three feet from the foot of her bed, arms folded over a bare torso.

Patricia kept the covers pulled firmly to her chin and looked back at him. He was tall and muscular and wore nothing but a cloth draped around his waist.

"Who are you?" Patricia asked him. She repeated the phrase in Arabic.

The man regarded her stonily, obviously not understanding her.

"I've seen this movie," she told him. "Don't even think about ravishing me."

She wasn't afraid, because it was all so absurd. The bed with its lush hangings, the fruit, the bath, and the half-naked man were all like something from a 1920s film. She admitted that it was better than huddling alone and afraid in the dark, but this was bizarre.

Music began, the wild, fast Egyptian music played at parties and weddings. The man started to dance in smooth, sensual waves, flowing and undulating with grace.

"I see," Patricia said. "You're the entertainment."

The man went on dancing, ignoring her. He was quite good, his body gleaming with oil in the subdued candlelight. His hips swayed enticingly, his movements strong and sensual.

Patricia watched him for a while before she realized he was not going to stop.

"You know, I'd much rather you told me where the door was," she said. "If you're getting paid to do this, I'll give you a bonus for pointing the way out."

The man continued to dance like he hadn't heard her. Patricia knew her Arabic wasn't good enough to make herself understood, so she lapsed into silence.

His body was like liquid sensuality, but Patricia felt only pain in her heart. It reminded her of how Nico had danced for her in his apartment, how he'd smiled as he'd slid his hands to her waist and swayed with her.

She understood now why he'd resisted staying with her. If his pain had been anything like what she experienced now, she knew why he'd tried to avoid it. Nico had lived through thousands of years of that pain.

"Damn you, Hera," she said. "You have so much power, and you waste it punishing a man who only wants to love." Patricia knelt upright in the bed, still clutching the blankets. "Do you hear me? I think you're nothing but a mean bitch. You punish others for your own hurting. So many people are starving or helpless in this world, and you obsess on petty vengeance."

She fell silent, half expecting the amenities to vanish and the walls to fall on her. But the music went on, and the oiled man kept dancing.

Patricia sank down to the pillows again. She wanted to get out of the bed, but the dancing man kept staring at her, and her dirty clothes were on the other side of the room.

Almost as soon as she had the thought, a silk robe appeared at the foot of the bed, along with what looked like a belly dancing costume.

Ignoring the sequined bra and gauzy skirt, she pulled on the robe and belted it before dropping the towel. The dancer ignored her, still undulating to the music like he was on automatic.

A mindless drone, she thought. Like the Dyons.

Patricia climbed out of bed and moved back into the alcove where the bath was, the area now containing benches strewn with cushions.

But as much as Patricia paced, she found no door or window, not even a ventilation shaft that communicated with the outside world.

She clenched her fists and let out a scream. It rang to the ceiling but was drowned out by the wild music.

The dancer whirled on, oblivious of her frustration. She watched him sway his hips and swirl around, arms and hands working, then she sat down on the cushioned bench and cried.

~ ~ ~

"IT was here," Ahmed said. "I think."

They stood on a dune at the end of the jeep road, staring out across the empty desert.

It was beautiful. Waves of sand flowed under the blue sky, a contrast of color and light. Behind them was the rocky desert, the oasis swallowed in the mist on the horizon.

"Sandstorm is coming," Ahmed said, sniffing the air. His brother Faisal nodded. "We can't start now."

Nico conceded. He could survive even the worst sandstorm, or he could easily fly away from it, but his human companions could not.

They took shelter in a rocky outcropping below the dunes, and Nico helped the brothers unroll the cloth top over the jeep. It wouldn't be much shelter, but would help keep out the brunt of the storm.

When it hit, the visibility disappeared within seconds. Nico huddled in the jeep with the brothers, who started swapping stories about other sandstorms they'd weathered. Nico sat silently and thought about Patricia.

He swore he'd heard her call out to him, in a voice ringing across the sands, but when he'd sat up, he'd realized that Ahmed and Faisal had heard nothing. He wanted her so much, so longed to hear her tell him that she loved him, that her voice had cut through his dreams.

He remembered the naughty look in her eyes as she'd fantasized out loud in the car on the way to Cornell. She'd described how she'd open his jeans and fondle him, then suck his cock into her mouth.

He remembered all the times she'd really done it. Patricia seemed especially fond of his cock, loving to simply hold it and gaze at it. She liked licking it and nibbling on it, and seeing how much of it she could take into her mouth.

Patricia had a skilled, wicked mouth. She'd always smiled at him afterward, pleased with herself.

He'd give anything to have her with him now, locked alone with him in this sandstorm. She'd look at him with her sexy eyes and whisper to him how much she wanted to pleasure him. Him, the slave that was supposed to be devoted to her pleasure.

She'd never tried to take advantage of his bondage to her, never tried to humiliate him. Everything she'd done or asked him to do had been loving, sweet, beautiful.

The sandstorm lasted several hours, and by the time it lessened, the sun was sinking. Ahmed and Faisal got out of the jeep, brushed away the worst of the sand, and started setting up a camp.

Nico helped them, then left to begin to explore the dunes.

~ ~ ~

REBECCA worried about getting to the oases quickly, until Demitri told her he had a private plane. They'd fly out to Dakhla and be there in a few hours.

Andreas hadn't spoken much to her at all. She'd cleaned up and dressed without seeing him, fuming that he hadn't tried to get into the shower with her.

In the plane, she had a seat to herself, with Demitri across from her and Andreas behind her. She pretended to ignore Andreas and talked to Demitri instead.

"So, you're a demigod, too?" she asked him.

He nodded. "My father was Apollo, my mother a magic woman from the Indus Valley. She could take the form of a tiger, and she taught me to as well."

"And you've been friends with Nico and Andreas since . . . ?"

"Since forever, as people like to say now. We met as young men. When Hera trapped the two of them with her curse, I wasn't there. I decided to stick around and help them as I could."

Rebecca saw guilt in his eyes that he'd been elsewhere when Hera had taken her vengeance. He'd stayed not only because he wanted to help his friends but to atone for escaping.

Andreas didn't contribute to the conversation, and when Rebecca looked behind her, he seemed to be asleep. She set her jaw and looked out of the window in silence.

They landed first at Bahariyya but found no evidence that Nico had come this way. Demitri insisted they continue to Farafra and then Dakhla. It was getting late by then, so they opted to stay in a small hotel and continue their search the next day.

Rebecca found it strange to walk on cool, green grass under palm trees when, not far away, the stark desert spread across thousands of miles. This was a beautiful place, an island in the desert, but it frightened her that Patricia might be lost somewhere in the endless sands.

Demitri discovered quickly that Nico had been there. The villagers here knew everyone, and everyone had heard the story of Ahmed shooting a godlike man out of the sky. They scoffed at the story but agreed that Ahmed's family had found a man in the desert and driven off west with him.

Demitri went to hire a car and guide, while Rebecca pored over a local map in her hotel bedroom, trying to decide which way they should go.

She heard Andreas enter and stand right behind her. He smelled of sweat and the diesel of the car that had brought them here, and his own male musk.

"Why did you come back?" he asked abruptly.

She kept her gaze on the map, pretending his nearness didn't unnerve her. "To help Patricia. It was ridiculous for me to stay home when I knew what the inscription on the wall said and maybe how to help her."

"No other reason?"

Rebecca turned around, suppressing a shiver as she looked up at his tall, powerful body.

"Do you want me to tell you I came back for you? After you fled the scene in the tomb?"

His blue eyes darkened. "I had to. I knew Hera would never let me go. She'd trick Bes into giving me back to her if I stayed. I went back to Olympus to talk to the other gods."

Rebecca had never thought in her life she'd be with a man who so casually mentioned that he talked to the gods of the Greek pantheon. "And what did you talk about?"

"I got a promise made that if Nico and I were free, we'd be free for always. And that Hera couldn't take her revenge on you. You are not to be hurt."

"That was nice of you."

Andreas growled, his leopardlike temper returning. "It wasn't *nice*. It was necessary."

"I meant it was kind of you to make sure I'd be all right."

"Damn it." Andreas grabbed her by the elbows and pulled her tight to him. "I'm not kind. I don't do things to be *kind*. I wanted you to be all right so when I saw you again, I could have you back. I want you to be all right because—I want you to be."

Why did he always take her breath away? No man had ever

wanted her like Andreas wanted her. It was a heady feeling, and frightening, too, because she didn't want it ever to stop.

"You're not under the curse anymore," she said, trying to hold her voice steady.

"No kidding." Andreas put his thumbs under her jaw and turned her face up to his. "I don't care about the damn curse. I just want to find out what it will be like with you without it."

Her heart hammered. "You mean like an experiment?"

"I don't care what you call it. I want you to be safe, but I want to be with you. It's driving me crazy. Why didn't you stay in New York?"

"I already told you why."

"How are you supposed to stay safe if you don't do what I tell you?"

She started to laugh. This tall, strong male had come to her in her little room at the B and B and made her take off her bra and give it to him. Then he'd pleasured her in a shower in London to wash away her fear of the Dyons. Her heart began to thump as she thought that maybe they'd finally consummate their relationship in this exotic oasis in Egypt.

She reached up to kiss him, intending a brief, tempting kiss, but he pulled her into it and took her mouth in hunger.

He always bowled her over with his extreme masculinity. Walking in to see him sticking his tongue into Demitri's mouth had only stoked the fires. Andreas was everything that was masculine and dominant and wild and exciting.

"Make love to me," she whispered. She'd gotten to the point where she wasn't above a little shameless begging.

He drew back with a hot smile, reverting to the Andreas she knew.

"How do you want me to do it? On your back, me on my back, me behind you? I can think of many exotic ways."

Rebecca's pulse sped. "However you want it."

He slid his arms around her and gently bit her ear. "Don't tempt me like that. I have a demigod's power, unrestrained now. The things I could make you do . . ."

"I mean that I can't decide."

"Hmm." Andreas stepped back, his ice blue gaze sweeping her body. "Why don't you let me call the shots, then?"

Her cleft was warm, aching, while her imagination spun. "That would be good."

"Strip."

The abrupt command made her blink, but in another second, Rebecca started tearing off her clothes.

Andreas pointed at the bed. "Lie down."

Rebecca breathlessly climbed onto the bed and bounced onto her back. When she looked up, Andreas was naked, his lovely body glistening with sweat. His hard face and cool eyes made a contrast to his thick cock lifting for her in wanting.

"Spread for me, baby," he said softly.

Rebecca spread her legs, bending her knees and sliding her feet to her hips. "Like this?"

"You're beautiful." Andreas climbed on the bed and positioned himself between her thighs, his body heavy and warm. "You're so beautiful."

His lips found hers. He playfully nipped them, but she sensed most of his playfulness had fled. He was all business now, all man, and he wanted her.

"Have me," she whispered. She lifted her hips, her pussy full and hot for him.

She felt his fingers swirl over her and dip into her moisture. "You're a sweetheart to be so wet for me."

"I've been wanting you for a long time. Ever since you came in my room and told me to take off my bra."

"You wanted me before that." His eyes sparkled. "You wanted me when I was licking your breasts."

"I thought that was a dream."

"Nope. It was real." He drew his hot tongue around her nipple. "You tasted good."

"You were a leopard."

"And you were a sweet thing. I wanted to bury myself between your legs and lick your pussy clean." He shrugged. "But I didn't want to scare you."

His words made the pool of heat inside her boil over. "Fuck me," she begged. "Please, Andreas. I'm dying for you."

"You look pretty healthy." He smiled, slow and sensual. "But all right."

He took her lips in a hard kiss at the same time he lifted slightly and pushed inside her. He was a tight fit, and he spread her and stretched her until she gasped.

"I can't take all of you."

"Yes, you can, sweetheart." His eyes were half closed, his voice ragged. "You're so beautiful, Becky."

She lifted her legs and wrapped them around his back. He pushed inside, farther, farther. He would tear her apart.

Andreas groaned. His eyes closed; his mottled white and black hair fell across his flushed face. "Damn," he breathed.

He started to ride her. They moved together, body to body, her hands on his back, his mouth opening hers in heated, bruising kisses.

"I love you," she whispered. "Oh, gods, Andreas, I love you."

"Love you, too, Becky," he said hoarsely. "You sweet, sweet woman."

She lay back, beginning to come under him, but he rocked into her for a long time. By the time he finished, she was laughing, sore, bruised, and happy.

Even if after they found Patricia, Andreas decided to disappear to his demigod world, or wherever he went, Rebecca would have this. She'd always remember.

They emerged from the bedroom hours later, dressed again, as Demitri returned to tell them he'd arranged for a car and driver to take them out into the sands.

23

AHMED drove the jeep to the end of the track at first light, and they proceeded on foot over the dunes. Ahmed had a stick that he kept running over the sand, swearing that it would point their way to the ruins.

Nico wasn't sure he believed that, but he let Ahmed lead the way. The brothers had grown up in this country and knew it, and Nico hadn't been this way in thousands of years, since Roman times. Amazingly, it didn't look much different.

After about half an hour of searching, Ahmed's stick thumped on something hard under the sand. He broke into a grin.

"It's here."

Nico and Faisal joined him on their knees to start scraping away sand. Nico's pulse quickened with sickening fear. Patricia couldn't be buried in a ruin here. She'd never survive.

The land was covered with sand as far as the eye could see, no outcroppings or man-made edifices poking through. If Patricia was under here, she'd have no way to breathe.

They dug quickly, the sand sliding and spilling back as fast as they moved it. Faisal had brought a shovel, which helped, but the final uncovering they had to do by hand. What they found was a square, flat stone that had obviously been hewn by an ancient chisel.

"You see?" Ahmed said. "I know where all the ruins are."

Nico lay down and put his ear to the hot stone. He could hear nothing, feel nothing. It was too damn thick.

"How big is this place?" he asked.

Ahmed shrugged. "I don't know. I've never uncovered all of it."

"I need to get inside this. I need to find her." He broke off in fear and frustration. "She might not even be here."

Yesterday, he'd heard her voice loud and clear, echoing across the emptiness. *I love you, Nico. Love you so much.*

He'd thought he'd imagined it, but now he wondered again. Patricia was psychic. What was to say she couldn't project strong psychic energy that his own magic picked up?

Ahmed suddenly screamed. Nico jerked his head up in time to see Ahmed leap from the top of the building, his face white with fear.

Nico and Faisal stepped hurriedly back into the sands, Faisal holding his shovel high. From the corners of the building, dozens of snakes had emerged: desert vipers, thin and deadly. Their yellow, slitted eyes beamed hatred.

"Stay back," Nico told the two men.

His first beat of fear turned to one of grim satisfaction. Hera had just signaled loud and clear that Patricia was here, unless this was another decoy.

He didn't think so. The snakes began to coil on the hot rock, then one by one rose into the forms of Dyons.

"Demons," Ahmed cried. He unshouldered his rifle, bringing it up in his hands. Faisal stepped behind him, eyes wide, shovel ready.

Nico wasn't quite sure of their odds against an army of Dyons, even with Ahmed's rifle. Dyons couldn't kill Nico, but they could tear him apart enough that he would be a bloody, useless wreck for some time, and of course they could kill his human companions.

Wind whipped up behind him and the two men, sand rising in a deadly cloud. But this was no ordinary sandstorm. It was something malevolent, a whirlpool of sand with the three men and the Dyons in the vortex.

"Go back to your jeep," Nico shouted at Ahmed and Faisal. "You'll die here. Go back."

Both men looked like they wanted to run but held their ground. "I'll not leave a friend to die," Ahmed said.

It would more likely be Ahmed who died, but Nico had no time to argue. The Dyons attacked at the same time the sands whirled to swallow them up.

Nico fought, reverting to his true form as the Dyons reached for him. His true form was mostly light, the shape of the winged man solidifying it. Nico was at his most powerful in this form, able to fuse the magic of his divine half into something deadly.

But keeping that form took its toll. He tired more quickly, which would leave him vulnerable, and the slave chain made everything more difficult.

Nico heard Ahmed and Faisal both cry out, and he did his best to defend them. The Dyons swarmed him, and sand stung and scoured him. The sand would rip his flesh from his bones, and the Dyons would finish the process. Only a god could kill Nico, but when the Dyons finished, he knew he'd wish himself dead.

Ahmed's cries turned to shouts. Dimly Nico heard the whirr of an engine, and he wondered who could have driven out here amid the sand cyclone.

Then new shapes entered the fray, a lithe, white snow leopard followed by a huge tiger rippling with muscle. Nico laughed, getting sand in his mouth, but he fought through Dyons to stand side by side with his friends.

"Join with me," he yelled over the storm.

Andreas and Demitri couldn't answer in their animal forms, but he felt their surge of magic. He joined his to it, and the Dyons closest to them crumbled into dust before the onslaught.

The other Dyons, mindless beings, converged for another attack. The three demigods struck again, breaking the first line.

But they'd keep coming, again and again, until Nico, Andreas, and Demitri were worn down. He couldn't see Ahmed and Faisal anymore and hoped they'd had the sense to run for safety.

The three demigods continued the battle without speaking, their magics fused into one. Nico loved the feeling, having his two best friends part of him, a bond unlike anything else. Sometimes the three of them got close to this during sexual play, their power flowing into one another through hands, tongues, and cocks, but mortal bodies were limited. *This* joining was joy.

He marveled that his mortal body and Patricia's could come together with the same joy. That's what love did, he decided; it expanded what was physical into something magical and powerful.

He needed that with Patricia even more than he needed his godlike powers, his immortality, and his wings.

Nico heard a grinding sound and gleeful shouting, and out of the corner of his eye, he saw Ahmed's jeep break through the sands of the cyclone. The jeep landed on a line of Dyons, breaking them down into their snake forms, which hurriedly crawled away.

Andreas and Demitri leapt forward, their big-cat forms taking down the last two Dyons. The whirling sand suddenly stopped, the last particles raining down on the gathered group and the jeep. The blue sky arched serenely overhead as though nothing had ever happened.

The jeep was full of sand, and sand piled on the heads of the grinning Ahmed, Faisal, and Rebecca.

"Whew!" Rebecca called, brushing sand from her face. "I didn't think that would work."

~ ~ ~

THE next problem was how to get into the ruin beneath their feet. The storm had dumped most of the sand they'd labored to sweep from the top of it back on.

With Andreas and Demitri to help, they cleared it again, only to be faced with a slab of blank stone.

"We could drill," Ahmed suggested. "Or get explosives."

"No!" Rebecca cried before Nico could. "This is an artifact. It needs to be properly excavated."

"Patricia might be in there," Nico snapped. "No explosives—or an excavation that could take two years," he added, looking pointedly at Rebecca.

"Of course I want to get Patricia out safely," Rebecca returned. "But if we could disturb this as *little* as possible?"

Faisal ruined that idea by banging on the top of the stone with the point of his shovel. Little chips of stone flew out, to Rebecca's distress, but it didn't make much of a dent.

"It will take too long without the proper tools," Faisal concluded.

"We'll have to dig down the sides," Ahmed said. "Find a door below the sand?"

"I could send for a backhoe," Demitri offered. He and Andreas had resumed their human forms and their clothes, which Rebecca had brought in the jeep. Rebecca winced at the word *backhoe* but kept silent.

"Could heavy equipment get here on these roads?" Andreas asked.

"I have to admit I don't know."

Ahmed looked off to the west and sighed. "It looks like another sandstorm coming. A real one."

Nico stood staring at the slab of stone, bright in the sunshine, his heart like lead.

Was this his test? What would he do in order to retrieve Patricia? Endanger his friends and strangers who tried to help him? Endanger Patricia herself trying to get to her?

"You need to go," he said abruptly.

Andreas started to snarl, his eyes flashing dangerously, and Demitri broke in. "Why?"

"Because this has to be me, alone."

"No," Rebecca said. "I saw the wall. You should be helped by a tiger and a leopard—"

"And I was. You helped me defeat the Dyons and Hera's defenses, but I can't endanger you any more for this. Please go."

"What happens if you can't?" Andreas asked. His eyes betrayed his worry.

"Then Hera destroys me."

"Like hell," Andreas said.

Nico faced him, his friend for an eternity, the man who'd struggled by his side all these years, never leaving him.

"I stay here until I find a way to save her," Nico said. "I won't walk away. If that means I stay here forever, chained to this place, then so be it."

"She'll never set you free," Andreas said. "That's the real point, isn't it? Hera will make you search forever, enslaving you forever."

"I don't care about that anymore." Nico put his hand on Andreas's shoulder, squeezing. "I want to make sure Patricia is all right. Hera can do what she damn well pleases: keep me a slave, kill me. I don't care anymore. I just want Patricia safe."

Andreas started to speak, then he saw what was in Nico's eyes and subsided.

He put his hand on Nico's shoulder and pulled him close for a brief, hard hug.

"Take Rebecca out of here," Nico said. "Go on."

Andreas nodded. He turned away, but not quickly enough for Nico to miss the tears in his eyes. Andreas reached for Rebecca and led her down into the sand.

"Yell if you need us," Demitri said. He gave Nico the same kind of heartfelt hug.

"I won't."

Demitri only nodded and followed the others, but Nico knew they'd wait for a long time before they gave up and went home.

Ahmed and Faisal were much easier to convince. If the story said the winged man had to save the great lady by himself, then he did. You didn't mess with a story.

They left him water and wished him luck, then spun the jeep around and ambled down the dune.

Once they were gone, Nico knelt on the top of the stone slab.

He spread his wings out, fanning the hot air, sweat trickling down his face and half-naked body. He crossed his wrists in front of him, as though offering himself to be bound.

"All right, Hera," he said in a conversational tone. "I'm here. I've found her. Do whatever the hell you want with me. Just let her go home and be all right."

For a moment, nothing happened. He felt only the soft breeze touching his hair, the threat of storm gone, heard only the slither of sand as it settled on the dunes.

He waited, knowing Hera could make him kneel there for years, but as he suspected, she was too impatient for that.

A shaft of light manifested from the sand, and Hera stood in its protective glow, her robes and dark hair not even stirring.

"Do you mean that, shallow demigod?" she asked. "You'd sacrifice yourself to me to save her?"

"Yes."

Nico refused to meet her eyes, refused to grovel and plead like she wanted him to. His only concern was saving Patricia, and to hell with anything else.

"Your life for hers?" Hera prodded.

"If necessary."

The goddess put her hands on her plump hips. "Well, I can't do that. Your father has made it clear that I am not to kill his offspring, even though he has followed the rules and not interfered with my vengeance."

Dionysus had always been an indifferent father as far as Nico was concerned, paying little attention to him after he'd fathered him. Nico wondered if things would have turned out differently if Dionysus had cared, or if Nico had tried harder to make him care. Lessons learned.

"Then do whatever you want," Nico said. "But let Patricia go safely home."

Hera watched him, her head tilted to one side, dark eyes curious. "You truly think you would do anything to save her, don't you?"

"I do," Nico said quietly. "I love her."

"You love nothing. This is a game. I am making you feel what you feel. *Me*."

"It doesn't matter."

Hera straightened up, her face softening into a smile. "He thinks he's learned something after all." She leaned to Nico, the glow still surrounding her. "What if I let her go, and she doesn't remember you? What if she's indifferent to you and doesn't love you? Would you still want me to save her?"

Nico knew in that moment that he'd lost Patricia forever. Hera had never intended to let Nico have her. She had spun out this test because it amused her, and because she'd wanted to remind Bes that she was far more powerful than he was.

"Yes," Nico said, his throat tight. "It doesn't matter what Patricia thinks of me."

"Hmm." Hera studied him a few moments longer, her eyes alight with glee. "Very well. She goes free."

She pointed her finger at the corner of the slab, and it broke open to reveal a dark hole beneath. As Nico dove toward it, Hera vanished.

~ ~ ~

The walls around Patricia started to shake. The music ceased like someone had flipped a switch, and the dancer vanished.

She gasped and clutched the bench she rested on, staring at the ceiling in terror. Was the whole thing about to explode, like the tomb? Was it going to come down and crush her?

The silent dancer had been boring and unhelpful, but at least he'd been company. Now she was going to die alone.

The bench vanished, and Patricia plopped onto the floor. She huddled into a ball, covering her head with her hands.

The beautiful tiles disappeared as did the bathtub and the table laden with food and drink. The candles dissolved, leaving her in darkness.

Her heart hammered. Why was it all being taken away? Had she not been appreciative enough? Was she supposed to have set up a shrine to Hera and groveled before it?

"You heartless bitch!" she shouted. Not a way to placate the goddess, but it made Patricia feel better.

She heard the walls close in on her, stone grinding against stone. The building rocked and moved for an excruciatingly long time, and then just as abruptly, it stopped.

Patricia rose. She put out her hands, her whole body shaking, and started to walk across her prison. She nearly cried when she touched a wall right away, realizing that she was again trapped in the six-by-six cell.

Tears rolled down her cheeks. Maybe she'd been asleep and dreamed the food and water, the bath and the bed. Maybe none of it had been real, and her mind had conjured everything up to keep her from going insane.

Except she still wore the silk robe, her own clothes having disappeared.

"Damn it." Patricia rested her head in her arms and let herself go. She choked on sobs, crying like she'd never cried in her life. She was lost here, and she'd lost everything.

A sudden light pierced the darkness, and she winced at the pain of it.

"Patricia?"

She didn't recognize the voice, but she didn't care. She dashed the tears from her eyes, trying to see.

"Here!" she shouted, her words strangled from weeping. "I'm down here!"

"Thank all the gods."

The man exuded relief, although Patricia still couldn't place him. Andreas's friend Demitri, maybe?

A block of stone not far above her slid out of the way, and blue sky appeared, sunshine pouring down through the hole.

"Is this real?" she asked shakily. "Not more weirdness?"

"This is real." The man reached down for her. He had dark hair and eyes and a sinfully handsome face, but she'd never seen him before.

She wasn't certain he could pull her out, but he caught her wrists and lifted her, then grabbed her under the shoulders and hauled her the rest of the way out. She landed facedown on top of a stone slab, sand all around her. Dunes marched to the horizon beyond the slab, knife-edged and perfect.

For a moment, all she could do was lie still and breathe the dry, ovenlike air, enjoying seeing sky above her and true sunlight. The breeze, though hot, spoke of freedom.

She sat up, pushing her curls from her face. "Where the hell am I?"

"The Great Sand Sea," her rescuer said. "West of the Dakhla oasis."

"Oh." She thought about the fact that she was literally in the middle of nowhere rescued by someone she'd never seen before.

Everything she knew was so far away, but that hadn't sunk in quite yet. "You speak English," she said.

The man smiled a little. "I speak many languages."

He certainly was a looker. His skin was tanned from bright sunshine, and his eyes were coffee-dark. He was wearing blue jeans and no shirt, letting her get a good look at his hard chest dusted with black hair. The sleek, oiled dancer in her cell had nothing on this man.

When he turned to fetch water, she saw that a tattoo of wings covered his back, the ends disappearing under his waistband. Nice.

"What are you doing out here?" she asked. "Not that I'm not grateful for you pulling me out, but how did you find me?"

He swallowed, his Adam's apple bobbing, and she was startled to see his eyes moisten. "Your friends came looking for you. They're not far. They have a jeep." He pointed down a dune that looked like all the other dunes.

"That's good news." Patricia pushed her hair from her face. "Are you all right?"

"Sand in my eyes, is all."

"Is everyone else all right—Rebecca, Andreas?"

"They're fine. They're waiting for you. Do you feel up to walking?"

Patricia started to climb to her feet, then winced as her bare soles touched the stone. "I lost my shoes."

"That's all right."

Before she could stop him, the man swept her up into his strong arms. He was powerfully built, muscles rippling on his arms and shoulders. If she had to be rescued, she didn't mind a gorgeous man like him doing the rescuing.

He stepped off the slab of stone, sinking a little into the sand, but easily carrying her down the side of the dune. She saw in the distance that the sand petered out, and rock took over. She could make out the outline of two vehicles against the rocks, and people around them.

She looked up at her rescuer again. His face was unshaven, and sand dusted his hair. His eyes haunted her: beautiful, dark eyes that held a world of pain.

"Have I met you before?" she asked. "You look familiar, but . . ." She shook her head. "No, I don't think I have."

"My name is Nikolaus. Everyone calls me Nico."

"Thank you, Nico. I can't tell you how happy I am to see you."

He flinched, jaw tightening, but he remained firmly upright. She daringly laid her head on his shoulder, loosely clasping his arm with one hand.

Nico didn't set her down all the way to the jeeps. As soon as her feet touched the ground, Rebecca flung herself at Patricia and hugged her tight, crying.

"I thought you were dead," Rebecca sobbed. "Are you all right?"

"I seem to be." Patricia took stock. The things in the ruin might have been illusion, but she felt hydrated, fed, clean, and rested. "It was the weirdest experience."

Patricia let Rebecca help her to sit in one of the jeeps. Patricia wasn't in a hurry to be inside anywhere for a while, but the canvas top of the jeep kept the sun from burning her.

"You must have been terrified," Rebecca was babbling. "I'm so sorry I didn't get here sooner, but Bes magicked me back to New York, and I had to fly all the way to Cairo again."

"It's all right," Patricia said, taking a long swig of water. It didn't taste nearly as clear and pure as the water in the tiled basin had, but Patricia found she preferred the ordinary plastic bottle. "I knew you'd find me."

"Nico did," Rebecca said, smiling happily.

"Yes." Patricia turned to the man, who was being greeted by Andreas and Demitri as though they knew him well. "And I'm grateful."

Rebecca looked puzzled. "Grateful? What do you mean, grateful?"

"Shouldn't I be?" She gazed at Nico, who avoided her eyes. "It couldn't have been easy to pull me out," she said to him. "I don't have a lot of money, but I'll find some way to repay you."

"Patricia," Rebecca began.

"She doesn't remember me," Nico said.

The others stopped and stared at him, looking stricken, and Patricia couldn't imagine why. If she'd met him in passing somewhere, they couldn't really expect her to remember that this instant, not after the trauma of her imprisonment.

"That was the price," Nico said to them. "I'm free, and she doesn't remember." He touched his bare, brown throat.

Rebecca looked from Patricia to Nico, her mouth open. Andreas and Demitri seemed shocked but somehow not surprised.

The two Egyptian men by the other jeep exchanged glances, and the younger said something in Arabic.

"He says it's a tragedy," Rebecca related. "They were hoping the story had a happy ending, but now they know it's a tragedy. They think it's romantic."

Patricia was relieved enough to laugh. "I think me getting out of there is enough of a happy ending for me."

"She needs to get out of the sun," Demitri said. "I'll have a doctor make sure she's all right, and once she rests, everything will clear up."

Rebecca looked worried again and urged Patricia to drink more water. The others piled in the jeeps.

Patricia found herself squished between Rebecca and Nico, who remained silent.

"I'm sorry I don't remember you," she said to him as the jeep bounced over the rocks to a more level track. "Where did I meet you, again?"

"It doesn't matter," Nico said in a bleak voice and looked away.

24

WHILE Patricia slept in the little hotel, Nico's friends tried to comfort him.

"It sucks," Andreas said. "And it isn't fair. You're free now. You should have what you want."

"I made the bargain," Nico replied. His chest ached as though someone had stepped on him. "Her life and her freedom in exchange for my heartbreak. But to me, it's more important that Patricia is alive and well than that she still wants me." He stopped, the words choking him. "I'll make sure she gets back to New York, then I'll leave her alone."

"But you passed the test," Andreas protested.

"No," Nico said. "That was the test. Would I sacrifice my own happiness for her life? It was an easy answer. Yes."

Andreas started to argue, but Demitri rested his hand on Andreas's shoulder. "Leave him be. Think about it. What if it had been Rebecca?"

Andreas's mouth turned down. "I know. I'd have done the same. I still think it sucks."

Nico left them and went for a walk, not able to take much more of his friends' sympathy. They were good to feel for him, but what he needed most was to be alone.

Nico's new friends Ahmed and Faisal had returned home, blessed with luck. They'd have a grand time telling the story of how they fought snake monsters side by side in the desert with three demigod warriors. They would likely tell the story over and over as the years went on, until they were famous for it. As to who would believe it, it was hard to say.

The hotel was situated near cultivated fields, the smell of green assailing him as Nico strolled along. Palm trees soared overhead, dates hanging in huge, golden brown bunches.

This was a beautiful place, a haven in the harsh desert, but Nico couldn't enjoy it. He could only see the blank politeness in Patricia's aquamarine eyes when she asked, "Have I met you before?"

Hera knew how to twist the knife. Nico's gut hurt, and the hurt only increased when he realized that what he'd felt for Patricia under the slave chain had been real. He'd loved her, and now that he was free of the curse, he loved her still.

He'd heard her tell Rebecca of the strange room that had given her more and more comforts, taking them all back as soon as Nico found her. He wondered if Bes had worked some magic to give her that. Hera likely wouldn't have. Patricia had been smiling, her eyes tired but unafraid. Her ordeal had not broken her.

Nico knew that no matter how much it hurt, he wouldn't take back his sacrifice. Patricia was safe, and that mattered. He would go away, and she could get back to her real life.

An Egyptian man in a business suit walked toward him, and Nico stopped to wait for him.

"Hello, my friend," Bes, in the guise of Mr. Ajeed, said. "All is well?"

Nico folded his arms over his borrowed caftan and fell into step with him as they walked along. "Patricia is well. Thank you for helping. Was it you who gave her the fruit and water and so forth in the cell?"

Bes beamed. "Yes, that was me. Every time you thought about how much you loved her—thought it from your heart and your gut—she received another benefit. Your love for her kept her fed and warm and rested while she waited."

Nico's eyes narrowed. "What was with the naked dancing man?"

"I thought she'd like it," Bes said innocently.

"I just wish she'd stop talking about it," he growled.

Bes gave him a sympathetic look. "I heard of your sacrifice. It was nobly done."

"I'll feel noble later. Right now I feel like someone hit me with a truck." He tilted his head back to stop the tears from leaking from his eyes. "I love her."

"Yes." Bes walked in silence a moment. "You passed the test; you are free. You will find your reward."

"I don't give a damn about rewards. I'll make sure Patricia gets home, then I'll go to Olympus. I need some peace about now."

"You could always guard the tomb in Amarna with me. That is peaceful."

"The tomb was destroyed."

"Yes, but the lord must still be guarded. Archaeologists will come soon and take him to a museum, and then I can go."

Nico gave him a look of new respect. "I wish all the gods were as loyal and steadfast as you."

"The Egyptian people were good to me, before the gods were forgotten. I guarded homes against snakes and other animals and made sure even the humblest of the people were safe. They paid me back in reverence."

"You helped Andreas and me, too. Why? We're not even of your people."

Bes shrugged. "I had several thousand years to study the wall painting. I knew you'd come eventually. It was very exciting, actually—the most excitement I'd had in millennia."

Nico smiled, his lips stiff. "I won't forget you, Bes. Anytime you want to come to Olympus, I'll make sure they let you in."

"A fine offer," Bes said. "I might pay you a visit. You do deserve a reward for your kindness, and you will have it."

Nico wished he'd drop the admiration. "I don't need anything. Just a little peace and quiet."

"Oh, yes, you do. You will get your reward. I'll make sure of it. Wait and see."

Bes smiled mysteriously, then he stopped, shook hands with Nico, and strode off the other way.

Back in Andreas's room, Nico found Demitri on his cell phone talking to people at his hotel and Rebecca sitting on Andreas's lap, kissing him.

Rebecca slid to her feet when she saw Nico, blushing. Andreas lounged back, a satisfied look in his blue eyes. A stray cat from the village sat on the windowsill behind him, purring.

"As soon as I'm back at Cornell, I'm putting in for a grant to dig out here," Rebecca told Nico. "I don't know what those ruins are, but the stone is older than Greco-Roman. Want to join us?"

"If you can find it again," Nico said absently.

"What? Why not? I can hire your friends to drive me out there. They seemed nice."

"It might not be a real place—maybe something Hera put together. Besides, what about your tomb in Amarna?"

"My ruined tomb," she said in a sad voice. "When we start excavating that, they'll be able to tell it was destroyed just last week."

"They'll think it was an earthquake," Andreas suggested, stretching his arms along the back of the sofa. "Or vandals. Which is true; it kind of was both."

"I'll find the ruins," Rebecca said stubbornly. "I need to make my name."

Andreas looked at her with a fond expression. "If you want it that much, I'll help you, Becky."

Rebecca looked surprised. "You'd stay with me?"

Andreas pulled her down to the sofa "You and I are going to be together for a long, long time. I have so much more to teach you, Becky."

Rebecca flushed with happiness. "I think I'm in love with you."

"I *know* I'm in love with you," Andreas returned. "How about that, Nico? Me, in love, and not because of the damn curse. For keeps."

"Congratulations," Nico said, happy for his friends even through the hole in his heart.

Demitri was still talking loudly to someone on the phone, not paying attention to the others. Nico left them, drawn to the door of Patricia's room.

He knew she was asleep. Rebecca had given her a sleeping pill to calm her down and had shooed everyone away from her, but Nico couldn't resist looking in on her.

The latch of her door clicked under Nico's touch, and he pushed it open. The shades were drawn to shut out the glaring sun, the room dim and quiet. A portable fan quietly hummed in the corner.

Patricia lay in the middle of the small bed, a sheet over her, her head pillowed on her arm.

Nico closed the door and softly approached the bed. Patricia lay with her eyes closed, her curls spilling over her shoulders.

He lifted a curl from her cheek, smoothing it back with a gentle touch. Knowing that the sleeping pill would have her slumbering soundly, he leaned over her and pressed a kiss to her cheek.

She stirred a little, her lips curving to a faint smile. Nico's heart leapt, then slowed again when her mouth smoothed back into sleep.

Time to go. Nico moved noiselessly to the door and turned the knob.

"Nico?"

Patricia's sleepy voice arrested him. He faced the door, unwilling to see the look of blank inquiry in her eyes.

"Sorry," he said. "I was just making sure you were all right. Go back to sleep."

He started to open the door.

"Nico."

The throb of love and longing was unmistakable. Nico let the door close and made himself look back at her.

Patricia was sitting up in bed, tears spilling down her cheeks. "Nico, I couldn't remember who you were."

She bit back a sob, and Nico's heart shattered. He was across the room, scooping her against him in an instant, burying his face in the curve of her neck.

"Why couldn't I remember?" she whispered. "I love you, Nico. It was all I could think of while I waited for you to rescue me. Why couldn't I remember you?"

Nico couldn't speak. He held her so hard, his hands shaking, tears spilling from his eyes.

She pulled away from him slightly but only to kiss him. Nico kissed her back desperately, hungry for her. She laughed, he was so frantic, her laughter spilling into his mouth.

"I love you," she repeated.

"I love you, too, Patricia." He held her against him, his lips in her hair, on her face, hands fervently undoing the buttons on her nightshirt. "I love you so much."

"Then why didn't I know you?"

Nico didn't want to talk, but she looked so perplexed, he explained what had happened. "It was the final test," he finished. "A test of my love. The hardest thing I've done in my long life: let you go."

"I felt so alone." She ran her hands across his shoulders.

"I think Bes gave you back your memory," Nico said. "He told me I'd find a reward, and this is what he meant. I don't know how he thwarted Hera."

"Maybe he didn't." Patricia pulled him down to her. "I was lying here, feeling so empty, and I didn't know why. It was like I'd lost someone I loved, someone I'd forgotten, but I didn't want to forget. I tried lifting my psychic shields to search, and I found a barrier there, one I hadn't erected. I pushed and pushed, and I started dreaming of you—a man with wings taking me to a strange place where we had incredible sex." She smiled. "And then when I woke up and saw you, I *knew*."

Nico's heart beat faster. "Remember the story Rebecca translated on the tomb wall? She said that pursuing lust for its own sake would return to punish the lustful, while true love is rewarded with happiness. I think this is what Bes knew, that our love would drive though anything Hera could throw at us. That love would win in the end." He held her close. "And I do love you."

"I love you, too," she whispered, tears in her eyes. "I'm crazy with it, Nico."

"I'll never leave you alone. Never again."

"Just be with me now."

Nico burrowed into the nightshirt, kissing her breasts, suckling each nipple into his mouth, unable to get enough of her. He ripped the shirt the rest of the way open and stripped it from her, his hands parting her legs even as she laughed.

His need pounded so hard it hurt. He felt her fingers at his waistband, trying to tug open his pants. He unzipped them and kicked them off, nearly tearing his shirt and underwear off in his hurry.

He kissed her as his cock found her opening, wet and slick for him. It took nothing at all to slide into her, his whole body rejoicing as he found his way home.

She lifted her hips, her face relaxing into the joy of him inside her. Her quim squeezed him tight as her hands closed on his ass.

"It's good," he groaned against her lips. "It's good to fuck you, love."

"One thing's missing," she murmured, her hips rocking to drive him even deeper into her. "Your wings."

Nico grinned. He let them slide out from his shoulder blades, feeling satisfaction as he stretched them to the ceiling and gently flapped them down.

He enclosed them in a black, feathery cocoon, the sensitive tips brushing against her warm skin. Patricia smiled and bit into his feathers, causing him to wince and laugh at the same time.

"Vixen," he growled. "Like it rough, do you?"

"I think I do."

"Well, then, sweetheart, get ready."

She looked innocent. "For what?"

"For me. I'm going to fuck you so hard you will beg for mercy."

"Will I? I don't think so."

"Don't tempt me, Patricia. I'll make you pay for being so cute."

"Oh, really? How?"

He showed her. She screamed and laughed as he made love to her, then spanked her ass until it turned cherry red. Then he fucked her all over again. She writhed and laughed and loved every minute of it.

"I love you, Nico," she said as she sank back into sleep. "Don't go yet."

"Never."

"But you're free of the curse now." Her eyes slid closed, even as she held him close. "You can go anywhere you want, be anyone you want."

"I'm right where I want to be," he said. "And who I want to be. Nico, with Patricia, the woman I love."

She touched his face. "Do you mean that?"

"I plan to spend a long, long time showing you."

"You're immortal, more or less," she said. Her eyes were sad. "And I'm not."

"I know. But Hera owes me something for this torture she's put me through. If she wants me to be true to one woman and love her and her alone, she can help me. She can let you come to Olympus with me, and become an immortal."

Patricia's eyes rounded. "An immortal . . ."

"It's nothing I'll force you into. You make the choice. Likewise, I can ask to be made mortal myself, so I can stay with you. It doesn't matter to me either way—as long as it's you and me together."

"That's a lot to think about."

"Take your time," Nico smiled. "I don't mind waiting."

She mused. "Of course, if I was immortal, I could become a fantastic antiques dealer. I could put things away for years and then make a killing on the market."

"You see? Advantages."

"Make love to me again." Patricia slid her arms around his body, tickling him under his wings. "So I can decide if I really want to take the step."

Nico's body warmed, his still-hard cock more than ready. "This will help you make up your mind?"

"Yes." Patricia smiled, her blue green eyes warm and full of love. "But I'll have to be completely certain, so you'll have to do it again, and again, and again."

"Oh, sweetheart," Nico said. He held her wrists against the pillow, loving how her eyes darkened as he slid into her again. "As many times as you want me. We'll have all the time in the world . . ."

ABOUT THE AUTHOR

Allyson James writes bestselling and award-winning historical, contemporary, and paranormal romances, award-winning mysteries, and historical fiction under several pseudonyms. She lives in the warm Southwest with her husband and cats and spends most of her time in the world of her stories. More about Allyson's books can be found on her website, www.allysonjames.com, or contact Allyson via e-mail at allysonjames@ cox.net.